BLUE ANGEL NIGHTS

BLUE ANGEL NIGHTS

MARGARETE VON FALKENSEE

CARROLL & GRAF PUBLISHERS, INC.
New York

First Carroll & Graf edition 1986

Carroll & Graf Publishers, Inc.
260 Fifth Avenue
New York, NY 10001

Library of Congress Cataloging-in-Publication Data

Von Falkensee, Margarete.
  Blue angel nights.

  I. Title.
PR6072.045B6   1986   823'.914   86-11775
ISBN 0-88184-283-4

Manufactured in the United States of America

Foreword by the translator

This remarkable novel by Margarete von Falkensee was first published in 1931 in a small edition by OBUS Verlag of Berlin, the original title being *The Pleasure Garden*. It is set in Berlin in the late 1920s.

Satire to the point of indecency was a well-established form of social comment in Berlin, the cartoons of George Grosz being a well-known example, while cabaret artists such as Werner Finck became notorious for their outspoken performances. In this tradition Margarete von Falkensee outdoes anything previously seen in print in her presentation of the politics of the Weimar Republic in terms of sexual activity in a group of people broadly representative of the times.

Some of the topical allusions in the novel have lost their meaning with time but the interest remains in a picture of a collapsing society and some of the characters are still easily recognised. Jutta von Loschingen, for example, is a caricature of the old aristocracy and Hildegard Buschendorf of the German middle-class zeal for authority. Magda Nebel symbolises a new menace, the emerging authoritarianism of National Socialism. It is needless here to categorise all the women in the novel; the reader will recognise them.

Two chapters may be referred to briefly as central to the author's thinking. In one, the elections of May 1928 are represented as a visit to a brothel and a choice between prostitutes. In the other, an account of an orgy in a Turkish

Bath, the religion of the times is mocked in a highly indecent way.

Those of a literary turn of mind may see some resemblance between the main character of the novel, Manfred von Klausenberg, and Voltaire's hero Candide. There is also a possible comparison with Kafka's hero in *The Trial* and *The Castle*, these two novels being published in Berlin only a few years before *The Pleasure Garden* was written. But whereas Candide withdraws from a world he finds unacceptable and Kafka's hero succumbs to forces he does not understand, Klausenberg fumbles his way towards an alliance with wholly unpredictable results. Whether the author was seriously proposing this as a solution to Germany's political and social problems is impossible to say. This is a novel, not a tract, however symbolic.

The years from 1924 to 1929 were regarded by most Berliners as the Golden Twenties, but this was a superficial view. The Republic founded in 1918 had survived Communist and Fascist attempts at revolution and it had survived the crippling hyper-inflation of the early 1920s. By 1925 the currency was stable, industrial production rising and employment growing. It was a time of dawning hopes and expectations, but events soon proved that there was no secure foundation under the new prosperity and no stability in the democratic system. The world recession heralded by the Wall Street stock market crash of 1929 brought bankruptcy and intolerable unemployment to Germany. The moderate centre in politics was eclipsed by the extremists and the National Socialist Party increased its representation in the Reichstag. In 1933 its leader, Adolf Hitler, was appointed Chancellor and the long night of barbarism fell on Germany.

Although this novel is set in 1928 it did not appear until 1931 and the delay killed off any prospect of success it might have had. It is very probable that the author had difficulty in finding a publisher, given the uncompromising nature of the content. OBUS Verlag was a small publishing house founded by the Hartmann brothers at the end of the

6

1914–1918 War and had a reputation for avant-garde work, Willi Klar, Gerd Fischer and Ursula Strauss being among its authors. By the beginning of the early 1930s OBUS Verlag was on its way to bankruptcy, its authors being more acclaimed than bought and by the time *The Pleasure Garden* came out Germany was in financial collapse and deep social turmoil. The catastrophe had happened and no further warning was required; *The Pleasure Garden* passed almost unnoticed.

Margarete von Falkensee was born in Potsdam in 1896 and was the daughter of a civil servant. After some experience in the theatre she worked in the film industry after 1924. Like many other writers, directors and performers, she emigrated to America when the Nazi Party took office. Her efforts to establish herself as a screen-writer in Hollywood met with only limited success, though her name can occasionally be seen in the credits of old black and white films. She died in a road accident in San Diego in 1948.

This English edition of *The Pleasure Garden* has been retitled *Blue Angel Nights* for reasons which may require some little explanation. Heinrich Mann's novel *Professor Unrat* was based on the same basic theme as Margarete von Falkensee's – sexual corruption as an image of the destruction of social values. It was filmed as *The Blue Angel* by Josef von Sternberg, with Marlene Dietrich as Lola and first shown in 1930. It treated the theme as tragedy, but Margarete von Falkensee treated it as vicious comedy. The new title for the English edition will, it is hoped, give it some of the flavour of those long-gone days and serve as an advertisement to the reader of what to expect.

It is not only the times that are long gone; the Berlin of this novel has also gone forever. Allied bombing reduced large parts of the city to rubble and Russian artillery and tanks destroyed much of the rest in 1945. Some of the sites in which the action of the novel takes place have vanished and some have been rebuilt; some lie on the far side of the Berlin Wall. Margarete von Falkensee's Berlin has disap-

7

peared from the earth as surely as ancient Babylon, but some of its spirit lives on in these pages.

Egon Haas,
Munich, 1985

The Birthday Party

On the morning after his twenty-third birthday party Manfred von Klausenberg woke with an aching head and a queasy stomach. The curtains were drawn and the room dim, for which he was grateful. He could hear the sound of quiet breathing beside him and there was a warm bare thigh over his waist. He slid out of bed cautiously, so as not to waken his partner, whoever she might be, and found that he was wearing only a sadly crumpled evening shirt and black silk socks. He stepped on an empty champagne bottle lying on its side on the floor and almost fell. The bottle skidded away under the bed, while Manfred stripped off his shirt and made his way to the bathroom.

Plenty of cold water on his face and the back of his neck helped to revive him a little. There was a bright red evening frock and one silk stocking draped over the side of the bath – the property of the woman asleep in his bed, he reasoned. He couldn't at that moment remember who she was. In fact, he couldn't remember going to bed at all. His head needed aspirin, but his stomach refused to accept it.

Naked but for his black socks, he padded round the apartment. The drawing-room was in semi-darkness and stank of tobacco smoke, stale drink and perfume. A man and a woman lay asleep in each other's arms on the zebra-skin sofa, the man without his trousers. *Poor Dieter, he never had much style*, Manfred thought, when he saw who the woman was. In an armchair two women slept together, Ulrika with her hand between the other woman's thighs. All the other guests seemed to have gone. The indications

9

were that the party had been a resounding success. About fifty friends had been invited and they had brought others with them so that it had been impossible to keep track of who was there – not that anyone tried. There had been a seemingly endless procession of pretty women and well-dressed men, talking, dancing and, above all, drinking.

He went back quietly to his bedroom for trousers, shoes and a thick ski-pullover and then out for a walk in the cold March sunshine to clear his head. He walked at random, trying not to be sick and hardly aware of his surroundings, his head throbbing unmercifully whenever a tram rattled past or a car hooted. Memories of the night before started to reassemble themselves, though chaotic and incomplete.

There had been a long and comic wrangle between Horst Lederer and Max Schroeder about Horst's style of painting. According to Max, it was outmoded, socially irrelevant and intellectually dangerous. Horst retaliated by insisting that the work of modern Expressionist artists was trash, the work of timid men who needed to distort reality before they could bear to look at it. Things livened up when Horst, as genially drunk as the rest of them, told his girl to show her backside to Max. Without demur she turned round, bent over and flipped up her frock to display a big fleshy bottom that was innocent of underwear. Horst patted it affectionately.

'There's reality for you,' he said, 'Rosa's backside. There's more life and truth in that than in all the rubbishy smears you pretend to admire.'

The little group of friends standing round to listen to the disagreement laughed. One of them prodded Max in the ribs and demanded to know how he answered that.

'Horst has a very *fundamental* view of art. He is the sole survivor of the peasant school of painting,' Max retorted.

'And I am proud to be so,' said Horst, 'it is the only school that will survive. Manfred – you're rich enough to buy pictures – what would you spend your money on – Rosa's backside or the degenerate daubs which Max promotes?'

10

'Give me Rosa any day! You have only to look about my walls to see that I never buy these modern problem-pictures to give myself bad dreams.'

Max threw up his hands in mock despair.

'I've looked at all your pictures, Manfred, and I am thoroughly depressed by your taste. Flat Prussian landscapes and family portraits! The plight of the intellectual has never been made plainer. We are trapped between the upper millstone of aristocratic ignorance and the lower millstone of bourgeois stupidity. Deep down in their hearts aristocrats and bourgeois are equally peasants.'

'I suppose that makes me a peasant too,' Rosa complained, her head still down near her knees.

'Yes,' said Max and Horst together.

'You can kiss my arse!' she replied, forgetting as she used the common expression what it was that she was showing.

Max and Horst grinned at each other and both bent over to plant a smacking kiss on the pink cheeks of Rosa's bottom, to the vast amusement and applause of the bystanders.

'As it is futile to discuss art with you, Horst,' said Max. 'Perhaps I may have the pleasure of discussing it with Fraulein Rosa.'

'By all means,' said Horst with a sly grin, 'if you kiss her backside enough times you'll come round to my way of thinking.'

There was another curious argument later on with Werner Schiele, which did not have so amusing an outcome. Werner was holding forth to two very pretty women in a corner by the piano.

'It is our moral duty to ourselves and to history to demolish this ugly city, this monument to militarism. We must destroy the Brandenburg Gate, the Royal Palace and all the relics of the shameful past.'

'I hope you'll leave the Opera,' said Manfred, 'I like that.'

Werner did not even pause for breath.

11

'When we have reduced to rubble these hideous monuments to barbarism, we shall build a new and modern city, shining and glorious, a symbol of the new Germany.'

'What sort of city, Werner?' one of the women asked.

'A wonderful city of glass and concrete. Walter Gropius is showing us the way to a new and magnificent expression of our national genius.'

'What about the Kranzler Cafe?' Manfred asked anxiously. 'There's no better place for a drink on the terrace while you watch the girls saunter past on a warm afternoon. I hope you're not going to knock that down.'

'You are a dinosaur!' said Werner fiercely, 'a fossil from a dead age. You will be swept away with the rubbish of the past.'

'What you overlook is that most Berliners like their city as it is. They won't thank you for knocking it down and building it in a different style.'

'The people are ignorant,' said Werner, 'they will be taught to respect the future instead of venerating the past.'

'He's mad,' said the woman who had spoken before, 'come away, Manfred, it might be infectious.'

'You are right,' said Manfred, taking her arm, 'against stupidity the Gods themselves struggle in vain.'

'Really? Who said that?'

'Schiller. Let me get you another drink.'

'You'll see!' Werner called after them, his tone angry.

Some time later, or perhaps it was earlier, for the sense of time was totally confused in Manfred's mind, he found himself perched on the arm of a chair in which two of his friends had become involved with each other. Nina was sitting on Konrad's lap, his hand was down the front of her low-cut evening frock and he was talking to her about politics.

'We lost our Emperor and became a Republic. But after ten years of this political comedy it must be obvious to everyone that we do not want democracy. It was forced upon us at bayonet-point by the Allies in 1918. The German spirit is not naturally democratic. What is democracy but the rule of the ignorant mob?'

'My husband would agree with you,' said Nina, 'but should you be doing this to me in front of him?'

'Manfred is not your husband. I know for certain that he is not married.'

'Not Manfred. That's my husband over there, dancing with the red-head.'

'The one with the monocle? Is he a jealous man?'

'I've never yet found out.'

'Manfred,' said Konrad, 'is this dear lady's husband a jealous person?'

Inside her frock his hand was moving slowly over Nina's breasts.

'I don't know either,' Manfred answered, 'he doesn't seem to object when Nina comes here to visit me. But then, she and I have known each other for many years and perhaps he thinks that we discuss books together. Do you tell him what we do together, Nina?'

'Idiot!'

'On the other hand,' Manfred continued, 'if you look closely at Gottfried von Behrendorf, my dear Konrad, you will notice that he has a duelling-scar on his cheek, from which we may deduce that he understands how to use a sabre. He also hunts wild boar whenever he gets the chance, so he is no stranger to fire-arms. Before you move your hand from Nina's charming breasts to an even more fascinating part of her delightful body, you have a difficult decision to make.'

'Nina, this is a matter we must talk about in private, away from this neutral fool,' Konrad declared.

The two of them got up and made their way between the dancers and out of the room.

'Poor Konrad,' said Manfred to no one in particular, 'Nina will drain him dry and then Gottfried will butcher him. Life is tragic sometimes.'

Then there was the American girl. Not that he knew she was an American at first; his attention was caught by the

13

way she was dressed. She wore a man's evening-suit, stiff collar, white tie, tails, the complete ensemble. Some of the smarter lesbians about town had been affecting this style since a well-known actress appeared on stage in it a year or two before. This girl, moving with great poise through the noisy party guests, was exceptionally beautiful. She had jet-black hair and an expression of disdain. Manfred bowed, kissed her hand and introduced himself, wondering who had brought her. They danced together and, though her German was fluent, her accent was foreign and he learned that she was from New York.

Manfred was as well-disposed towards Americans as most, and for good reason. American money had refloated German industry and stabilised the country. American bankers were very welcome in Berlin, especially if they had beautiful daughters. But how terrible, Manfred thought, that so wonderfully attractive a girl should be interested only in other girls. What a loss to men! What a loss to himself! *'Life is tragic sometimes'*, he repeated aloud.

She thought he was talking to her.

'Only if you laugh,' she answered mysteriously.

She drifted away from him after the dance. A girl dressed in shiny white satin rose from between two men on a sofa and flung herself into Manfred's arms, bursting into tears.

'Make them stop, Manfred! I can't stand it!'

'Good God, what are they doing to you?'

'Nothing. I've been sitting there with my skirt up to my belly-button for twenty minutes and neither of them has even looked at my legs. All they do is argue about books.'

'They're strange creatures, the intelligentsia. I'll save you from them.'

In his fuddled state he was not sure what to do next. Instinct propelled him towards the bedrooms, the tearful girl clinging to his arm. He pushed a door open a little and peered round it, wondering what he would find. The room was in darkness but there was enough light round the door to reveal two couples making use of the bed. Across the middle he could see a bare and hairy bottom pumping up

14

and down in full spate. At the bottom of the bed a pair of silk-stockinged legs pointed straight up in the air, their thighs clamped round the head of a man kneeling on the floor.

'I know those legs,' said Manfred, 'they're Nina's. In you go, my dear, someone will take care of you.'

He pushed her towards the bed, backed out and closed the door silently, feeling that he had done his duty as a host.

After walking for an hour in the streets, Manfred found that his headache was gone and his stomach settled. He was in Friedrichstrasse, surrounded by window-shoppers. The other side of the street looked less crowded and he dodged across two lanes of cars and took refuge on a central island. Eventually he reached the other side and kept going until he came to the railway station.

A small comic scene was being enacted there. Two men were collecting money outside the station for their political movements. One wore the brown military uniform, the jack-boots and swastika armband of the National Socialist Party. The other wore a shabby overcoat and a workman's cloth cap and held a placard on which was lettered *RED FRONT*. Both were shaking their collecting-boxes aggressively at passers-by. They stood about five metres apart and ignored each other ostentatiously.

Manfred was hungry. He walked past the collectors, giving each of them the same glare of disapproval, and went into the station restaurant. It was warm and comfortable after the chill of the streets and smelt pleasantly of food. After pig's knuckles and sauerkraut and a glass or two of cold beer he felt much better and decided to take a taxi home.

It was well after midday when he let himself into his apartment. The married couple who looked after him and cooked and cleaned had done their work well. The rooms had been aired out, the mess removed and the furniture put back into place. Frau Geiger was in the kitchen, washing up glasses and plates.

'Good day, Herr Manfred. Did you enjoy your party?'

'It was very good. I've been out for some fresh air. No problems?'

'Nothing serious. We waited till ten o'clock, as you said, before we came in to clear up. There were two people asleep on the sofa in the drawing-room and I made coffee for them before they went. My husband found a young lady in the dining-room, asleep under the table, and put her in a taxi. He lent her one of your overcoats.'

'Why was that?'

'She was stark naked and we couldn't find her clothes anywhere.'

'Was she pretty?'

'If you like thin redheads. My husband couldn't keep his eyes off her. She said her name was Schwabe and that she'd send your coat back.'

'Yes, I know her. Where's your husband now?'

'Getting rid of the empty bottles. Will you dine in this evening, Herr Manfred?'

'I don't know yet. I'm going to shave and have a long soak in the bath.'

The telephone calls began about three that afternoon. The first caller was Nina von Behrendorf to thank him for a marvellous party and to congratulate him.

'I'm glad you enjoyed the party, Nina. I noticed that you and Konrad continued the political discussion in my bedroom. Evidently he has a persuasive tongue. But why the congratulations? My birthday was yesterday.'

'Congratulations on your engagement, darling, what else.'

'Engagement? What do you mean?'

'I'm sure you'll be blissfully happy together, just like Gottfried and me. Must rush now. Auf wiedersehen.'

She hasn't sobered up yet, Manfred thought. Engagement indeed! But in the next hour more friends telephoned to offer their congratulations and he became completely bewildered. He telephoned Wolfgang, whom he trusted, to find out what was going on, but there was no answer. Eventually he managed to extract some sense from Konrad.

'You mean you don't remember?' said Konrad in open disbelief. 'You couldn't have been that drunk. You've got cold feet and want to call it off.'

'Konrad – who am I supposed to be engaged to?'

'Mitzi, of course, you made a big enough scene of the announcement.'

'But I don't know anyone called Mitzi.'

'As you wish. But it's a damned strange way to behave. The girl will be broken-hearted by such callousness.'

'But who is she?'

'I don't know. I'd never seen her before last night. But she is very pretty.'

'Who brought her to the party – do you know that much?'

'No idea. I was a bit drunk and didn't take everything in.'

'You managed to take Nina in – or part of her, at least.'

'Whatever passed between her and me was in private. Your performance was both public and vulgar.'

'What do you mean?'

Konrad chuckled.

'No one will forget that engagement in a hurry. After all, you stripped your fiancée naked in front of us all and danced a tango with her.'

'Oh my God!'

'Then you dragged her off to the bedroom and that was the last we saw of you. Didn't she remind you of all this when you woke up together this morning?'

'There has been a dreadful mistake, Konrad. I must speak to this young lady at once. Do you know where I can find her?'

'She's your fiancée, not mine.'

'But did you see her with anyone last night who might know her?'

'I hardly noticed her before you played your big scene. I was too busy with Nina. After you'd paraded her naked round the room everyone wanted to talk to her – but you

17

rushed her off to bed. Wait a minute, though, I think I saw her in the dining-room earlier on having something to eat with Werner. But I wouldn't swear to it.'

Manfred cut him off with a brief 'thank-you' and telephoned Werner Schiele.

'Werner – do you know a girl called Mitzi?'

'That's good, coming from you! I've half a mind to come round there and punch your thick head. Of all the cheap stunts to get her away from me!'

'Werner, there's been a misunderstanding. We can punch each other some other time. Just give me her telephone number.'

'Were you too ashamed to ask her this morning? My God, when I think what you put that poor girl through – you ought to be flogged in public!'

'We can go into that later. Just give me the number.'

'She's not on the telephone.'

'Then where does she live?'

'You couldn't be bothered to take her home? You'll tell me next you forgot to ask her name. What a cheap and rotten trick to get a girl into bed!'

'Everything will be explained eventually. What is her name and address? I must talk to her at once.'

In tones of high indignation Werner at last gave him what he wanted. Manfred consulted a street-guide and drove himself to the address. It was in a far from fashionable part of Berlin, a grey and shabby apartment building in an unknown street of grey and shabby buildings. The caretaker informed him that Fraulein Genscher lived on the first floor. In fact, when Manfred walked up the unswept stairs, he found that she had a room in a large old apartment. A landlady in a worn and shiny black frock opened the door and showed him the room he wanted, knocked for him and ushered him in.

It was a fair-sized room, but filled with heavy old-fashioned furniture and a divan-bed half-hidden beyond a wardrobe. Three young women sat at a table, drinking coffee and eating little cakes. They looked up at Manfred's entrance, smiled, and the middle one came quickly across the thin carpet to throw her arms about him and kiss him on both cheeks.

'Darling! I didn't expect you until later. I was telling my friends about the wonderful news. Come and meet them. You already know Rosa Vogel – and this is Ilse Kleiber.'

Manfred bowed over their hands. He remembered Rosa as the plump and jolly model who had been with Horst at the party. She was pretty, in a fleshy way, and so was the other woman, Ilse. Mitzi herself was easily the best-looking of the three, a tall, yellow-haired beauty in her early twenties, with a round, doll-like face and a complexion like fine porcelain.

'Let me present my fiancé,' she said in breathless pride, 'Herr Manfred von Klausenberg.'

'Ladies,' said Manfred, bowing again.

Mitzi took his hat and overcoat and asked him to sit down.

'He is so handsome,' said Rosa, 'isn't he, Ilse?'

'So distinguished,' said Ilse, a tinge of envy in her voice.

'And so rich,' Rosa added, 'you should see his apartment!'

Manfred was out of his depth. He took the cup of coffee he was offered and sat in silence, trying to look pleasant.

'Mitzi has been telling us all about the party,' said Ilse, 'it is like a fairy-tale come true.'

'The guests were so elegant,' said Mitzi, 'I was in my old red frock that I've had since before Christmas. I felt terribly out of place, as you can imagine. Then, out of the blue, Manfred took me in his arms and said the most charming things to me.'

'So romantic,' Ilse sighed, 'and you were there to see it, Rosa.'

'What made it even more romantic,' said Rosa, 'was something very common that happened earlier on. That mad Horst made me show the whole company my backside and kissed it. And one of his friends!'

That was something which Manfred definitely remembered from the chaos of the night before.

'I think it must have been that which gave Herr Manfred the idea for what he did later on,' Rosa continued. 'Of course, being a gentleman, what he did wasn't common at all.'

'Tell me,' said Ilse breathlessly.

Mitzi took up the tale.

'His strong arms held me and I trembled like a little girl. I looked into his handsome face and it was like a dream. Then it happened, the most wonderful moment of my life.'

'What happened?' Ilse asked quickly.

'He called for silence in a great ringing voice and announced to all his friends that he had fallen passionately in love with me.'

'Fantastic!' said Ilse.

'He took this ring from his finger and put it on mine as a token of love until he could buy me the biggest diamond in Berlin.'

She held out her hand. With a sinking heart Manfred recognised his heavy gold signet ring, engraved with the family coat of arms. Until that moment he had not missed it.

'Ah, and then came the best part of all,' said Rosa, 'the dance!'

'The dance,' said Mitzi, 'even now I can hardly believe it happened.'

'He made her strip off,' Rosa said solemnly, 'every stitch! They danced a tango with all of us looking on. You should have seen the men staring at Mitzi. Their eyes were sticking out on stalks. You could hear trouser-buttons popping right round the room.'

'Rosa!' said Mitzi in reproof. 'You make it sound like a cheap cabaret act. It was supremely romantic. I felt like a goddess floating in the arms of some great hero of old. Love had transformed us and put us beyond shame or modesty at that moment. We were in love – and we were divine!'

20

She smiled lovingly at Manfred, who sat appalled at these revelations.

'I could refuse you nothing,' she told him proudly, 'you swept me into your bedroom and showered me with kisses.'

'And the rest,' said Rosa.

'Fiancés have their rights,' said Ilse, her face pink with emotion.

'Mitzi, I must talk to you alone,' said Manfred awkwardly, 'if these ladies will graciously permit?'

'Come on, Ilse,' Rosa said at once, 'these two have private matters to discuss.'

'Yes, you must leave now,' Mitzi agreed, her pale blue eyes aglow, 'my fiancé wants to be alone with me.'

'And we can guess why,' said Rosa with a giggle.

Manfred stood up and bowed as Mitzi's friends left. He had no idea of how to extricate himself from the predicament in which he found himself without being brutally discourteous. He must have been insane last night!

He was still on his feet when Mitzi closed the door and came back to him. To his amazement she flung herself at his feet, wound her arms round his thighs and pressed her face to his belly.

'Darling! I am so pleased you are here. I have been longing to see you all day.'

'The thing is,' he began uncertainly, 'you and I have something of importance to sort out between us.'

'So many things,' she agreed, 'so many arrangements to make for the wedding. But first . . .'

Her fingers were busy with his trouser-buttons and before he had time to say more, her hand was into the slit of his underpants and held his dangler.

'I think I must be going mad!' he exclaimed piteously.

'Yes, mad with passion, like last night,' she said, her warm hand fondling what it held, 'three times you drove me to the madness of ecstasy before you let me sleep.'

'Three times – did I really?'

'You were magnificent. When I woke up this morning

21

in your bed I felt that I was already a bride on her honeymoon. But I was alone. Where were you, my darling?'

'I needed air. I went for a walk.'

'Do you want another walk now? Or do you want something else?' she teased him.

Manfred's stem stuck out of his trousers like a steel rod. He took Mitzi under the arms and raised her to her feet. She was tall, nearly as tall as he was, and strongly built. He snatched at her dove-grey frock and pulled it over her head. Her satin slip went the same way, flung across the room, and she was naked except for her stockings. In Manfred's circle the smart young women had given up wearing underclothes years before and it came as no surprise to find Mitzi without, even though she was very obviously from a different social level.

'Ah,' he said in appreciation.

Her body was strong and well-proportioned, very pleasing to the eye. And also to the hand, he confirmed, as he ran his palms over her weighty breasts and down over the very smooth skin of her sides and hips. He looked into her eyes and saw an expression of eagerness.

'Mitzi . . .' he began, and stopped.

He wanted to explain that what had happened at the party was no more than a drunken frolic, for which he now felt ashamed and apologetic. He also wanted to make love to her now that the delights of her naked body were open to him. Desire struggled with shame and he wavered.

'Manfred, I am yours,' she whispered, 'do what you like with me.'

His mind urged him to stop before he became involved deeper in an absurd misunderstanding, but the part of him sticking out impudently lower down insisted that he should go on.

'You were not so hesitant last night,' Mitzi told him, 'did you over-exert yourself? Can't you do it again yet?'

'Three times you said?'

'If you can't decide, I will!'

She whirled away from him, very light on her feet for a

large woman, and seated herself on a low stool upholstered in faded red plush. Her feet were together, the heels of her white shoes touching, and her knees wide apart. The hair between her legs was almost the same yellow colour as the hair on her head. Manfred regarded it in silence, admiring its aesthetic appeal.

'It's yours to do as you please with,' she said, and ran her middle finger up between the pink-brown lips to open them.

'Dear God!' Manfred breathed and threw himself to his knees, though not in prayer.

Mitzi's feet moved apart, her hand reached for his stiffness and tugged him towards her, he shuffling on his knees until she had him at the right spot. He held her by the thighs, up above her gartered stockings, and pushed slowly into her. His eyes were on her round doll-face, enjoying her expression of simple adoration.

'So big and strong!' she murmured, 'I can feel you right up inside me.'

Her legs were round the small of his back and her arms about his neck. To maintain her precarious balance on the stool Manfred put his arms round her waist and supported her. He bestirred himself with slow deliberation.

This was not a pleasure to hurry through, he thought. Explanations could come later and, when they did, that would be the end of it, with hard words and tears. But until then, this marvellous life-size blonde doll was his to enjoy.

Her responses were keener than his own, he shortly discovered. His stately stroke was not long established before her legs tightened round him like a vice, her body shook in his arms and she gasped out 'Oh, oh, oh!' Manfred maintained his rhythm unbroken. He could not recall when he had last enjoyed making love so consciously as now and it was far too good to spoil. Before long Mitzi cried out again in another crisis and half-choked him by the grip of her arms round his neck.

He felt the heat of her body right through his clothes.

23

The part of him inside her experienced her warmth and softness even more directly and revelled in it, like a king in his castle. The moment came when Manfred could restrain himself no longer. His steady thrusting became a frenzy of short strokes and he poured his passionate offering into her. Through his own ecstasy he heard her gasping and moaning.

'Darling,' she said when she could speak rationally again, 'do you truly love me? I want to hear you say it.'

The horrible moment had arrived and could be evaded no longer. Manfred held her closely to him, to restrain any violent reaction to his words and, still embedded in her wonderful body, made his confession.

'There has been a most unfortunate misunderstanding, Mitzi. The fact is that I was too drunk last night to know what I was doing. I must apologise to you for the distress I have caused by my regrettable behaviour. It is not possible for us to be engaged.'

'What?' she exclaimed shrilly. 'You take advantage of my good nature and then tell me you were drunk when you asked me to marry you? I've never been so insulted in my life – never! Don't think you can slide out of it that easily – I've got witnesses.'

'I don't doubt it. But what did they witness?' Manfred asked reasonably. 'A drunken frolic at a party, that's all. And perhaps the witnesses were drunk too. Listen to me, Mitzi, I think that everyone was confused about what happened last night. You're a very nice person but I don't love you and not for one moment do I believe that you love me. Would it not be more sensible to let the matter end like that, with a suitable present from me to you as a token of respect?'

'Am I a whore to take money for letting you make love to me!' she said in outrage.

'Certainly not. I would not insult you by offering money after the tender exchange that has just taken place between us. What I had in mind was a fur coat.'

To his surprise she began to laugh. She laughed so hard

24

that his now limp affair was ejected from its warm hiding-place by the constriction of her muscles. He felt it safe to let go of her now that her rage had subsided and sat back on his heels, still fascinated by her big naked body.

'A fur coat,' she said cheerfully, 'I like that very much. Though to be fair to you, it seems a lot for one quick go.'

'And the three times last night, of course.'

'Last night you were so drunk when they carried you to bed that you were past it,' she informed him, 'I tried to rouse you but you were dead to the world.'

Manfred grinned at her. She was a good-natured woman, as he had thought.

'It's too late to go shopping today,' he said, 'I will call for you tomorrow morning at eleven, if that is convenient.'

'You really mean it, don't you?' Mitzi said, half-surprised.

'You have my word. And I would like you to return my signet ring when I come for you tomorrow.'

'Take it now – I trust you.'

'Thank you,' and he accepted it from her and slipped it back on to his little finger.

Mitzi sat up straight on the stool, knees together, and looked at him seriously.

'There is one thing,' she said.

'And what is that?'

'Until I am wearing the fur coat you promised I have every right to regard you as my fiancé.'

'If you choose,' he answered, wondering what she intended.

'Fiancés have privileges. You heard my friend say so.'

Manfred stared at her big and beautiful breasts.

'Fraulein Ilse was correct,' he said, 'since our engagement will be a very short one, I ought to make full use of my rights while I have them.'

'It would be a pity not to,' Mitzi agreed.

She rose from her stool, offered him her hand to rise and led him to the divan-bed by the wall.

★ ★ ★

25

Punctually at eleven the next day Manfred called for her in his impressive maroon-coloured Mercedes tourer and took her shopping along the Kurfurstendamm. Her pleasure in being taken seriously in expensive shops was so engaging that Manfred let her indulge it to the full. He sat quietly smoking cigarettes in shop after shop while assistants brought coats for Mitzi to look at and try on. It occurred to him eventually that he had never in his life given any woman so much pleasure as Mitzi was experiencing in trying on coats and staring at herself in long mirrors and twirling round in front of him to let him see the effect and give his opinion.

Eventually she chose a red fox coat, magnificent in appearance, which set off her blonde colouring admirably. Her old cloth coat with the rabbit-skin collar was neatly folded and wrapped by a smirking shop-assistant who knew all about men buying fur coats for pretty young women. Manfred tucked the parcel under his arm, led Mitzi to his car and decided to take her for a light lunch to Kranzler's Cafe. He was in an extremely good mood and ordered champagne as soon as they were seated.

'A toast, Mitzi. A brief engagement but a happy one.'

'That's worth drinking to. If only all engagements could be like that!'

'Tell me what happened at my party. It's still a blank to me.'

'About two in the morning you were blind drunk. You danced with me and you were muttering to yourself. I couldn't make out what, but you were unhappy about a woman. I felt sorry for you – you were really suffering – so I tried to be nice to you. Then you decided that you were madly in love with me and told everybody. You didn't even know who I was and I don't suppose it made any difference, the state you were in.'

'Who had made me unhappy? Did I say?'

'No, but I guessed later. You asked me to undress and I was drunk enough to do it and we danced together. It was a sensation – your friends were clapping and shouting.

26

In the middle of the dance you passed out and half a dozen of the men put you to bed. After that they put their heads together, a few of them, and dreamed up this story. You were supposed to wake up with me in bed and find out that we were engaged. Then they'd confirm the story. Only it nearly went wrong when you got up and vanished while I was still asleep. So they did it the other way round by telephoning you and letting you come to find me. Understand?'

'My God – they really put one over on me. All of them who telephoned me were in on it – Konrad, Nina, Werner – and Rosa, of course. Whose idea was it?'

'The lady.'

'Nina von Behrendorf, you mean?'

'She was hanging on to that Konrad and she wanted to get at you. And she was the one you were unhappy about, I think, when we were dancing. Something went wrong between you, that was obvious.'

'Nina and I were in love for a long time, but she married that idiot Gottfried. It was my fault, I suppose. We were happy as we were and I saw no reason to change things by getting married. So she married him to spite me. Then at the party Konrad was making up to her and I didn't take her away from him, which is what she wanted. I let them go off to the bedroom together.'

'Why? If you love her and she loves you, why are you trying to hurt each other? It doesn't make sense. She marries another man to hurt you and then you let somebody else drag her off to bed when you want her yourself, so that you can hurt her. It's too complicated for me. Are you sure you were in love with her?'

'To distraction! We had wonderful times together and we did marvellous and crazy things. The winter before last, we were skating one afternoon on the little pond in the Tiergarten. It was just getting dark and there was hardly anyone about. Shall I tell you what Nina did? She stripped off and skated naked to please me. She was so beautiful in just her tall fur hat. Her body was the colour of mother-

27

of-pearl – my heart was beating so fast that I had to stand still and watch her. Then a nurse-maid came by with three children and the woman shouted to the children to come away at once, as if the sight of so much beauty would harm them! And an old man with a big moustache rushed out on the ice waving a walking-stick at Nina, and he slipped and went sliding across the pond on his backside. His indignation was incredibly comical – I was aching with laughter. Nina skated a circle round him as he sat there croaking at her. Then she came to me and kissed me and I wanted to throw her down on the snow and grass and make love to her.'

Mitzi smiled and reached across the table to stroke his hand.

'You should have married her, Manfred.'

'Maybe. What about you, though – Werner brought you to the party but he didn't mind having you go to bed with me as part of the joke.'

'He'd had enough of me. I knew that before he did. There was only one thing he wanted from me, and he didn't want that for long. He told me that you were soft-hearted enough to see me right if I made you believe the story they cooked up about being engaged.'

'Something must be done about Werner,' said Manfred. 'He meant that I'm soft in the head, not the heart. And the coat you're wearing is proof of that.'

'Look,' said Mitzi, 'it was only a joke for me. I didn't know about the ill-feeling or I'd never have agreed to it. Take the coat back to the shop and get your money back. I don't want it now I know how I was used.'

'No, you keep it, Mitzi. I like you and you've been honest with me. Besides, it suits you and every woman should have a fur-coat.'

'If we're talking about honesty, there's something you don't know about me.'

'I'm sure there are many things I don't know about you. But it's not important and you don't have to tell me.'

'You've been straight with me and I want to be the same

28

with you. You see, even if you'd fallen for the joke and really believed that we were engaged, it wouldn't have meant anything. I'm married already.'

'But you don't wear a ring.'

'I pawned it ages ago. My husband is in prison, the dirty pig.'

'What did he do?'

'He's a cheap swindler. They caught him selling dud insurance policies to old women. He went inside and left me penniless. That was two years ago and I was twenty.'

'How have you survived since then?'

'As best I can. Once or twice I've found a job for a few months, but I'm not really any good at anything and sooner or later the boss starts feeling my backside, so I move on. Most of the time I find a nice young man who wants to pay the rent and take me out. I'm not a whore, you know, but there is one thing I'm good at.'

'Have there been many before Werner?' Manfred asked sympathetically.

'Five or six since I've been on my own. This will make you laugh – the first one was my husband's brother. He couldn't wait to get his hands on me. That was all right – I liked him – but his wife found out that he was keeping me and that was that. I thought my troubles were over with Werner. I mean, he's got plenty of money and lives the way he wants to. It's all parties and dancing and nice restaurants. He took care of the rent, but he was too mean to buy me any clothes, except now and then.'

'What will you do now?'

Mitzi winked at him across the table.

'Someone else is interested in me,' she said happily. 'He's been after me since he saw me strip off at your party. He's biding his time till the engagement joke is over. That's now, I suppose.'

'So it is, dear Mitzi. And while my best friends may be laughing at me behind my back, the truth is that I've enjoyed the joke more than they have.'

'Have you?'

She stared at him, her pale blue eyes shining with amusement, a little grin on her doll's face.

'Oh yes – the thing that you are good at, as you put it, you are very good at. Shall I tell you what I'd like to do this afternoon?'

'Go on, then.'

'I'd like to take you back to your room and take all your clothes off and kiss you from head to toe.'

'We're not engaged now, you know,' she said, her grin getting wider.

'Then I'd ask you to put your new fur-coat on, so that the silk lining is against your naked body, and the fur against my naked body, and then I'd roll you around on your bed until we both go nearly crazy with sensation and I'd open the coat and throw myself on top of you and make love to you like a madman, time after time. What do you think of that?'

'Why are we sitting here talking?' Mitzi asked, 'Let's go!'

Backstage at the Theatre

To celebrate the successful first night of Oskar Branden-stein's new comedy *Three in a Bed* there was the usual glittering party back-stage. Oskar, a burly man in his mid-forties played the impressario most convincingly, accepted congratulations with an air of world-weary politeness and told everyone about the even more sensational new comedy he intended to put on in the autumn. Actresses and actors flitted about, kissing each other repeatedly, and assuring each other that their performances had been marvellous. Oskar's backers and the other non-theatrical guests drank champagne and tried to look important.

In this heady atmosphere of euphoria and bright promise, Manfred von Klausenberg circulated happily. He told everyone who would listen that Oskar would soon displace Max Reinhardt as the leading figure in the theatre. Everyone agreed enthusiastically, especially Oskar himself, who clasped Manfred's hand in both of his own and almost shed tears of joy. The only person who did not agree was the young American lady who had appeared at Manfred's birthday party.

'Oskar has talent,' she informed Manfred, 'he would do well on Broadway. But Reinhardt has genius. There is a difference.'

Her name was Jenny Montrose, Manfred ascertained, for he couldn't recall asking her name the first time he met her. She was more conventionally dressed for Oskar's party, in an elegant frock of cerise taffeta that left her arms and shoulders and much of her bosom bare.

'I don't see your fiancée,' she said brightly, 'Isn't she here?'

'I have no fiancée, Miss Montrose. That was a silly joke by some of my friends.'

'But it was you who ripped the girl's clothes off and danced with her.'

'That was a different sort of joke,' he said uneasily.

'What a strange sense of humour you Germans have.'

Her companion was the star of Oskar's play, Hugo Klostermann, a handsome matinée idol over whom young girls and middle-aged matrons had been swooning for years. The story told about him, as Manfred knew well, was that unless he made love at least every four hours he developed a raging head-ache. Perhaps it was no more than a publicity story, but in theatrical circles it was open gossip that he invariably had a woman visit him in his dressing-room half an hour before the curtain went up. If none of his countless girl-friends turned up to oblige, the female members of the cast took the duty in rotation.

Manfred saw that his first impressions of Miss Montrose must be revised. The male evening dress she had worn at his party could have been no more than affectation, for she and Klostermann were clearly on the best of terms. It was to be seen in the way he touched her arm as he talked and the way she smiled at him. Her taste was for men, after all, and with the actor that taste was surely being indulged to the full.

Manfred had been brought to the back-stage party by an actress who played a minor role in *Three in a Bed* and who had of late been playing a leading role in Manfred's own bed. But sometime after midnight, when large amounts of champagne had been consumed, the allegiances of many of those present began to shift. It dawned upon Manfred that Anna had deserted him. She was sitting on Oskar's lap, stroking his bald patch and evidently auditioning for her next role. Manfred shrugged and grinned. He wished her well in her career now that he had, when all was said, fairly well exhausted her repertoire.

So it was that he cultivated the acquaintance of another of Oskar's minor players, Magda Nebel. She was in conversation with a fat old man who looked like a financier and probably was. It proved easy enough to detach her from him, so easy in fact that Manfred concluded that she had been instructed by Oskar to be nice to the money-man and had no relish for the task.

She was about twenty-five, dark-haired, and wore a short evening frock of bright green with little tassels round the hem. Her hair was cut dramatically short and brushed back from her forehead and ears, but her most striking feature was her sulky mouth. Manfred found her charming. As simple logic indicated that Anna was not likely to accompany him home that night, being too deeply engrossed with Oskar and her future on the stage, he applied himself to making a good impression on Magda. He was flattered to find that she already knew who he was and pleased to observe that she gave every sign of being well-disposed towards him. When the party began to lose its interest for both of them, Magda accepted his offer to drive her home. Even better, when they got there she invited him in for a drink.

Her apartment was not large, but modern in its furnishings and colours. Manfred settled himself in a square arm-chair upholstered in oyster-satin, a glass of brandy in his hand, while Magda left him for a few minutes. He was well content. More than that, he anticipated a rewarding night, which might perhaps prove to be the start of an interesting new friendship.

His heart bounded when Magda returned. She had changed into a short négligé of white lace and, from the glimpses of pink flesh it afforded through its open pattern, she was obviously naked inside it. In addition to his heart, another part of him bounded when she took a chair opposite him and tucked her bare legs under her.

'I suppose you think I brought you here to make love to me,' she said casually.

33

'Dear Magda, no such presumptuous thought entered my head.'

Her thighs were very smooth where the short négligé parted a little to reveal them. She stared at him thoughtfully.

'Why not? Don't you find me attractive?'

'Of course I do! You have a dark and sultry beauty which I find irresistible.'

'Is that so? You seem to be resisting very well.'

The hint was clear enough. Manfred moved across to the arm of her chair and kissed her. Her mouth was passive, even when he slipped a hand down her négligé to cup a soft breast.

'It takes a lot more than that to get me started,' she told him, 'and when I do – look out! There aren't many men who can cope with me.'

'I've never yet met a woman I couldn't please. Nor one I couldn't arouse.'

Her fingers touched his trousers to ascertain his condition and then pinched hard through the cloth.

'Men know nothing about women,' she observed, 'they think that if they grope about for five minutes any woman will open her legs and beg them to stick it in her.'

She sounded almost angry and there was no point in arguing with her. Although Manfred was still fondling her breast with an expert touch, its bud remained soft and unresponsive to his attentions.

'There is a mystery here to be solved,' he said, 'you have a secret which I cannot even guess at. Yet I feel that if you were to allow me to share your secret, the experience would be exceptionally enjoyable for both of us.'

'It might be more than you bargained for.'

'That makes me even more interested.'

'Don't say that I didn't warn you. Come with me.'

She led him into her bed-room. It was square, white-walled and had a low divan-bed. The only note of colour in the room was a dark wolf-pelt spread over the bed itself. Without a word she removed her lace négligé and stood, hands on hips, for Manfred to look at. Her expression was beyond him to define, part defiant, part sulky, and part something for which no adequate word occurred to him just then. It was easier to stare at her heavy breasts, her narrow belly and the small triangle of curls between her thighs. These features at least presented no complications and required no elaborate interpretation.

'You are superb,' he praised her, 'provocative and dangerous!'

Magda cupped her breasts in her long-fingered hands and pushed them upwards. The reddish-brown halos around her buds were larger than on most women and contrasted sharply with her clear skin tones.

'The other girls at the theatre say they are too big for the style today,' she remarked, 'do you think they're too big?'

'Not at all. I like women who look like women and not like boys. I think your breasts are luscious, Magda. Let me see your bottom too.'

She turned about to display a pair of round cheeks, well-proportioned and very appetising.

'Are you sure you don't prefer boys?' she asked. 'Is my bottom good enough for you?'

'Perfection!'

Before he had time to give her bottom a fond squeeze, she walked across to a white-painted wardrobe, opened it and rummaged inside. When she turned back towards him she held a coil of crimson cord, of the kind used for bell-pulls in old-fashioned houses.

'There!' she said almost fiercely. 'My secret. Do you understand it?'

Manfred's imagination raced as he stared at the coil. This was a new bedroom game for him. He nodded, words failing him, and Magda held the coil out to him.

'Prove it,' she said sharply, 'what kind of man stands dumb-struck with a naked woman and does nothing about it?'

He seized the heavy coil with enthusiasm, weighed it in his hands, found one end of the cord and tested it. It was smooth and supple and probably almost unbreakable. Before Magda could taunt him again he spun her away from him, pulled her arms behind her back and tied her wrists together.

'NO!' she cried out when her wrists were securely bound, 'Let me go!'

He had no experience of tying up naked women, but the idea had a certain appeal. Improvising as he went, he looped the crimson cord from her wrists over one shoulder, under one breast and back over the other shoulder. Interest and ingenuity made up for lack of experience and in a minute or two he had Magda on her knees on the fluffy white rug, the cord between her legs and pulled tight, her ankles bound and a length of cord round her waist and cutting into her belly. Through it all she struggled and complained and, when he stepped back to view his handiwork, she said with every appearance of anger that unless he released her at once she would scream for the police.

Manfred smiled and flicked the silk handkerchief from his breast-pocket to gag her.

'Scream all you like. No one will hear you except me.'

The criss-cross of the crimson cord over her pale flesh was very exciting to see, as was the way in which she squirmed against her bonds. Manfred sat on the rug and felt her trussed breasts to his heart's content and Magda made hoarse noises through the silken gag. Her buds were standing very hard now and had flushed a darker red. On a sudden inspiration he gripped her by the shoulders and put his mouth to the nearest breast to suck at the swollen tip.

'So, it seems that I have succeeded in getting you going, dear Magda. As for satisfying you, I see no problem there.'

He rolled her on to her back, the bonds keeping her knees up towards her belly, and examined her between the thighs with feverish intensity. Under the dark curls the lips had been forced apart by the cord between her legs. He moved the cord sideways into her groin and forced his middle finger inside her to tickle her pink nub. It was very slippery and it needed only a little stimulation to set her belly twitching.

The game had aroused Manfred as much as it had her. He rolled her over on to her knees as if she were a big parcel, her face down on the rug and her bottom in the air. It was the work of a moment to kneel behind her and open his trousers.

'Now comes the moment you dread, Magda! You are about to be savagely raped and you are helpless to move or to beg for mercy. What a nightmare of torment for you!'

He pressed the ball of his thumb against the little knot of muscle between the cheeks of her behind and his finger into the lips lower down.

'Two warm little holes,' he teased her. 'Which one of them is to be violated? Something hard and brutal will force itself into one or the other. Do I prefer boys or girls, you asked me. This is when you will find out.'

He heard her gurgle through the gag as he touched the tip of his swollen stem to the tight little entrance in her bottom, let her tremble in fear for some moments, pretending to be pushing into it. Then with his thumbs he pried open the proper entrance and slid in quickly.

'You are relieved that I prefer girls,' he gasped, 'But your relief is only temporary. I am going to treat you viciously.'

With his hands on her hips to steady himself, he plunged briskly in and out. It was no time for tenderness – Magda had shown that rough handling excited her. He intended to give her enough of it to satisfy her.

She had left the wardrobe open and it had a long mirror on the inside of the door. Manfred could see his own reflection and could hardly believe what he was seeing. He was still in his elegant evening clothes, black bow-tie perfectly in place and a white carnation in his button-hole. Magda's bare rump, on which he was mounted, was in full sight, but her head, down on the rug, was out of sight in the mirror. Manfred grinned at the image of his own face and the image grinned back, red with excitement and exertion. So bizarre a view of himself spurred him on to harder endeavours, which brought louder gurglings from Magda and an explosion in his own belly that flung an ecstatic stream into her. He pounded away until at last the pleasure faded and left him panting for breath.

When he was calm again he released Magda from her bonds and lifted her on to the bed. Her skin was marked where the cords had constricted it.

'Brandy?' he asked.

She nodded, her eyes closed and her legs still trembling. He fetched the bottle and glasses from the sitting-room, exhilarated by the grotesque game in which he had taken part. On his return he found her sitting cross-legged on the wolf-pelt, rubbing her breasts upwards.

'Do they hurt still?' he asked, pouring brandy for her.

'No, they feel good. I like stroking them. I do it all the time when I'm alone.'

Manfred sat on the bed, facing her, and poured brandy for himself. The night still had a long way to run.

'Did I do it right?' he asked.

'You're a fast learner, if that was the first time.'

'It was the first time I've tied a woman up.'

'Did you like it?'

He raised his glass to her in salutation.

'It was fantastic.'

Magda emptied her glass and put it down. Her hand went between her legs to pluck at the dark curls there.

'Now you know what it takes to get me started. But you still don't know what it takes to finish me off.'

'I think I can guess.'

'You think you're clever, don't you? But you may be in for a surprise.'

Manfred was fascinated by the way in which she was stroking the dark-haired lips between her thighs. She saw the direction of his glance and grinned wickedly.

'Do you like my Fotze?' she asked him.

'It's a beauty – and very hospitable.'

'Then you have no objection if it welcomes you again?'

'Far from it – I shall insist on another visit when I've finished my brandy.'

'Finish it then. I'll show you a different game to keep your interest up. It wouldn't do for your attention to slacken halfway through. Why don't you take your clothes off?'

Manfred stood up to undress. He had guessed that Magda would want to reverse roles and bind him this time. The prospect was amusing and strange enough to be exciting.

'Kneel on the floor and let me tie your hands,' she said when he was naked.

She bound his wrists behind his back with the skill of long practise. She did not truss his body, as he expected, but linked his wrists to one ankle. And that, he realised, was all that was needed to make him helpless, for he was unable to get to his feet or free himself. Magda stood back to stare at him, her head tilted to one side and her hand still caressing between her legs.

'Good,' she said, 'now for the surprise.'

He watched with keen interest as she went to the open wardrobe and bent over to reach into the bottom of it. Her rump was thrust towards him and, between her spread thighs, he could see the dark-curled mound he had ravaged. Its long pink slit was agape and the impression the sight made on him was so lubricious that his limp stem stirred again. His interest turned to surprise, as Magda had promised, when he saw her pull on black knee-length riding-boots. Surprise became astonishment when she buckled round her narrow waist a black leather belt, complete with pistol-holster on one hip. And finally, astonishment was overwhelmed by incredulity when he saw her put on a military helmet with a badge on the front and a spike on the top.

Attired in this incongruous manner, she posed before him, a long and thin riding-crop in one hand. She stood arrogantly, legs apart, head back and her fists on her hips, glaring down at him.

'Now, you swine – it's time you found out what happens

to scum like you! Straighten your back! Stop drooping like a bag of rubbish!'

Her voice was harsh, her expression cold. Manfred knelt up straight, intrigued by her change of personality and wondering how this version of the game was played.

'Look at you!' she said, 'good for nothing! What use are you to a woman with a shrivelled little thing like that?'

'You found it useful enough a little while ago.'

'Silence!'

She reached down to prod him between the legs with the end of her riding-crop, none too gently.

'As much use as a punctured balloon.'

'It's resting,' Manfred told her, 'like a boxer between rounds.'

'Boxer! That miserable thing couldn't punch its way through a paper bag. One quick sneeze and it's done for! I've seen better on six-year-old boys.'

She poked the end of her crop under his limp equipment and started to flick it upwards as she harangued him.

'Up with it! I'll have no laziness here. Do you think I brought you here to doze off?'

The rough jerking had its effect. Manfred's disabled limb began to grow strong again.

'About time too,' Magda commented brutally, 'I thought it had died of shock after its little performance.'

Manfred gazed down fondly at his growing stiffness. His pleasure was cut short by Magda flicking at it hard with her crop.

'That hurts!' he complained.

'Hurts! My God, what a weakling!'

She flicked repeatedly at his uprisen projection, cutting at it from each side in turn. Manfred twisted his body to escape the stinging little blows, but in the end the only way to protect himself was to bend forward, his head down on his knees. At once Magda changed tactics and flicked him across his upraised bottom.

'Kiss my boots,' she ordered, 'quick – or I'll really lay into you.'

She planted one jack-booted foot on his bent knee so that Manfred could kiss the shiny black leather.

'Now the other.'

She changed feet and he obeyed her meekly.

'Now you know who is in control here,' she said heavily.

Manfred raised his head slowly, his gaze travelling up her booted legs to her smooth thighs and at last to the dark triangle of curls where her legs joined. She resumed her former pose, feet apart, back straight and hands on hips.

'Yes, stare at my Fotze,' she said scornfully, 'that's all men ever think about – how to get their miserable length of gristle between a woman's legs. You're all the same! No sense of decency, no dignity, no higher emotions, no sensitivity, no culture! You've got nothing but a silly prong sticking out in front.'

Kneeling up straight again, Manfred found his face on the level of her groins. Magda moved closer, twined her fingers in his hair and pulled his face to within a hand's-breadth of her curly fleece.

'As you're only interested in what happens below the belly-button, now's your chance to get a good look. That's what you want, isn't it? Let me tell you something, you brainless rapist – what you see there between my legs is far too good for you.'

'You forget that I've tried it out already. It was nice but no more than that.'

'It's the most beautiful thing in the world,' she said furiously, 'kiss it!'

Her clenched fingers tightened painfully in his hair and he had no choice but to press his mouth to the warm lips between her straddled legs.

'That's all you're good for,' she said contemptuously, 'that's all any man is good for. Lick me!'

This new version of Magda's game had aroused Manfred sharply and the scent of her hot eroticism drove him further. He forced his tongue between the pouting lips and found her slippery nub.

41

'You swine!' she gasped. 'How dare you try to excite me like that!'

All the same, she kept his face clamped to her. Manfred's tongue flickered and in a surprisingly short time she screamed thinly and her legs shook until she almost fell.

'More, more!' she moaned, her finger-nails digging into his scalp.

Her orgasmic throes passed quickly and Manfred found his cheek pressed against her perspiring belly and the big metal buckle of her leather belt.

'So fast!' He murmured, proud of himself.

'Too fast,' she answered weakly, tremors still running through her belly, 'you spoiled my game with your clumsiness. You're going to pay for that.'

Manfred was thoroughly into the spirit of the game. He knew now that what excited her so quickly was not the physical stimulation alone but the sense of domination she experienced from having him at her mercy, bound and unable to escape from her. And perhaps not domination alone, but the contempt for her partner that sprang from it. He set out to provoke her.

'You talk of culture and higher emotions,' he said with a laugh, 'what higher emotions were you feeling when my tongue was in you? Was it a high aesthetic experience? Did it promote a philosophical insight?'

Magda pushed his head away from her belly and glared down at him. Her mouth was beautiful, he thought, sulky and dangerous.

'The philosophical insight was mine,' he continued, 'while you were squealing and shaking I remembered what the great Schopenhauer said about women. Shall I tell you?'

'What is it to me what some crazy old professor said?'

'He said that only a man whose mind is clouded by sexual desire would think that women are beautiful, for in reality they are undersized, narrow-shouldered and broad-hipped.'

'So!' she hissed. 'You insult me! Suddenly you've got your courage back.'

'My mind is not clouded by desire,' he taunted her, 'I

see nothing special about the little slit you call your Fotze. I've seen plenty of them and you can take it from me, dear Magda, yours is no different from any other.'

'You're brave now because you saw me in a moment when my body betrayed me into weakness,' she said with awful and menacing deliberation. 'You blockhead – that was nothing to do with you. It was an accident.'

'A cultural accident,' Manfred sneered, 'the sort of accident you arrange for yourself three times a day. The only culture you understand is a *prong* in you.'

Magda's face turned dark red with rage. She put one booted foot against his upright stem and pressed it hard against his belly.

'Be very careful what you say to me or I'll tread it flat!'

Manfred looked down from her furious face to the join of her thighs and the dark-furred entrance he was becoming desperate to get into.

'You needn't look at me there,' she said angrily, 'you'll never touch that again.'

'No great loss,' he answered calmly, 'it was boring when you had your bottom up in the air and I was thumping away to give you satisfaction. I almost got up and left, but I thought I ought to be polite.'

'I'll show you what's boring,' she shouted hoarsely.

She raised her boot to his chest and pushed hard. He toppled over backwards on his tied hands and lay awkwardly. Magda, a monstrous sight in her spiked helmet, dumped herself down on his belly and her bent knees clamped into his ribs.

'In case you are too ignorant to know,' she said icily, 'these are cavalry boots I'm wearing and this is a cavalry helmet.'

He winced as her hand groped for his hard stem and forced it between her legs. She sat down abruptly on it, driving it in deep.

'Untrained colts have to be broken,' she said. 'Trot!'

To her own command she rose and fell on him at a controlled pace, flicking at his nipples with her riding-crop.

43

Manfred stared up at her flushed face and saw that below the metal edge of the helmet her dark-brown eyes were glinting with the emotions of power.

'Follow my movements,' she ordered.

He obeyed willingly, pushing upwards to her rhythm as far as his constricted position would permit. The feeling was so agreeable that he was soon moving faster than she intended.

'Halt!' and she pinned him to the rug with all her weight.

'Magda – don't stop!'

'What do you think you're doing?' she roared. 'You're here to learn, not to enjoy yourself. One more twitch out of you and I'll thrash you until you bleed.'

'I can't control myself – it's too exciting!'

'I'm controlling you. Lie absolutely still. Understand?'

'Yes," he whispered, sensation swirling in his belly.

'You will now be taught how to canter.'

She bounced up and down on him, faster than before. Manfred clenched his fists behind his back and willed himself to lie still. It would take very little more of this to finish him off.

'That's better, you're learning,' Magda gasped, 'don't move a muscle. We're going to gallop now.'

With bulging eyes Manfred stared up at her big breasts bobbing up and down to her rhythm. Her eyes were only half-open and her breathing was loud and ragged as she pounded at him hard and fast. But the gallop was a short one. Manfred felt his belly contract and with a loud cry he jolted his essence into her, not feeling in his delirium the riding-crop slashing across his chest, nor hearing Magda's scream of 'No!'

His spasms lasted a long time, but at last he lay still and opened his eyes to see her staring down at him with an expression on her face that made him shiver. She looked so cruel that he wondered, for the first time, just how far the game might go.

'Poor little horse,' she whispered thinly, 'he was beginning to learn his lesson but he tripped and fell. His leg is broken and he's done for. There's nothing for it but to put him out of his misery.'

She threw away her riding-crop and unbuttoned the flap of the holster on her belt. Little tremors ran over the skin of her belly and thighs, Manfred saw, the tips of her breasts were hard dark-red points. It was obvious that she had not shared his violent ecstasy.

The pistol she pulled out of the holster was large and looked dangerous. With the end of the long barrel she tickled her nipples, one after the other, smiling thinly.

'When this one fires his shot,' she said, her voice distant, 'you really know about it. It's not just a quick squib for him, it's a great roaring fiery burst.'

'Magda, put that pistol away!'

'Poor little horse, he's whimpering in pain. I must do my duty.'

Manfred stared in real alarm as she cocked the pistol, gripped it with both hands and leaned forward to press the cold muzzle to his temple.

'Magda, for God's sake!'

'Goodbye, little horse,' she said shakily.

'No!' he shouted in terror as her finger tightened on the trigger.

The pistol clicked emptily and Magda writhed on him in a stupendous orgasm, her bottom grinding into him and the grip of her knees almost cracking his ribs.

'Ah, ah, ah!' she was screaming.

It went on and on. The heavy pistol fell from her hands and almost broke Manfred's nose before it slid off his cheek to the carpet. Still she rocked and squirmed, her finger-nails clawing at her own breasts. Then without warning, she pitched forward and Manfred twisted his head out of the way to dodge the heavy steel helmet. Even so, he got a hard knock on the corner of the jaw that made him swear. Magda lay heavily on him, very still, hardly breathing. The sheer force of her climactic release had overloaded her nervous system and she had fainted.

Trapped in this ridiculous position, there was little that

Manfred could do. He heaved his shoulders to try to roll her off, but with his hands bound behind him her weight was too much for him to move. He shouted her name in her ear, again and again, but it seemed a long time before she twitched and began to recover her senses.

'Magda,' he said in relief. 'Are you all right?'

'Oh yes . . . that was incredible. I passed out.'

She took his face between her hands and kissed his mouth, his eyes and his temples, telling him between kisses that she could easily fall in love with him. The prospect made him shudder, but he kept his voice cheerful.

'That's the nicest thing any woman has said to me for a long time. Untie me and let's have a glass of brandy. We both deserve it.'

She climbed off him and hauled him to a sitting position to free his hands. They got into bed together, under the wolf-skin, and Manfred drank a whole glass of brandy in one swallow.

'Did you enjoy the game?' she asked affectionately.

'You certainly kept your promise to surprise me.'

'The look of fear on your face was so convincing that it did for me instantly.'

'I didn't know whether the pistol was loaded or not.'

'Nor did I. I thought I'd unloaded it but I couldn't really remember. That's what made it so interesting.'

Manfred thought it over and decided it was time to leave her.

'No, don't go,' she cajoled him, stroking his bare chest, 'Stay here tonight. I know another game we can play when we wake up.'

'With the pistol?'

'No, it's completely different. You'll love it. I'd show you now but I'm finished for tonight after what you've just done to me.'

'I had the impression that you were doing it to me. If I stay, promise there'll be no weapons tomorrow.'

'No weapons and no rope, I promise.'

'What then?' he asked, yawning, 'I can't imagine that you'll want to lie on your back and do it the usual way.'

'I can't get excited like that,' she said sleepily, 'I'll give you a hint. I've got a lovely little leather restraint harness that fits round the waist and controls your pink tail when it starts to stand up.'

Manfred was already asleep, the results of strong emotions and brandy, and he missed her description of the delights to come in the morning.

He was enjoying a light breakfast, two days later, when Oskar Brandenstein telephoned him. Oskar sounded hoarse.

'How is that little actress friend of yours,' the producer asked after they had exchanged greetings.

'Which one do you mean?' Manfred asked cautiously.

'Anna Kindt. Is she well?'

The question was puzzling and Manfred thought quickly before he gave an answer.

'She's in your play, Oskar, you must know better than I do how she is.'

'I'm in bed with a wretched cold – have been ever since the first-night party. I haven't been to the theatre.'

'I haven't seen her since the party either. I spoke to her on the telephone yesterday, but that's all.'

'How did she sound?'

'Oskar, what is this? I have no doubt you took her home after the party. If you haven't heard from her since, then perhaps your style of entertainment failed to please her.'

Oskar chuckled.

'I was asleep when she left and so I had no opportunity of asking her.'

'Who needs to ask?'

'To tell you the truth, Manfred, I got very drunk and I have only hazy recollections. But I think it was all right. I woke up stark naked in my own bath and I've had this awful cold ever since.'

Manfred laughed.

'It's time I had visitors,' said Oskar grandly. 'Come round and see me after lunch. I'm beginning to feel lonely without someone to talk to. Bring me grapes and chocolates to make me feel better.'

About the middle of the afternoon Manfred drove to Oskar's apartment in Mohrenstrasse, behind the State Theatre. He was taken by surprise when the door was opened not by a servant but by Magda Nebel. She was oddly dressed in a short skirt of chamois leather dyed scarlet and a coloured shawl round her bare shoulders.

'Magda dear, my apologies. I've obviously arrived at an inconvenient time. I see that you're playing games with Oskar. Tell him I'll come back tomorrow.'

'Don't be silly,' she said, her smile welcoming him, 'you haven't interrupted anything. I'm helping Oskar read new scripts, that's all. Come in, he's expecting you.'

Manfred stepped inside, closed the door behind him and took Magda in his arms to kiss her warmly. His questing hands confirmed his impression that she was naked above her skirt and had put the shawl round her shoulders only to answer the door-bell.

'But you're dressed to play games,' he said, squeezing her bare breasts.

'You're wrong.'

The bedroom was hot and stuffy. Oskar, his nose red and swollen, lay in a vast modern bed that had a framed oval mirror as head-board. In black silk pyjamas he looked like a beached whale. Half a dozen manuscripts bound in cardboard covers lay scattered about the bed.

'Manfred, my dear friend, how good of you to visit me on my bed of pain. Don't come too close – I should never forgive myself if you caught my cold. Magda, give him a drink. I find schnaps very good for colds.'

Without going close enough to shake hands, Manfred took a chair and accepted a glass of schnaps from Magda. She at least had no fear of catching Oskar's cold, for she discarded her shawl and sat on the bed with her back to the

48

big mirror, so that Oskar could rest his head comfortably on her bare bosom.

'A man needs his comforts at a time like this,' said Oskar, 'have you ever heard of Karl Kessel?'

'No, who is he?'

'I'd never heard of him myself until the other day, but he writes plays and it seems he's had some success in Munich. Not in the real theatre, or I'd know about him. Probably in a beer-cellar or students' club. He's sent me a play to read and it's very funny.'

'Good enough for you to produce?'

'Well, it couldn't be put on in Munich and it may be too obscene even for the Berlin stage.'

'I never thought to hear *you* say that. What's it about?'

'Little girls, mostly. I think the man's a pervert. I'll outline the plot so that you can judge for yourself.'

Manfred tried to concentrate his thoughts on what Oskar was saying, but his eyes were drawn to Magda's big bare breasts and his thought followed in the same direction. He remembered all too clearly her black leather restraining harness which buckled tightly round his waist and held his wrists strapped to his sides and another part of him strapped tightly at a right-angle to his body, with a thin steel chain that ran between his legs and various metal loops and fasteners sewn into the leather that enabled Magda to create curious sensations and ecstatic results. Oskar droned on, sniffling every now and then, and Manfred crossed his legs to hide the reaction in his trousers to the sight of Magda's breasts and his own memories of their violent games together.

He had no doubt that Oskar had deliberately planned this scene to get his own back. Magda too was enjoying his discomfiture – she was smiling cruelly at him and her hand moved lightly and slowly over the soft leather of her skirt, exactly above the object of his desire.

An idea struck him. Magda's pleasure lay in humiliating men, as he knew from first-hand experience of her games. By her standards Oskar's little revenge was hardly amusing

49

at all. If it were possible to reverse the roles and get her to turn her attention towards Oskar, that might be far more interesting. He waited patiently for the summary of Kessel's comedy to end.

'I see what you mean, Oskar. It would not be easy to find little girls to do that on stage. Perhaps with grown-up girls? Would that work, dramatically?'

'Stupid question, my boy! The whole essence of the comedy is that the girls are all under twelve years old.'

'But how exhilarating to see dear Magda on stage doing those things. What a lucky man you are, Oskar, to have her as your friend. She is enchanting and has great talent. She's easily the best actress in *Three in a Bed*.'

The surest way to make Oskar disagree was to praise anyone else.

'Magda? She's a good enough little bitch,' said Oskar dismissively, 'I've trained her personally, you understand, otherwise she would be nothing.'

'I disagree totally. Without her the play would be nothing – a farrago of semi-humorous dialogue, a patch-work plot and a cast of not very inspiring actors. Hugo Klostermann is dreadful, of course. The only part he can play is himself – the idol of elderly ladies and schoolgirls. No, you have to agree that Magda brings life and piquancy to the play. She makes it work.'

'Nonsense!' said Oskar. 'It's a first-class comedy. Magda is nothing – I gave her the part out of charity. Without me she would be just another little whore of a would-be actress with no future.'

His puffy face screwed up as he sneezed loudly into his handkerchief. While he was so occupied, Manfred stared into Magda's dark eyes and gave her a hard grin. She returned his stare, took the handkerchief from Oskar and wiped his nose tenderly, kissed him on the bald spot on his head and slid a hand into his black pyjama jacket to stroke his chest.

'Another little whore of a would-be actress,' Manfred said slowly, 'those are cruel words, Oskar. I can only think that your cold has made you feverish and you don't know what you are saying.'

'Of course I know what I'm saying. I know all about would-be actresses. Every little whore in Berlin thinks she has only to open her legs for me and I'll make her a star. As if I cared whether they open their legs or keep them together! I have no interest in that, have I, Magda?'

'Certainly not, darling Oskar,' she answered, her bare arm further down inside his pyjamas, obviously stroking his paunchy belly, 'that's for fools who know nothing about the real pleasures that you enjoy.'

'You are one of the few women who understand me. Well no, no one can really understand the complexities of my personality, but you have some faint glimmering.'

Oskar's voice was shaky, perhaps from the effects of his cold. Or perhaps, thought Manfred with gentle malice, from the effects of what Magda was doing to him under the silk sheet. It was moving in a manner which made it all too obvious which part of him she was now stroking.

'Shall I ever understand you, Oskar?' she asked.

'As much as anyone else – perhaps more than most. I am not an ordinary person who can be diverted by the tedious acts which ordinary people regard as pleasures. At least you understand that much about me.'

Manfred found it difficult not to smile openly at Oskar's discomfiture now that Magda was using him as the object of her game. He almost laughed aloud when Oskar exclaimed in a quavering voice:

'Give Manfred another drink.'

'Yes,' she said at once, continuing her secret massage, 'Is the schnaps to your liking, Manfred, or would you prefer something else?'

'Let me think,' he said, playing along with her, 'it is very good schnaps, no question of that. But how much of it should one drink in the afternoon, that is another matter.'

Oskar's face had turned a dull red. He grabbed at Magda's arm to stop its movement, but she had a firm grasp on him and continued what she was doing inside his silk pyjamas.

'For Oskar's cold, schnaps is an excellent medicine,' Manfred said slowly, 'But as for me, I do not have a cold and it may not be the appropriate drink. There is much to consider here.'

'Magda, stop it!' Oskar groaned.

'Is something wrong, Oskar?' she asked calmly. 'Has your temperature gone up again? Perhaps I should fetch the thermometer and check. Maybe I should telephone Dr Feinberg. You are looking very hot and flushed, my poor darling. How do you feel? Tell me.'

The outburst she had been provoking took place. Oskar's bulk heaved upwards under the bedclothes and he gave a gurgling cry.

'Oskar, what is it?' she exclaimed, her arm moving in short and fast jerks.

'Uh, uh, uh . . .' he gurgled.

'Manfred's visit has been too much for you,' she said, withdrawing her arm from the bed. 'You are over-tired and you must rest. I'll see him out while you try to sleep.'

She eased herself from under his head and settled him on the pillows. His eyes were closed and he was breathing heavily.

'Auf wiedersehen, Oskar,' said Manfred.

Magda made no attempt to cover herself with the shawl as she led Manfred out of the bedroom, bare-foot and in only her red leather skirt. The moment the door was closed, Manfred stepped close behind her and put his arms about her to take hold of her heavy breasts.

'You really turned the tables on the old devil,' he said admiringly.

'There's something hard against my bottom,' she said, pressing back against him, 'I wish I had my harness here to restrain that wicked thing of yours.'

'It doesn't need restraint just now – it needs freedom.'

Her hands moved between their bodies, between her

skirt and his trousers, to undo his buttons and pull out his hard stem.

'So it has freedom,' she said, 'but restraint is more amusing.'

Her hands moved away and Manfred pressed against the soft chamois leather of her skirt. The sensation was extraordinary. He clasped her closer and rubbed himself slowly against the leather.

'Be very careful, little pig,' she warned him, 'I don't want stains on this skirt.'

They were still standing outside Oskar's bedroom door.

'Where shall we go?' Manfred whispered in her ear.

'The servants are in the kitchen. Don't make too much noise, unless you want an audience. Come with me.'

He followed her into the dining-room. There was a table big enough to seat a dozen, made of highly polished sycamore. Magda pushed aside one of the chairs and turned to face Manfred, her bottom resting on the edge of the table. She grasped him by his conveniently uncovered handle and pulled him to her.

'You're just like Oskar – one feel of my balloons and *this* is sticking out like a crow-bar. His was standing up for hours because I took my blouse off. It didn't take much to finish him off. As for you, if I had my riding-crop with me a few smart cuts would soften it for you.'

'But as you haven't,' Manfred countered, his hands busy fondling her *balloons*, 'we must find some other way, dear Magda.'

He winced as her red-painted finger-nails scraped along his out-thrust stem.

'What awkward things men have,' she said contemptuously, 'hard and swollen – very ugly. When did you ever see a statue of a man with his tail standing up stiff? Never. No artist would give himself the embarrassment of depicting it. But in great art no part of a woman's body is hidden. That's because every part of a woman is beautiful.'

The touch of her nails on his flesh had ceased to be slightly painful and had become pleasurable.

'Some women have very beautiful bodies,' Manfred agreed.

'Especially the part between their legs,' she informed him.

The words took him back to the first time he had entered into her games, when he knelt before her and she had made him kiss her between the legs. Was she repeating herself already – were there no more variations she could devise? She let go of him and used both hands to wriggle her skirt up her thighs so high that he saw she wore no underwear. No doubt Oskar had amused himself by resting his head on her dark curls while he read his scripts.

She knocked Manfred's hand away roughly.

'You are allowed to admire my Fotze,' she said coldly. 'You have no permission to touch it. Keep your hands to yourself. My God, such disrespect!'

It was much the same game as before, but without the crimson cord, Manfred decided. She was goading him and herself into a fury that would end in cataclysmic release. He fell into the role required of him, put a hand on each of her bare thighs and forced them apart, his fingers digging deeply into her flesh.

'What am I to admire?' he sneered. 'A slit with brown hair round it. A few Marks will buy me one as good as that on any street corner.'

'You swine! How dare you insult me like that!'

He moved in closer, his legs between her knees to keep her accessible while he steered the tip of his stem to the pink lips and pushed slowly. Magda's nails clawed at his face, but he managed to catch her wrists before she could scratch his cheeks more than once. He used his strength to force her arms behind her back and hold them there.

'I won't let you do it to me!'

'You have no choice whether to let me or not. It's for me to decide if this toy you prize so highly is interesting enough to make me want to use it. Tell me what is so special about it, Magda.'

'Let go of me! I refuse to be raped by that long ugly thing. Take it away!'

'Refuse as much as you like – the decision is mine. And as I can see nothing exceptional about your dearest possession, I must explore further.'

He pushed forward, in spite of her struggles, until he was settled comfortably inside her.

'It feels like any other,' he told her. 'Lie on your back.'

'No!'

He took the risk of letting go of her wrists long enough to put his hands on her bare shoulders and force her backwards. Her feet left the floor and her hands struck at nothing as she went over on her back on the dining-table. He took her under the knees and flung her legs up and over his shoulders and held them there tightly to stop her kicking his face.

'You never expected to be flat on your back with something hard inside you, did you? Do you find the position ordinary and boring?'

'I forbid you to do it!' she said through gritted teeth.

'Consider this – the next time Oskar has a dinner-party here you can entertain his guests by telling them what happened to you right here on the table.'

'You're raping me!' Magda gasped, her face mottled red with anger.

'That's right,' and Manfred stabbed hard and fast.

His deliberately brutal pounding at her body fired her anger to incandescence. Her mouth opened in a soundless scream of mad rage as her violent emotions exploded into shuddering ecstasy. For Manfred it was as if he had been struck by lightening and his high excitement discharged itself in a cloud-burst of passion.

When at last, after a long time, he disengaged himself from her, she sat up on the table and dried his limp part on his shirt-tail for him before tucking it back into his trousers.

'I really like you, Manfred. You play so well. You understand me.'

55

'In the same way you understand Oskar?'

'Him? There's nothing to understand. He can't do it properly with a woman. His only pleasure is to be shamed. He's pathetic.'

'You shamed him thoroughly this afternoon. He won't want to see me again after that.'

'Don't be an idiot. That was probably his wildest dream coming true. Now that he's been humiliated in front of you, he'll be your friend for life.'

To be a part of Magda's sexual fantasies was strange enough, but to find himself included in Oskar's was simply ridiculous. Manfred burst out laughing.

Madame Filipov

It started for Manfred as an evening at home, a pleasant pause in the round of dining out, theatre-going, taking girls to dance and the other amusements that made up much of his life. On this one fine evening in May he planned to relax at home and go to bed early and alone. Frau Geiger prepared an excellent light dinner for him: a soup with croutons, followed by chicken breasts stuffed with melted butter lightly seasoned with garlic, with golden sliced potatoes and red-currant jelly. After that there was a dish of black cherries with vanilla ice-cream, with a dash of Kirsch over it. Geiger waited at table, in his black suit and white cotton gloves, bringing in his wife's cooking and serving it expertly to Manfred, who sat at one end of the long table, his glass constantly replenished with a good white wine from the Rheinland.

Afterwards, in his gold brocade smoking-jacket with green velvet lapels, Manfred reclined on the chaise-longue in the drawing-room, coffee and brandy on a low table at his side, and set himself to read until bed-time. His domestic idyll was not fated to last. Soon after nine o'clock Geiger announced the arrival of Herr Schroeder. Max was elegantly attired in a new dinner-jacket, a flower in his button-hole. He sat down and accepted the brandy Geiger poured for him.

'To what do I owe this unexpected pleasure, Max?'

'There is no particular reason. I had arranged to take someone out to dinner, but she cancelled at the last

57

moment. I ate alone and thought I'd come here and see if you were at home.'

'You were lucky. I'm hardly ever at home in the evening.'

'I was passing the end of the street anyway, so I took a chance and told the taxi to drop me here. What are you reading?'

Manfred passed him the book.

'Collette,' said Max, 'amusing, but no substance. There never is in French novels.'

'I wasn't looking for substance. We have more than enough of that in our own novelists – misery, suffering, symbolism, social purpose – all that rot. Did you know that Ernst's new novel is to be published in the autumn? It will be dreadful. I prefer a little frivolity in a book.'

'For you life is a frivolous affair,' said Max with a smile, 'but for many it is a long and losing struggle.'

'I'm sure you mean well, but I can't feel guilty about the state of Germany today, Max. It wasn't my doing – or yours. You and I were still in short trousers when the War started and still at school when it ended and the Republic appeared out of nowhere.'

'But don't you feel any responsibility for changing things?'

'That's for the politicians. It's their trade.'

'Politicians!' said Max scornfully. 'What do they know?'

'Democracy means that every idiot has the right to vote for whichever idiot he prefers. That is our new system,' said Manfred, bored by the turn of conversation. 'You said you were passing by – that means that you were going from one fixed point to another fixed point and I am somewhere between.'

'Your logic is faultless. Since the young lady I invited to dinner did not appear, I had it in mind to visit Madame Filipov.'

'Who is she? I've never heard of the lady.'

'For good reason – she remains anonymous to all but a select band of admirers.'

'That conjures up a great many possibilities. How select is her band of admirers?'

Max grinned.

'Her talent lies in the organisation of unmentionable depravities – does that answer your question?'

'You mean she keeps a brothel?'

'That is a very crude description of what she does. A brothel is a place where you hand over your money and a fat young whore lies on her back for you. Madame Filipov does things very differently.'

'But Max, you know plenty of girls – why go to a brothel? There's a telephone in the hall – all you have to do is ring any one of a dozen or score of girls we both know. One of them will be at home. Have you been with Magda Nebel? She'll show you new ways of doing it, if it's a change you need.'

'That's not the problem. Listen, do you ever get bored by going to bed with the sort of women we know?'

'What a strange question! Let me fill your glass for you – I see that the girl who let you down tonight has made you thoroughly miserable. Who was it? Anyone I know?'

'Jenny Montrose.'

'The beautiful American!'

'We've been going out together the past few weeks, since Oskar's first-night. I thought she was a lesbian, but when I saw her with Hugo Klostermann I knew she couldn't be. So I called on her the next day and invited her to dinner and we went dancing afterwards, and so on.'

' "And so on" means that you have made love to her, I suppose.'

'Naturally.'

'Is it the same as with a German girl?'

'She's very strange in bed. She is very beautiful when she takes her clothes off and she has a sharp appetite – I could almost say greedy. But somehow she isn't there.'

'What on earth do you mean?'

'I find it hard to explain. Even in the wildest moments, the impression she gives is that her spirit, her inner self,

59

has withdrawn to some secret hiding-place. From its secure place it watches her body shake with pleasure, but never takes part in the enjoyment. Do you understand what I mean?'

'You are too imaginative, my dear Max. Some women are noisy in their passion and some go very quiet at the big moment, though they enjoy it as much as those who scream and bite. Obviously Jenny is one of the silent ones, that's all. There's no mystery about that.'

'You're wrong. I've been with silent women and I know the difference. In a way I cannot define, Jenny is still a virgin in spirit, whatever her body has experienced.'

'How morbid you are tonight, Max. Are you feeling well?'

'I'm perfectly healthy, but I'm not very pleased with life. Tell me something – when you walk along a street, do you notice how many people look thin and hopeless? Do you really look at them, or do you just rush on to the next restaurant or bar as if they were just a part of the scenery? They're real people too, you know, and their lives are lived in abject poverty and despair.'

Manfred was becoming alarmed by his friend's pessimism.

'What can any of us do about it?' he asked. 'We can only go on electing idiots because there is no one else.'

'I don't know what we can do and that is what worries me.'

'Look here, Max, this won't do. What you need is a visit to this fancy whore-house you mentioned. A bottle or two of champagne and a frolic with a girl and tomorrow you'll see that the world isn't such a bad place after all.'

'If only it were that simple!'

'It's a damned sight better than turning Bolshevik or marching with those thugs in the brown uniforms. Tell me what's so special about Madame Filipov's house. The women are young and pretty, I suppose.'

'More than that. It's a place where you can do anything you like with a woman. Or two or three, for that matter, all at the same time. Everything is possible, nothing is forbidden.'

'My imagination recoils in horror from the nameless depravities we might commit there,' Manfred said with a cheerful grin.

'I wish I had your eagerness. The truth is that even nameless depravities become wearisome after a time, believe me.'

Manfred was on his feet, determined to rescue Max from his black mood.

'Pour yourself more brandy. It won't take me more than a minute or two to change and we'll be off. You must introduce me to this remarkable place.'

'As you wish,' said Max, with no enthusiasm. 'Bring plenty of money with you.'

Ten minutes later they were in Manfred's car and on their way, across the city centre and west along Stralauerstrasse.

'Turn right at the next corner,' Max instructed him, 'Then the second left and look for number 19.'

The entrance to number 19 looked like the entrance to any large family home. The door-keeper who opened the door when Max rang was plainly-dressed, like any servant, though his height and the bulge of muscles under the shoulders of his black jacket suggested that he had duties beyond those of an ordinary servant. His nose had been broken and had set crooked. He bowed to Max and addressed him ironically as 'Your Excellency', obviously recognising him, but he stared hard at Manfred.

'The gentleman is with me,' said Max.

They went upstairs and into a large room, very dimly lit by small shaded lights on the walls. It was furnished with a number of ottomans and low tables and about half a dozen men and rather more young women sat and drank together. No sooner had Max and Manfred taken seats on an unoccupied ottoman than a tail-coated waiter, elderly and frail, placed an ice-bucket with a bottle of champagne on their table.

'The drink of the house,' Max explained, 'there is no point in asking for anything else.'

'Where is Madame Filipov?' Manfred asked.

'She never makes her entrance before midnight. But there will be other company.'

The words were scarcely out of his mouth before three young women detached themselves from a group on the other side of the room and sat down uninvited, one between the two men and one on either side of them. Without a word said, the waiter set glasses for them and poured champagne.

'Good evening, dear ladies,' said Manfred.

'Bring another bottle,' Max said to the waiter, 'that one's done for.'

The woman on Manfred's right was fair-haired and had a prominent bosom. She might be eighteen at most, he thought, though the dim lighting was deceptive. She sat half-facing him, one bare arm along his shoulders while she sipped champagne and told him that her name was Trudi. The woman on the other side of him was no older. She was very slender, dark-haired, and tiny pointed breasts made twin peaks in her frock. She too sat close to Manfred, resting a fragile-boned hand on his thigh while she chatted as chirpily as a bird. Her name, he learned, was Frieda.

Manfred lay back comfortably on the big cushions covering the ottoman and let things take their course. So far it was not very different from other expensive brothels he had visited and he could not imagine how Max's promise could be fulfilled. Trudi pressed her fat breasts against his face and his hand found itself under Frieda's frock to rest on her furry mound.

'That's what he likes,' said Frieda approvingly, 'his hand up a girl's clothes. But what does he want next? That's the big question. What do you think, Trudi?'

'He's a handsome boy,' said Trudi. 'He must have had his hand up plenty of girls' clothes before. He's come here for something he can't find anywhere else.'

'But what might that be?' Manfred asked, looking from Frieda to Trudi and back again.

He felt fingers glide over his trouser-front.

'This says you're ready for something new,' Frieda told him, 'and this part of a man never lies. There was a gentleman who came to visit us last week – he looked something like you, except that he had a moustache as soft as silk. You remember him, Trudi – the one who was so bored lying on top of girls that he'd even tried it with boys. But he didn't like that.'

'And he discovered something new here?' Manfred asked, wondering if she was telling him the truth or whether it was just a story to arouse his interest.

'Everybody finds what he's looking for here,' said Frieda with a giggle.

'There's a gentleman who comes here very regularly,' said Trudi, 'And he always asks for me. Do you know why? Because he thinks that I look like his daughter. He brings a little suitcase with him, with some of her clothes in it. We go up to one of the private rooms and I put the clothes on – very stylish, I can tell you! He calls me Gerda – that's his daughter's name you see.'

'Wicked old man!' said Manfred with a chuckle. 'But at least it keeps him out of trouble.'

'The things that man wants to do to his daughter!' said Trudi, chuckling too. 'You wouldn't believe it. I call him Papa and play with his thing and suck it. Then he . . .'

'Spare me the details, please,' said Manfred, 'Family life is not to my taste.'

'Do you know what he gives me when he leaves?'

'A suitable token of his gratitude, I'm sure.'

'A thousand Marks!' she said triumphantly. 'And always a box of chocolates. What do you think of that?'

'I've been given that much, more than once,' said Frieda immediately.

'For special services, of course,' said Manfred.

'Very special. The last time was only a day or two ago.

63

There was a gentleman from Munich who wanted to make use of both entrances.'

'But hardly at the same time.'

'One after the other,' she said, wriggling her warm and furry mound against his hand, 'face up and then face down. I think he was an Army officer, though he wore civilian clothes.'

'If you had been old enough to be here five or six years ago, when you were still at school,' said Manfred, 'he would have given you thousands of millions of Marks – and it wouldn't have bought you a new pair of shoes.'

'Don't talk about those times,' she said at once, 'they're gone, 'My mother was a widow with four children to feed. All we ever had to eat was potatoes, and not much of that. Give me another drink, for God's sake – you've given me the shivers.'

As Manfred sat up to fill her glass, there was a muted wail from the other side of the room. In the dimness he saw a man in a dinner-jacket jerk suddenly upright from the cushions, like a steel spring released, clutching at his trousers with both hands. The girl who had been lying beside him burst out laughing and the two girls with Manfred giggled.

'That stupid Maria!' said Trudi, 'She didn't even get him upstairs. He won't want to pay after that and there'll be a row.'

'What could she have said to him to bring that on?' Manfred asked.

'Some men are like that,' said Trudi, settling beside him again, 'As soon as they whisper their really secret wishes into your ear and you touch them a bit to make them feel good, it's too much for them. They just go off pop in their trousers. It's telling a sympathetic girl what he's kept hidden for years that does it. He'll be all right the next time he visits us – Maria will get him straight upstairs and he'll be doing it instead of talking about it.'

Before the threatened row could develop, a short and stocky woman waddled into the room, summoned by some mysterious system of signals. Her hair was cropped as short as a man's and her arms were as thick as thighs. She took in the scene at a glance and made straight for the unfortunate man, now complaining loudly. She stood pugnaciously in front of him, hands on her hips and silenced him with a glare. The girl with him stopped laughing and looked uncomfortable.

'Come with me,' she said to the man, took him by the arm and hauled him to his feet and out of the room.

'She'll make sure he pays the house, even if Maria gets nothing,' said Trudi. 'Shall I tell you about a foreign gentleman who was here not long ago and what he wanted me to do?'

'Other men's dreams and needs are not mine,' said Manfred, 'let's get another bottle from the waiter. Max, old friend, you are curiously silent – how are you now? Better pleased with life?'

Max was on his back on the cushions, his girl half on top of him, one of her legs between his, her mouth close to his ear to whisper to him.

'Life is a nightmare,' said Max, 'one day I shall wake up from it.'

'But until then?'

'Until then there are worse ways of passing the hours than lying here with this young lady, who has been telling me the most extraordinary things about herself.'

That squat woman with the cropped hair came back and clapped her hands together for attention.

'Gentlemen, Madame Filipov is ready to receive those who wish to pay their respects to her.'

The announcement surprised Manfred, who had assumed that the muscular woman was Madame Filipov herself. He removed his hand from between Frieda's legs and leaned across her thin body to tap Max on the shoulder.

'What do you think, Max, you know the rules of the house.'

'You should go,' said Max, 'Madame puts on quite a show.'

'And you?'

'I have reached an arrangement with this charming Oriental blossom and intend to accompany her to a private room.'

'She doesn't look Oriental to me.'

'She tells me that she was born in China, where her father was a Lutheran missionary. You would be amazed by what she has told me of the antics they practice in the East. You go and pay your respects to Madame and I'll see you back here later – much later.'

'If you will excuse me, ladies,' said Manfred to the girls on either side of him, 'I have the honour to attend on Madame Filipov.'

They both smiled at him.

'We'll be waiting for you,' said Frieda.

With two other men Manfred followed the short-haired woman along a passage towards the rear of the house, through a door panelled in faded red leather, which clearly marked the division between the public and the private parts of the building. Like Manfred, the other men wore dinner-jackets and were well-groomed and presentable. One was not much older than Manfred himself, a slenderly-built young man with narrow shoulders and a pale over-refined face. The other man was in his forties, heavily-made, with lines on his face and grey in his hair. He seemed to be embarrassed and his face was shiny with perspiration.

'Courage, my dear man,' said the narrow-shouldered one, 'we have been here before.'

The other man glared at him and made no reply.

'Not I,' said Manfred cheerfully, 'this is my first visit to Madame.'

They were ushered into an elegantly decorated room in which the main piece of furniture was a dressing-table with a large mirror. A chair stood close to it and, behind that, three other chairs, at about arm's length from each other.

'Madame will be with you shortly. Please sit down,' said their guide.

'Thank you, Fraulein Dunke,' said the pale young man courteously.

They selected seats and Manfred took a cigarette from his gold case and lit it. The older man pulled out a leather cigar-case and chose one. No one spoke, for it hardly seemed a moment for light conversation. In a few minutes the door opened and in swept Madame Filipov, followed by a girl dressed as a maid in black frock and starched white apron and cap. The men rose to their feet and bowed.

Madame Filipov was perhaps forty years old, of middle height and with raven-black hair worn long and piled up on top of her head in a very old-fashioned style. Her face was smooth and attractive still, not with the prettiness of youth, but with character and a touch of humour. She wore a long silk négligé in blush-pink, with a trim of marabou feathers round the neckline. Altogether a formidable woman, Manfred thought, when it was his turn to kiss her hand.

She addressed the other young man first, evidently knowing him well.

'Baron von Stettin – how nice to see you again so soon. You are always a most welcome guest. And Herr Krill, your business has brought you back to Berlin again. I am most pleased to see you.'

She smiled at Manfred.

'You are very welcome, Herr . . .?'

'Manfred von Klausenberg, Madame,' he said, bowing again.

'It is such a pleasure to make new friends. I have been informed by my staff that there was an unfortunate disturbance earlier. I apologise, gentlemen.'

'There is no need to apologise, Madame,' said the Baron quickly, 'the fellow was an ill-bred boor who should have been thrown downstairs, neck and crop.'

'Thank you, your words make me feel better. What exactly did happen? I was given only the vaguest account.'

Manfred was amused by Madame Filipov's poise, and impressed by it. She conducted herself as if she were a

67

Grand-Duchess receiving members of the aristocracy and the contrast between that and the reality was very piquant. Seeing the Baron and Herr Krill hesitate to put into words that would be acceptable to Madame the ridiculous affair of ten minutes ago, he took it upon himself to answer and, by doing so, show that he could match her style.

'A wretched-looking fellow in a ready-made suit was in conversation with Fraulein Maria,' he said, 'and as is often the way with such people, he allowed his enthusiasm to overcome his sense of propriety and finally disgraced himself by doing what is not done in polite company.'

Madame Filipov nodded graciously and looked at him with a new interest. She knew very well what had happened in the drawing-room and was using the incident to cause a tingle along their nerves.

'We must make allowances,' she said, 'I believe that it was the gentleman's first visit. The conversation of Fraulein Maria can be very stimulating to those unfamiliar with it.'

'It is also my first visit,' Manfred reminded her.

'The first of many, I hope. Perhaps you should converse with Fraulein Maria and learn to appreciate her style of sympathetic understanding.'

'Do you think so, Madame?' he asked, smiling at her boldly.

She fluttered her hands in an appealing little gesture.

'To speak truly, Herr von Klausenberg, it would surprise me to learn that Fraulein Maria's conversation was of much interest to a superior person like you. But who can say? Please sit down, gentlemen.'

They waited until she seated herself on the chair at the dressing-table, her back towards them, before resuming their own seats. Any one of them could have reached out to place a hand on Madame Filipov's silk-clad shoulder, but such a familiarity was unthinkable. The little maid-servant stood at Madame's side and handed her a crystal jar from the array on the dressing-table. Madame applied a thin layer of face-cream to her cheeks and forehead and stroked it in lightly with her finger-tips.

'Tell me what important affairs of business you have been engaged in, Herr Krill, since you were last here,' she said conversationally.

Herr Krill launched on a lengthy and tedious account of his dealings, his lined face shinier than ever with perspiration as he watched Madame Filipov making herself up. Indeed, both Krill and the Baron appeared to be utterly fascinated by what she was doing and had eyes for nothing else. Manfred found as much diversion in watching the two men as in watching Madame. While Krill rambled on, talking of deals, loans, contracts, hundreds of thousands of Marks, competition, imports, exports and other rubbish dear to the heart of his sort, Madame Filipov casually opened her pink silk négligé, threw it back from her white shoulders and applied face-cream to her neck. In the mirror Manfred had a perfect view of her uncovered breasts, as did the other men, and as she intended they should. He liked what he saw – they were still firm and well-separated and their rosettes were small and red-brown.

He caught her eye in the mirror. She saw his little grin and pouted at him. When she had creamed her neck to her satisfaction, she leaned back in her chair, her long-fingered hands resting on its padded arms, for the maid to apply a fine apricot-coloured powder to face, neck and breasts, with a big and fluffy powder-puff.

Krill broke off his recital to watch in adoring silence. Baron Stettin exclaimed nervously:

'Madame is exquisite!'

'It is sweet of you to say so, my dear Baron. But the words are mere flattery and not from the heart, I fear.'

'I swear I spoke from the heart! If it were permitted, the greatest honour in the world would be to kiss your adorable little slipper – I dare not say your foot!'

'So delicate an emotion deserves its reward,' she answered in a coquettish tone.

The little maid put down the powder-puff, took the silk slipper from the foot Madame raised and conveyed it to the Baron, holding it on the out-stretched palm of her hand.

The Baron received it as if it were an objet-d'art of enormous value and pressed it to his lips with reverence. Madame Filipov watched him in her mirror.

'Ah, Baron, you are one of my dearest friends,' she said fondly, 'I miss you when you stay away from me. And you, Herr von Klausenberg, do you also wish to kiss my foot?'

'That goes without saying, Madame,' he answered lightly, 'but I must tell you that we Klausenbergs are by tradition more inclined towards conquest than acts of homage.'

'The old Prussian spirit,' she said with a broad smile, 'how exciting to meet it again! I thought it had been lost forever in these modern times.'

Baron von Stettin was lost in rapture, stroking the pink silk slipper with his finger-tips and pressing a kiss on it from time to time. Manfred concluded that he was deranged in his wits and looked away to meet Madame Filipov's eyes in the mirror again.

'No, you are not likely to kiss my foot,' she said, 'but I am sure that my dear friend Herr Krill is dying to.'

'Yes,' the man answered hoarsely.

'Then do it!' she said, her voice sharp and commanding.

Krill rose from his chair to kneel at her side and take her bare foot in his clumsy hands.

'Kiss it!' she ordered him.

He bowed his head low and pressed his mouth to her foot.

'Herr Krill is from Lubeck,' she said for Manfred's benefit, 'but his spiritual home is here in Berlin, in my house. It is only here that he can cast off the restraints of his provincial and family life and indulge himself in the pleasures for which his soul is hungry. But you, Herr von Klausenberg, you seek something else from me, I think.'

Manfred was enjoying the play-acting.

'It would be an honour to drink a toast to you in champagne from your slipper,' he said.

'Of course!' she answered, her eyes glowing, 'it is far too many years since a handsome young gentleman did that.'

With her bare toes she kicked at the face of the man at her feet and spoke harshly to him.

'We need champagne, Herr Krill, so that the gentleman can drink a toast to me. Am I to be kept waiting?'

Krill scrambled up awkwardly and pressed a bell-push on the wall by the door. In a very short time the elderly waiter appeared.

'Champagne!' Krill ordered brusquely. 'And fast!'

At once he was back on his knees, caressing Madame Filipov's foot and kissing it.

'This tradition you spoke of,' she said to Manfred, 'I would like to hear more of it. It brings back pleasant memories of how things were once, before all this modern nonsense ruined Germany. You have a large family estate, I suppose?'

'The estate is very considerable, Madame, but it is not mine. My brother lives there with his wife and children. And my mother. I idle my time away in Berlin.'

'And why is that?'

'In the words of Goethe, "*Two souls dwell, alas, in my breast.*" '

The waiter returned with the champagne. He ignored Krill at Madame's feet, opened the bottle and filled a glass for her. The maid removed the tiny slipper from Madame's other foot and held it for the waiter. He filled it without the flicker of an eyelid, looked doubtfully at the Baron, who was lost in his dream, set the bottle in its silver ice-bucket on the dressing-table and took his leave.

The maid carried the slipper to Manfred, holding it in both hands so as not to spill a drop of the contents. Manfred stood up to take it from her, called out 'To you, Madame!' and poured the champagne down his throat in one. She raised her glass to him in the mirror and inclined her head gracefully.

'You must explain what Goethe's words mean to you,' she said, leaning towards the mirror to apply scarlet lipstick.

'Half of me is of the old stock. Like you, that part

71

respects our great national traditions and history. But the other half of me is drawn towards the new Germany that is emerging. Alas, the two halves do not fit comfortably together.'

The look of interest on Madame Filipov's face vanished abruptly as she glared down at Krill.

'Enough!' she said angrily. 'You go too far! I gave you permission to kiss my foot. I did not reprove you when I felt your lips touching my knee. It seems that I am too soft-hearted with you.'

'Forgive me!' Krill gasped, his face flushed dark red.

'Your manners are deplorable,' she answered coldly, 'God knows what you would have tried next! Your crude attempt on my modesty is shameful and unforgivable. Gretchen – bring me the stick!'

'I try to overcome my failings,' Krill moaned, 'you know how hard I try . . . but to be allowed to approach you so closely is more than I can bear without becoming desperate for a small sign of your esteem . . .'

'You shall have a sign of my esteem,' she said, her tone languidly cruel.

She got up and turned her back towards him while she opened her négligé fully and removed the only other garment she wore – a pair of silk knickers cut in the French style, with an edging of lace round the wide legs. Manfred was treated to a view of her body, breasts, belly and the patch of dark hair between her pale-skinned thighs. Meanwhile the maid had pulled out from behind the dressing-table a long and flexible cane. Madame Filipov dropped the silk underwear she had taken off on to the seat of her chair and turned to take the cane from her maid.

'Now Herr Krill, since you are so anxious to obtain a token of my regard and because I am a good-natured and obliging person, there before you lies something of mine – something more intimate than you dared to hope for.'

Krill shuffled on his knees to the chair and put his face down on to the silk garment.

72

'Oh!' he moaned loudly, 'I can feel the warmth of your body, Madame!'

Presented with so easy a target, Madame Filipov swung her stick and laid it with a crack across the seat of his trousers. To Manfred it sounded most painful, but he had not the least doubt that Krill was enjoying it. The energetic way in which Madame Filipov applied herself to thrashing her admirer's broad backside made her open négligé swirl about her and showed off her naked body to Manfred and the Baron to very fine advantage.

'Oh . . .' the Baron whispered, hugging the silk slipper to his heart, 'the delight of this stern Amazon destroying her victim . . . I shall faint with the joy of it . . .'

Herr Krill bore his punishment in silence, only his heavy body jerking slightly at each crack of the stick on his rump. Eventually Madame Filipov tired of beating him.

'There! That will improve your manners, Herr Krill. Whenever you are here I take a great deal of trouble with you and one day you will be truly grateful to me.'

'I am, I am,' he babbled, raising his purple-flushed face from the chair.

'I am pleased to hear it. You may take your leave of me and go to the room where Fraulein Ellie is waiting for you. She will soothe your pain with her cool hand and relieve your distress in ways that suit you.'

He kissed both of her bare feet, rose and bowed stiffly, her silk knickers in his hand, and hurried out of the room. Madame handed the cane to her maid and resumed her seat, to examine her hair in the mirror in case it had been disarranged by her vigorous exercise.

'He's a dear man,' she said, 'so devoted to me! His visits here are the high points of his life, you know.'

Baron von Stettin spoke in a quavering voice.

'I would die if you beat me like that!'

'You, my dear Baron? What a terrible idea! You must put it right out of your mind. Herr Krill requires very firm treatment – it is the only thing he understands. But you are a high-born and sensitive person and you could never forget your manners. Isn't that right, Gretchen?'

'The Baron is a most correct gentleman,' said the maid.

'Of course he is. His blood is very different from the coarse peasant blood of our dear Herr Krill. Therefore he deserves our respect and consideration. For him we reserve our tenderest concern.'

'Oh Madame, you are too kind,' he replied in so soft a voice that Manfred could only just hear the words.

'I must show you how dearly I admire and cherish you,' said Madame Filipov, 'Gretchen, let the Baron see how completely devoted to him I am.'

How many times, Manfred wondered, had this little comedy been played with the anaemic Baron and the dreadful Krill? Evidently Madame Filipov knew the most furtive wishes of her clients and indulged them at a price, while remaining to all appearances a gracious lady.

Gretchen seated herself on the Baron's lap and Madame continued with her make-up.

'If the Baron will permit,' said the maid and without waiting for a reply she unbuttoned his evening trousers and pulled out his stiff stem. She took the little silk slipper he was clutching and fitted it over his fleshy projection. When Manfred saw her agitating the one inside the other, he turned away from the scene to stare at Madame Filipov's face in the mirror.

'There, dear Baron, dear kind friend,' she cooed over her shoulder, 'I hope that this expression of my highest respect and admiration for you is not unpleasing.'

'Oh Madame, the delicacy of your sentiments is . . .' came the Baron's soft murmur and Manfred missed the last word.

As if nothing out of the ordinary were taking place behind her back, Madame Filipov turned her attention to Manfred.

'So you are torn between past and present, Herr von Klausenberg?'

She took a large crystal bottle from her dressing-table and was perfuming herself. She dabbed it behind her ears and under her chin, then parted her négligé wide to perfume her skin between her breasts.

'I am not torn between them,' said Manfred, 'I am trying to enjoy the best of both worlds.'

She spread her négligé wider and stroked perfume into her groins with her finger-tips and then behind her knees.

'The past has gone forever,' she observed, 'the future may be terrible. Only the present is of any importance.'

'In that I cannot agree with you. There are some ideals from the past which are worth maintaining in the present.'

'For example?'

'Philosophy in the boudoir,' said Manfred with a chuckle.

The sight of her body naked and in violent action as she swung her stick at Krill's backside had excited him. Her deliberately langorous movements as she perfumed herself added to his arousal. This she knew, of course, and now she sat still, négligé undone, to give him a full view of her breasts in the mirror. His stem jerked inside his trousers when she took up her lip-stick again and carefully tinted her nipples scarlet with it.

The Baron whimpered '*Oh, oh, oh!*' but Manfred kept his eyes on the mirror.

'One thing my father told me,' said Manfred, 'horses and women like a rider with a strong knee-grip.'

She nodded and smiled and spoke to her maid without looking round.

'Is the Baron satisfied with my demonstration of respect, Gretchen?'

'Yes, Madame, I believe he is.'

With this assurance, Madame Filipov spoke to Baron von Stettin in tones of warm friendship.

'I am so pleased that you were able to visit me this evening, Baron. I look forward to your visits, as you know. I hope it will not be long before you are here again. Friends should see each other often, to keep their friendship growing.'

The Baron was on his feet, his trousers decently fastened by the maid. He kissed Madame's hand, bowed slightly towards Manfred, and left. The maid flopped the spoiled slipper into a gilt-painted wicker waste-basket beside the dressing-table, collected the other one from which Manfred had drunk his toast and disposed of it in the same way. *On the Baron's bill*, Manfred thought. In the mirror he saw Madame Filipov looking at him thoughtfully.

'The next time you are here I shall know how to please you,' she said.

'How so, Madame?'

She laughed and told her maid to give him a proper glass of champagne. That done and the maid back beside her, Madame leaned back in her chair and studied her reflection. She was pleased with what she saw and smiled at herself appreciatively.

'The visit of my dear friends has made me quite agitated,' she said, 'you must attend to me, Gretchen.'

The maid knelt between Madame Filipov's parted legs, folded back her négligé with great care to expose her body completely, and kissed the tuft of dark hair where her thighs met.

'Good girl,' said Madame lazily, 'I become so flustered by the whims of my visitors that I don't know what I would do without you to soothe me.'

How will you know what pleases me if I come to see you again?' Manfred persisted.

'Unless you are as cold-blooded as a fish you will not leave my house before you have had a private interview with one of my young ladies. They are very clever, dear Herr von Klausenberg, in fact they are selected for their skill in pleasing gentlemen in unusual ways. You will be able to express yourself fully, even if your way of doing so is eccentric.'

Between Madame Filipov's thighs, the maid's head with its little starched cap bobbed busily up and down.

'Whichever young lady you converse with, I shall hear about it,' Madame continued, her words soft and interspersed with little sighs, 'so when you are here next time,

I shall know better than you do yourself what will truly please you.'

'Not everyone who comes to your house has the honour of being received personally,' said Manfred, 'most of them are content with your young ladies, I imagine.'

'As you say, only a few attend upon me. Herr Krill . . . I guessed what his secret desire was after he had been with one of my staff a few times. He still goes to her, but he calls upon me first . . . our meeting raises his spirits so he can enter fully into the conversation with Fraulein Ellie.'

'And the Baron, of course.'

'He is a dear, sweet, gentle person . . . too much so for his own happiness . . . he would find it impossible to approach a woman in the way most men do . . . but delicacy and tenderness and a proper regard for the proprieties – these are what he responds to . . .'

'With me there is no need for these roundabout methods,' said Manfred, hotly excited by what he saw the maid doing to Madame Filipov, 'I will tell you in plain words what I want.'

'Ah, a man who is not afraid of his secret desires . . . tell me – whatever it is . . . I will arrange it for you at once . . .'

He got up, stood behind her chair and reached over her shoulders to take hold of her bare breasts.

'I want *you*. Little games like those you played for Krill and the Baron may be amusing sometimes, but at this moment I want to make love to you in the simple old-fashioned way.'

Her eyes were half-closed in enjoyment of the emotions rippling through her body from the maid's busy tongue between her thighs.

'This is outrageous,' she murmured, 'I am not at the disposal of anyone who walks into my house.'

'You said that whatever I wanted would be arranged for me at once.'

'Oh, Gretchen . . . faster!'

He gripped her breasts tighter as her body writhed on

77

the chair in hot release. The maid ceased her attentions and her face turned up to grin lewdly at Manfred.

'Madame is satisfied?' she asked.

Without waiting for an answer, she took a bottle of eau-de-Cologne from the dressing-table, soaked a soft pad and gently wiped over Madame's belly to cool her and remove the faint sheen of perspiration.

'With the gentleman's permission,' she said, and pushed Manfred's hands away to wipe under Madame's breasts and up between them.

'Thank you, Gretchen,' said Madame Filipov faintly. 'It seems that I made a promise without thinking. Are you so inconsiderate of my feelings, Herr von Klausenberg, to hold me to it?'

'I am determined,' he answered.

'You understand that to converse with me is a more serious matter than a private interview with one of my young ladies?'

He understood well enough what she meant – it would cost him more to enjoy her than one of her employees. He answered equally obliquely so as to preserve her pretence of gentility.

'Believe me, Madame, when a Klausenberg makes up his mind, nothing deters him, not blows, blood or gold.'

'There speaks the rider with the strong knee-grip! Gretchen, prepare the bed.'

The little maid scrambled up and trotted out of the room. Madame Filipov leaned further back in her chair and rested her head against Manfred. He put his hands over her shoulders again and stroked her cool breasts.

'How old are you?' she asked.

'Twenty-three. My birthday was in March.'

'A good age to be! I wish I were twenty-three again.'

'If I may ask, what were you doing when you were twenty-three?'

'I was married and travelled with my husband. We lived in Paris sometimes and in St Petersburg. But the War and the Bolsheviks finished all that.'

'And your husband?'

She laughed briefly, but did not reply. Manfred thought it better not to enquire further, in case he was told that Filipov lived up in the attic and counted the takings.

'Come with me,' she said, smiling at him in the mirror.

Her long négligé wrapped around her, she took him into the next room. Manfred thought it very elegant, decorated in the style of the French Empire, with pale walls, gilt mirrors and bow-legged furniture. The bed was magnificent, an antique piece of taste and value. From a gold-embossed plaque set high on the wall, ivory silk drapery descended in soft swags to form a canopy round the carved bed-head.

Gretchen had already turned back the cover to reveal sheets of silk the same colour as the drapery. Hands folded in front of her, she stood at the foot of the bed, the very picture of the attentive servant. Madame Filipov dropped her négligé casually to the honey-coloured parquet floor and arranged herself seductively on the bed, one knee raised, as if in modesty, to hide what lay between her cream-skinned thighs.

'Assist the gentleman, Gretchen,' she ordered.

The maid helped Manfred to undress. She took his jacket and then went down on one knee to unbutton his trousers, while he pulled at the ends of his bow-tie to undo it. She helped him out of his shirt, knelt again to remove his shoes and socks and grinned up at him as he stood in only his silk underpants, his stem sticking out rigidly. She took hold of the waist-band and divested him of his final garment, stood up and clasped his protuberance firmly, as if to assess it.

'The gentleman is ready for you, Madame.'

By now Manfred was very excited indeed. He jumped on to the broad bed and used Madame Filipov with vigour. He rolled her about in his arms, rubbed himself against her, handled her breasts and bottom so firmly that she soon sighed and scratched at his chest with her finger-nails. He put his hand between her thighs and explored her slippery

79

entrance briskly and she gasped and sank her teeth into his shoulder. In short, it more resembled a wrestling-match than an act of love, but that was the mood that her games had put him in. Wise in the ways of men, she went along with his mood. It was not long before he rolled her on to her back, spread her knees and was on her and in her. She clasped her hands on the back of his neck and urged him on with cries and thrusts of her own hips and Manfred rode her as if he were galloping a good horse over the countryside of his boyhood. Madame Filipov moaned and heaved, her movements growing wilder in time with his, till everything dissolved in ecstatic convulsions that rocked the bed.

It took her some time to recover herself after so energetic a bout. Manfred lay beside her and smoked a Turkish cigarette he found in a Sevres porcelain box on the bedside table. It was only then that it occurred to him that Gretchen had remained in the room throughout, sitting on a gilt chair by the door, her hands folded in her lap, a silent witness to Madame's passionate interlude.

In another minute or two Gretchen came to the bedside with a very large bottle of eau-de-Cologne and refreshed Madame by wiping the cooling spirit lightly over her entire body, round her neck, down between her breasts and over her belly and down the insides of her thighs, much as she had done earlier, this evidently being a regular part of her duties.

'Thank you, Gretchen,' Madame Filipov murmured, her eyes opening slowly, 'and thank you too, Herr von Klausenberg – you made me feel myself twenty-three again.'

The maid had finished with her mistress. She moved round the bed and with her little palm smoothed eau-de-Cologne over Manfred's chest and belly. The sensation was most pleasant and the effect was cooling, but the touch of her hand in his groins had an unintended result. Manfred's limp stem quivered and began to grow longer again. Gretchen grinned at him and stroked the insides of his thighs upwards.

'The gentleman is ready again, Madame,' she announced.

'Great God!' Madame Filipov exclaimed, turning her head on the silk pillow to stare at him, 'you are determined to kill me with your brutal Prussian ways. No, it is out of the question!'

'I remember a certain promise,' said Manfred, amused by her response.

Privately he wondered how many times the girls of the house were expected to entertain clients each night, while Madame cried off after once.

'Promises are sacred,' said Madame, 'you must help me, Gretchen.'

The maid stood at the foot of the great bed and faced them while she took off her starched cap, her apron and black frock, her stockings and cheap underwear. She clambered on to the bed and crept up between Manfred and Madame Filipov, lying on her back with her arms at her sides. Madame put an arm under the girl's thin shoulders and, with her other hand, caressed her slack little breasts.

'She is such a good girl,' said Madame, 'so loyal!'

Manfred raised himself on one elbow to look at the girl and stroked her thin legs, up past the pink marks her garters had left on her thighs, to the few wisps of mousebrown hair that decorated the surprisingly well-developed and protruding lips of her sex.

'Has she been in your service long, Madame?' he asked.

'Five or six years now. She was a wretched orphan of fourteen when I found her in the street selling herself to drunks for the price of a crust of bread. I am sure you remember the hungry years well enough, though you never went without food or new clothes. I took pity on little Gretchen and saved her from disease and death, and she loves me for that and takes care of me.'

A sly smile appeared on the little maid's face as Manfred stroked between her parted legs, his finger exploring between the warm lips there.

'Do you like that, Gretchen?' he asked.

'Yes, it's very nice,' and she opened her legs wider for him.

'She is almost like a daughter to me,' said Madame Filipov fondly, 'I have never let her become one of my young ladies and converse with gentlemen who have eccentric tastes. She attends upon me and she is the best lady's-maid I have ever had in my life.'

'Her duties seem more comprehensive than those of the average lady's-maid, Madame. For instance, the service she performed for you earlier on, when you were agitated. And at this moment too.'

'The gentleman is ready, Gretchen,' said Madame Filipov firmly.

The maid turned on her side to face Manfred and threw her leg over his hips, her hand reaching for his stem to tease it with nervous little tweaks. Not knowing what to expect in this extraordinary household, Manfred slid towards her until he was close enough for her to steer his stiffness into her fleshy little socket. He pushed and wriggled closer and embedded himself comfortably in her until his belly touched hers.

Madame Filipov also turned on to her side and was close up to the maid's thin back. Her hands gripped Gretchen's hips and held her firmly against Manfred's slow thrusts.

'Oh Madame!' the maid murmured. 'He is so strong!'

'Oh Gretchen!' Madame gasped. 'So strong!'

As Manfred grew more excited he became unsure of which of the women he was doing it to, the mistress or the maid. His arm was over Gretchen and his hand was squeezing Madame Filipov's warm breast; Madame's hand was over the girl to stroke his face and push her thumb into his mouth. Her belly was bumping against the maid's bottom, to make her respond to his thrusts, and both women were sighing and moaning. When he discharged his turbulent passion, both women cried out at the same moment.

After a pause, the maid eased herself away from him and slid down to the foot of the bed and off it. Manfred was left gazing at Madame Filipov's face on the pillow.

'It has been a great pleasure to make your acquaintance,

Herr von Klausenberg,' she said, 'I hope to see you again before very long. But now I must ask you to excuse me – I have matters to attend to. Please stay here with Gretchen if you wish, for as long as you like. Now that I know you I have no hesitation in entrusting her to you.'

'Thank you, Madame, but I must take my leave.'

She remained on the bed, posing gracefully, while Gretchen assisted him to dress. She was expert as any valet, even to tying his bow-tie neatly, and her nakedness added a certain pleasure to the proceedings.

'Auf wiedersehen, Madame,' he said, bowing politely towards the bed.

'Auf wiedersehen, Herr von Klausenberg. When you come to see me again I shall have a very special way of pleasing you.'

Gretchen opened the bedroom door for him. He patted her bare bottom and gave her five hundred Marks, being in a generous mood. She smiled and curtseyed, her bare breasts bobbing in a way that was faintly comic.

Outside, beyond the red-panelled door, he found the squat and short-haired woman waiting for him and he learned from her that the services of Madame Filipov cost him very much more than the gratuity he had given her maid.

Ulrika's Celebration

'Thank you for inviting me, dear Ulrika,' said Manfred into the telephone, 'but surely you don't want men there. What would be the point?'

'I'm asking a few men friends so that they can see what they're missing.'

'You mean that you want to tantalise us with forbidden fruit. Anyway, what are you celebrating? it isn't your birthday until October.'

'I'm celebrating being me – what better reason? Will you come and help me to celebrate that? After all, I came to your birthday party and watched pretty young girls being pawed by men. Now it's your turn to suffer a little.'

'Ulrika, you did not suffer at my party. I saw you the next morning asleep in one of my armchairs with your hand up a girl's skirt. Don't pretend that nothing happened before you fell asleep.'

'That was a little flirtation,' said Ulrika with a laugh. 'She came home with me and stayed a couple of days but after that she became boring and I sent her back to her regular girl-friend.'

'There you are – you found her boring! How do you know I won't find your celebration boring?'

'It won't bore you to be surrounded by naked women, even if you can't touch them.'

'How so, naked?' he asked with more interest.

'Because I'm having my celebration in a Steam-bath.'

'That's very original. It will be like a visit to a Turkish harem.'

'And there will be slaves on guard to stop any unauthorised interference with the women of my harem.'

'I can see it now! Frustrated men wandering about with huge projections sticking out under their bath-towels and your girl-friends laughing at them. It sounds more like a torture-chamber than a harem.'

'I wouldn't be so unkind to you, Manfred. I've invited some other women – the sort who prefer men, though God knows why. And you can bring a girl of your own.'

'Thank you, but if I brought a girl, you'd eat her alive.'

'As you wish. There'll be enough others to keep you happy.'

Even with that assurance, it was with mixed feelings that Manfred arrived at the Steam-bath on the evening of the celebration. Ulrika Heuss was a cousin of his, five or six years older than himself, and he had known her all his life. He liked her – her parties were a different matter.

A large notice fixed to the door of the Steam-bath said CLOSED TO THE PUBLIC. Ulrika's money had talked. Inside, a muscular male attendant checked names against a list before passing anyone through – there were to be no gate-crashers, which was not in the least surprising. Five minutes later, his clothes stowed away safely in a wooden locker, Manfred strolled into the main room of the Steam-bath, wearing only a towel round his waist. There were at least thirty women in the hot and steamy room, some with towels round them, some completely naked, glasses in their hands and chatting away as if they were at an ordinary party and wearing their most elegant clothes. There were one or two men in the throng, all sporting bath-towels like himself, he noted with some relief.

'Manfred darling – at last!' Ulrika called to him.

As befitted her reputation for caring about nothing. Ulrika was stark naked, though she had a long string of matched pearls round her neck – so long that it looped down to her belly-button. She kissed Manfred on both cheeks and told one of the young women hanging round her to get him a glass of champagne. Manfred had never had the honour of seeing his cousin naked before and was taken by her elegance of form. She had kept her body slim and supple and, though approaching thirty, her breasts were pointed and firm. What was very striking about her was that the light brown hair between her thighs was neatly trimmed into a heart-shape.

'There's lots of people here you know,' she said, 'and your dear friend Nina is coming later.'

'And her husband?'

'Don't be silly. Gottfried is too boring for words. Did I ever tell you that he offered Vicki Schwabe a thousand Marks at your birthday party?'

But why? Vicki does it for nothing.'

'She doesn't do what he wanted, the filthy beast! It proves what I've always said about him. Why do you have that ridiculous towel round you, Manfred? You're not ashamed of anything, are you? Take if off – this is a celebration, not a prayer-meeting.'

Manfred had drunk a bottle of wine with his dinner and a good quantity of brandy afterwards. Consequently he felt no qualm about unwrapping the towel from his waist and handing it to the girl who at that moment came back with a glass of chilled champagne for him. She looked startled.

'Don't be afraid, Gerda,' said Ulrika with a wicked grin, 'you're not about to be raped. At least, not by Manfred. I'm the one you should worry about – I might drag you into a corner and ravage you until you scream.'

'Oh Ulrika!' the girl murmured, her eyes down-cast and a smile on her pretty mouth.

Manfred raised his glass.

'I celebrate *you*, dear Ulrika. May you never change!'

'You may rely on it. I'm glad you decided to come – you know I have a soft spot for you.'

He was conscious of her gaze, particularly on that part of him for which she had no use.

'You've grown up to be a very handsome man. And well-equipped too. It's grown a lot since you and I played together when we were children. It was a tiny little thing then.'

'I don't remember that. Are you sure it was me?'

'One summer in the country. You were about four. That was before I found out what really interested me.'

'Such a shame,' he said, smiling at her, 'you are a beautiful woman and if you had any interest in men, I'd take you to bed for a week. Did you really play with my dingle-dangle when I was a child?'

Ulrika laughed at him and padded away on bare feet to greet more guests. Manfred looked round for more champagne and poured himself another glass. Over on that side of the room two girls sat on a long wooden bench, both pretty and neither more than eighteen. They were giggling, exhilarated by what they had been drinking, and in a mood for anything. But even as he strolled towards them, the plumper of the two began to stroke the other girl's bare breasts and he knew that he was wasting his time. All the same, it was interesting to watch them. The plump girl lifted a leg over the bench and straddled it, exposing her brown thatch, and her friend turned to face her and put her legs round her waist. Manfred's stem stood to attention at the sight of their loving caresses and he turned away, to find himself face to face with Werner Schiele and Vicki Schwabe. Werner had a bath-towel round his waist, with a bulge under it. Vicki wore nothing, and the sight of her bouncy little breasts and reddish-ginger tuft was not only entrancing but probably accounted for Werner's condition.

'I got my clothes back after your party,' she said brightly, 'it was that idiot Dieter who took them. He said it was a joke, but I'm not so sure. Maybe he wanted to try them on.'

'Anything is possible with Dieter,' said Manfred, 'he has no style.'

'You should find yourself a towel,' Werner advised him, 'you are indecent like that.'

'Shame is for little minds,' Manfred retorted grandly. 'Have you seen Mitzi lately?'

87

'Your fiancée,' said Werner, with a malicious grin, 'No, not I.'

'I'm relieved to hear it. She seemed to me a very nice person, far too good for you.'

'If that were for me,' said Vicki, staring at Manfred's out-thrust limb, 'I'd take it as a compliment. But as you're alone, a swim might help to reduce the swelling.'

Manfred nodded and headed for the pool. Vicki followed him, leaving Werner dumbfounded. On the edge of the pool, Manfred stood with arms raised, in addition to what else was raised, curled his toes round the tiles and dived. He surfaced gasping for breath in the very cold water, just in time to see Vicki leap in, bottom first and legs flying. They splashed around for a while, flicking water at each other, until Vicki said she was freezing. They climbed out together and went into the hottest room, shivering as the water trickled down their skin.

They found a marble slab and lay side by side, warming up. They could hear voices in the room but caught only occasional glimpses of anything at all through the billowing steam.

'Look over there!' said Vicki.

Manfred raised himself on an elbow and saw, across the room, a tableau which made him chuckle. There was Werner, flat on his back on another marble slab, his towel discarded to let his meaty flag-pole point skywards. There was a woman with him, massaging his belly with both hands.

'He's lost no time, has he?' Manfred asked.

As the steam-clouds drifted across to conceal the scene, he saw the woman squat over Werner's face and lower herself on to his mouth.

'Anita Lenz – the slut!' said Vicki.

'Of course – I didn't recognise her now that she's bleached her hair.'

'Pity she didn't bleach her tuft while she was about it. It looks silly being blonde on top and mud-brown below.'

88

'Werner doesn't seem to object to the colour, and he has the closest view.'

'He's an artichoke-eater,' said Vicki, a note of hostility in her voice.

'I'm sorry,' said Manfred, 'is there something between you and him?'

'If there was, it's just evaporated. We've been going about together for a few weeks, that's all. He's nothing special.'

She turned on her side towards Manfred and put a hand on his thigh.

'He's a joker, Vicki. I owe him something for that little affair he arranged at my birthday party, when I thought I had got myself engaged to Mitzi. All in all, I am not very fond of Werner.'

'Nor am I. I'd rather be with you.'

Her hand closed round his stem.

'The cold water didn't cool you down for long. When we got out of the pool this was so small and shrivelled like a baby radish. Now look at it!'

'I can think of a good use to put it to,' he said, pleased that he'd got her away from Werner.

'I can think of ten good uses at least,' she answered.

Manfred fondled her breasts. Their pink tips became firm almost as soon as he touched them, which bore out all that he had been told about Vicki by friends who knew her better than he did. He put a hand between her thighs and found how warm it was there.

'The problem is,' she said, 'that this slab we're on is so hard that I'll be covered in bruises.'

He had to admit that she was right. She was slender to the point of thinness and the lines of her ribs were discernible below her breasts. Her hips were angular and were made even more prominent by the narrowness of her waist. He ran his hand along her pale-skinned thigh and felt her bottom. The cheeks were small and taut.

'You don't have much flesh on your bones, Vicki. Do you eat properly or do you diet to stay slim?'

89

'I eat like a wolf and it has no effect at all. It's because I am so energetic.'

'You like sport?'

'Only one sport, but I play it a lot.'

'We mustn't let you be bruised. Everyone would think I'd been beating you.'

'Some of them would find that amusing. You don't beat women, do you?'

'Hardly ever,' he answered, grinning at a sudden recollection of Magda's games with ropes and harness. 'Now if you were to get up on your hands and knees . . .'

'Do it like dogs in the street? That's disgraceful!'

'Or like a stallion and a mare in a field,' he suggested.

'Or like parrots in a cage,' she giggled, and positioned herself as he had proposed.

'Parrots! What do they know about it?' he asked, grinning.

From behind her rump he surveyed the ginger-flossed peach she was presenting to him, split it with his thumbs and pushed his stem into it swiftly. From all accounts this delectable part of her had been used more than was usual for a woman of twenty-two, but this was his first encounter with it.

The temperature was very high in the hot-room. Vicki's back was slippery with perspiration as he lay along it and tried out his new toy. His hands were under her to stroke her breasts, and they too were slippery. Quite soon he learned something which no one had bothered to mention to him – Vicki was a noisy lover.

As her excitement grew with his, she started to sob loudly in pleasure. Not that Manfred cared – it tickled him to know that she was enjoying what he was doing to her. He carried on with great enthusiasm and, when the critical moment arrived, his delight was magnified by Vicki's ear-splitting shrieks of ecstasy.

An instant later, while his belly was still convulsing and she was still screeching, all the delight was spoiled by a sneering voice close by. It was Werner.

90

'So! You've stolen another girl from me! First it was Mitzi and then, as if that wasn't enough, I find you sticking it up Vicki! This is getting to be a habit with you – a bad habit! I shall have to put a stop to it.'

Manfred turned his head to glare at Werner, who was standing within arm's-reach of him, staring and grinning unpleasantly. Anita was beside him and she too was grinning. Werner's flag-pole was down and Anita looked flushed.

'The fact is that women prefer me to you,' said Manfred, not wanting to start a quarrel, 'Leave Anita here when you go, there's a good fellow.'

'They can't like you for your style,' said Werner, 'I thought it very unimaginative – crude, in fact. Of course, Vicki is easily pleased, but even so, I think it must be your money they prefer. Someone told me that Mitzi got a fur coat out of you. Will Vicki get the same, or does she do it for less?'

Manfred was strongly inclined to pull free from Vicki and punch Werner in the face. Before he had time to translate the thought into action, Vicki spoke up.

'Go away, Werner, or I'll tell everyone about that little episode with the beer bottle. You didn't demonstrate much style yourself then.'

Werner's face turned a dull red. He seized Anita by the hand and dragged her away. Manfred freed himself from Vicki and turned her round to kiss her.

'What about a beer-bottle? What did he do with it?'

'If I tell you, everyone will know and I'll have nothing to threaten him with if he starts being tiresome again.'

'He's always tiresome.'

'I know,' she agreed. 'How about a cold shower together?'

Some time later, back in the big room, Manfred spotted the beautiful American, Jenny Montrose. But beautiful was an inadequate word, he thought; she was heart-stopping! She was naked and she gave no sign of embarrassment as she talked to Ulrika. Manfred stared at her as if to photograph her on his memory – and with good reason. Jenny was long-legged, round of hip, with a neat black tuft where her thighs joined. Her breasts were perfect, but most ravishing of all was her face, long, patrician and with an expression of slight disdain. She wore diamond ear-clips which shone against her jet-black hair like stars in the night-sky.

Manfred started towards her, only to be stopped in his tracks by the sight of Ulrika putting an arm round her waist and kissing her on the mouth. It did not seem much like the ordinary friendly kiss with which women greet each other – at least, not on Ulrika's part. Yet Max had made love to Jenny – he had said so, and Manfred did not doubt his word. But Max had also said, he recalled, that she was strange in bed, as if her spirit was elsewhere.

The two women turned away and walked slowly towards the massage-room, each with an arm about the other's waist. Manfred stared at two long and elegant backs retreating from him and he saw that Ulrika was stroking the American's bottom.

Damnation! Manfred swore aloud, and if Werner had been in sight at that moment, he would have beat him to a pulp to relieve his frustrated emotions.

Over by the wall, on the wooden bench, the two girls he had seen earlier were still caressing each other slowly. The plump girl was lying full length, legs astride and her feet on the tiled floor. The other girl sat with her knees up, tickling her friend between the legs with her big toe.

'Isn't that sweet!' said a well-known voice behind him. 'Someone should photograph it and make it into a Christmas card for Ulrika.'

Manfred turned to smile at Nina von Behrendorf.

Naturally, Nina was naked to show off her charms. Not quite naked, she had knotted a pale orange chiffon scarf round her waist, the loose ends floating in front. The chiffon was transparent enough for her triangle of brown curls to show through and the effect was more provocative

92

than if she had worn nothing at all. Konrad Zeitz was with her, a bath-towel round his waist.

'There's an old friend I haven't seen for a long time,' said Nina, reaching out to touch Manfred's hanging part briefly, 'is this an invitation?'

Konrad looked displeased.

'Manfred's an exhibitionist,' he said, 'it would not surprise me to hear that he visits nudist clubs and parades himself around among the fresh air fanatics.'

'Better to wear nothing than a worn-out towel with someone else's name on it,' Manfred replied. 'What are you hiding, Konrad?'

'Yes, why are you hiding it, darling?' Nina asked, 'You've nothing to be ashamed of.'

'I'm sure you know,' said Manfred, 'I'm glad you're both here at last. There's less than a dozen of us who support the traditional method. All the rest are wild women chasing each other round the swimming-pool.'

'Each to his own – or her own,' said Konrad, 'so long as they don't try to include Nina in their frolics.'

'Surely that's Nina's choice,' said Manfred.

Konrad scowled, Nina laughed and patted his cheek.

'Don't look so angry – I'm a supporter of what Manfred called the traditional method. What I don't understand is why Ulrika invited us.'

'She gets a thrill from flaunting herself and her little friends,' said Manfred.

'Where is she?'

'Around somewhere, amusing herself – the champagne is over there.'

They drifted away and Manfred was free to go in pursuit of Ulrika and Jenny. Why he wished to do that he was not entirely sure. He told himself that it was an opportunity to settle the question of whether the American girl was a lesbian or not, but why that should be important to him he had no idea. He searched through the whole Steam-bath, witnessing scenes of love taking many forms, and at last tried the only place left – the store-room. There were voices inside, so he opened the door quietly and slipped round it, to conceal himself behind a cupboard against the wall. There were seven women in the room, including Ulrika and Jenny, and there Ulrika's celebration of herself was well advanced.

She lay on a wooden table, cushioned by dozens of folded bath-towels, her legs apart and her head pillowed on Jenny's thighs. Olga Pfaff, a very pretty blonde woman with whom Manfred had once been on terms of intimacy for a few weeks without discovering her interest in other women, lay cross-legged between Ulrika's raised knees. The other women stood around the table, close up to it, engrossed in what was going on. All attention was concentrated on the heart-shaped tuft of light-brown hair between Ulrika's thighs. It graced a plump mound, split by fleshy lips, with a little bud at the top from which the opening descended vertically until it disappeared into the shadow below.

Blonde Olga was leaning forward, her red-nailed hands busy with Ulrika's exposed treasure, stroking it upwards again and again with deliberate slowness. Ulrika's thighs were trembling and her head rolled restlessly on Jenny's bare thighs. As the finger stirred her emotions, the women standing round the table uttered tiny sighs and drew in their breath swiftly. Ulrika was in seventh heaven, revelling in sensation and in the total exposure of herself to her little congregation of friends, hiding nothing, pretending nothing, joyously celebrating being herself.

'Darlings!' she said, speaking to no one in particular, to all who could hear and to herself, 'this is my body, my beautiful living body, given freely for you. Whenever two or three of you are gathered together, do this in remembrance of me.'

Her gleaming belly contracted when Olga's finger probed deeper and touched something of special interest. Ten or a dozen upward caresses caused the fleshy lips to open by themselves within the heart-shaped brown fur, to expose the pink skin within. Ulrika's breathing quickened and her breasts rose and fell to the rhythm, her long rope of pearls

94

sliding over her moving flesh. Olga brushed blonde hair from her forehead with the back of her free hand and leaned closer to stare into the tender pink vestibule in which her fingers were playing.

'Look at me closely, little ones,' Ulrika breathed, 'feast your eyes on my secret and sacred heart.'

Her raised knees parted wider, descending in opposite directions towards the table on which she lay, their movement pulling her open to the full. Her head rolled a little on Jenny's naked thigh and Jenny smoothed her hand over Ulrika's flushed cheeks.

The other women standing round the table to observe Ulrika's long act of surrender and triumph were fondling each other, hands squeezed breasts, palms stroked bellies, fingers caressed between thighs. On each face was the same rapt expression. Now that Ulrika was open for all to see, Olga concentrated her attentions on the tiny pink bud that stood revealed. Her finger-tips touched it delicately and Ulrika's sighs grew loud and insistent.

'There is a great and lasting love for every one of you in this secret heart of mine,' she murmured, 'you know that – you have all touched it! You know what it is to be in my arms and to be loved by me. You have felt the true ecstasy that I give to those I love . . .'

All of them, Manfred thought feverishly, his stem straining at full stretch. That included Jenny. He tried to imagine her in Ulrika's arms, their naked bodies pressed close together, their breasts flattened against each other's breasts, their mouths joined in a long kiss and Ulrika's hand between Jenny's long legs, inducing ecstatic sensations.

'Oh Ulrika, I love you!' Olga moaned, her fingers fluttering between the spread thighs, 'I love you, darling! Give yourself to me!'

'And I love you,' Ulrika answered, her voice shaky with emotion, 'as I love all of you.'

'Give yourself to me!' Olga cried, almost hysterically.

'Freely!' Ulrika gasped.

In a flash Olga's legs were uncrossed and her body twisted about until she lay face-down, her blonde head between Ulrika's thighs. Her wet pink tongue flickered over Ulrika's little bud. Manfred, concealed behind the cupboard, bit his knuckles hard to top himself from crying out. He saw Ulrika's legs shake to the urgent swelling of delight in her and then her fingers clutched at her own breasts, plucking at the upstanding nipples. The little group of women seemed to have crept in closer around the table, arms tight about each other, the sound of their breathing harsh as they waited for Ulrika's moment to arrive.

Manfred's stem was so swollen that he thought it might squirt involuntarily. Trickles of sweat ran down his forehead and chest, his legs trembled. Then Ulrika announced the moment of consummation with a long shriek of joy, her mouth wide open to show her teeth and her body bouncing up and down on the scattered bath-towels. Olga's arms were tight around Ulrika's thighs, her face pressed deep into the heart-shaped tuft.

Manfred could stand no more. Before Ulrika's cry of triumph died away, he backed quickly out of the store-room, leaving the door open, and ran, holding his raging stem in his hand to stop it from shaking painfully about as he raced through the large room where the drinks were, scattering young women left and right without even seeing them. He was looking for Nina and he found her in the massage-room. She lay on one of the massage-tables, her chiffon scarf pulled to one side so that the knot was on her hip and her tuft was uncovered. Konrad was not with her.

'Nina – help me!'

'My poor Manfred, what has happened to you?'

There was no time to explain. Manfred flung himself on her, but her legs closed at once, denying his desperate need.

'What are you doing?' She demanded. 'Konrad will be back in a minute. He's gone to get me a glass of champagne.'

By then Manfred had her soft breasts in his hands, the balls of his thumbs tickling her buds and it was like the old times again, when he and she had been lovers. Nina's blue eyes stared up at him, amused, and her legs parted in welcome. One fast push took him deep into the flesh he knew so well and before he had time to realise that the deliciously wet and velvety feel of it was due to Konrad's ministrations, the raging torrent inside him burst its banks and he was gasping and jolting in release.

'My God, that was quick,' said Nina.

'Thank you, Nina, thank you, thank you . . .'

'Does this mean that we are good friends again?'

'We shall always be good friends,' he said, recovering himself.

'That's not what I mean, as you know very well.'

'Why are you with that dreadful Konrad?'

'Are you jealous? That's a good sign. But until you make your mind up whether you and I are close friends again, you'd better get off me before he sees you.'

Manfred rolled off her and lay at her side, to stroke the soft skin of her shoulder. Her legs moved close together and she adjusted her scarf to bring the knot into the middle, just below her belly-button, and the trailing ends covering her tuft of curls.

'You shouldn't have married Gottfried. That spoiled everything.'

Before she could reply, there was a shout from the doorway. Konrad was back, carrying two glasses of champagne.

'What's going on?' he demanded, 'I leave you alone for two minutes to get you something cold to drink and I find this Casanova making up to you.'

Manfred rolled off the table and stood up, his deflating stem hidden by the table itself.

'Konrad, you've been hours getting me a drink,' said Nina, unruffled. 'We were talking about the old days.'

Konrad glared suspiciously at Manfred.

'The old days are over,' he said. 'Go and find yourself a girl somewhere. There's plenty of them about, running round without a stitch on. Nina is with me – understand?'

97

'I enjoyed our little reminiscence of the old days,' Manfred said to Nina with a broad grin. 'We must talk again like that sometime when this bad-tempered fellow isn't with you.'

An hour or more later Manfred was lying on the tiled floor of the big room, his head resting across the thighs of Anita Lenz, who sat half-asleep and propped against the wall. He was in the process of persuading Anita to accompany him into the massage-room, to spite Werner, but she had drunk a little too much and was disinclined to make the effort, though she gave him to understand that she had no objection in principle. Vicki Schwabe appeared, sat beside him and rested her head on his shoulder.

'You look very pleased about something, Vicki,' said Manfred. 'Who have you found to join in your favourite sport this time?'

'This party is a bore. Most of the women are groping each other and the few men there are have had so many offers that they're worn out.'

'I'm not worn out. Let's find a comfortable place and I'll prove it.'

'I knew I could rely on you, Manfred. But not just yet – I don't want to miss what's going to happen.'

'What is going to happen?'

'Wait and see,' she answered mysteriously.

It was very comforting to lie with his head on Anita's lap and stroke Vicki's belly. Manfred thought he might doze for a while until Vicki was ready to accept his invitation. Or perhaps Anita would come to life again and then he would try to get both women with him in some secluded corner and really pay Werner back for his rudeness. With these pleasant possibilities in his mind, he drifted into a light sleep, to be awoken by a noisy and violent commotion. He could hear men's voices shouting in anger and women's voices raised in alarm.

'Come on – there's a fight!' Vicki exclaimed, jumping up.

Manfred followed her at a more leisurely pace. The noise was coming from the pool. Gottfried von Behrendorf, in a grey suit and a homburg hat, confronted a naked Werner Schiele and, but for the two men holding him back, would have been at Werner's throat. Around them were a dozen naked men and women, including Nina, adding their cries to the hubbub.

'What's going on?' Manfred asked the woman nearest him.

'I don't know. This madman rushed in and tried to murder Werner.'

One of the men restraining Gottfried was Konrad, his face red with the struggle. The tumult subsided when Ulrika strode in, her hair untidy from whatever she had been doing, but still magnificently in control.

'Gottfried! What are you doing here? You were not invited.'

'How dare you ask my wife to a disgusting affair like this where she is molested by a degenerate!' Gottfried raved.

Manfred grinned at that. Whatever molestation Nina had been subjected to was by her whole-hearted consent. Konrad had molested her, that was sure, besides himself. How Werner came to be accused was a mystery, but a highly enjoyable one. Fortunately for her, Nina was still wearing the chiffon scarf round her waist and she was the only person present to wear anything at all, jewellery not counting.

'Nothing disgusting is going on here,' Ulrika said forcefully, 'this is a celebration of health and beauty for a few friends. I must insist that you leave at once.'

'Nina, put your clothes on,' Gottfried said sharply, 'We're leaving.'

Without a word Nina walked towards the changing-room, making certain that her little scarf did not flutter as she went and expose anything which might further infuriate her husband.

'As for you,' Gottfried snarled at Werner, 'you haven't heard the last of this. You are a despicable swine.'

'But you've got it all wrong,' Werner protested hotly. 'It was a mistake – I thought she was someone else.'

Gottfried stared at him as if he were a particularly unpleasant insect who had just emerged from under a stone and Werner, trembling visibly, made things worse.

'I thought she was Anita, I swear!'

'Who did you think was me?' asked a voice at Manfred's side.

It was Anita, who had woken up and at last joined the crowd by the pool.

'Anyway,' she continued innocently, 'I've been sitting out there for ages talking to Manfred.'

'That's true,' said Vicki Schwabe with a touch of malice, 'the three of us were together.'

'So!' Gottfried shouted, his eyes popping from his head, 'you are a dirtier swine than I thought! You try to lie your way out of the consequences. I shall deal with you. Goodnight, Ulrika, I apologise for interrupting your health and beauty assembly.'

The men holding him released him and he turned on his heel and marched out. Vicki linked her bare arm with Manfred's and led him towards the massage-room.

'I don't understand any of this,' he told her, 'what brought Gottfried here unexpectedly and why did he find Nina with Werner instead of Konrad?'

'How do I know. I was with you.'

'Not all the time. I suppose you telephoned Gottfried and told him that his wife's honour was in danger. But the rest of it?'

'Who knows? Strange things can happen at parties like this – you should know that. And that fool Werner has been hot for Nina for ages.'

The massage-room was fully occupied, each rubbing-table bearing a couple uninterested in the affray by the pool. And all the couples were women.

'This is a bigger bore than I thought,' said Vicki, 'let's go home.'

'Your apartment or mine?'

'Mine. Believe it or not, I like to wake up in my own bed.'

In the dressing-room they found Werner putting his clothes on, his expression one of utter dejection.

'Going so soon, Werner?' Manfred asked, with a grin.

'I hardly touched her and that lunatic ran in and half-strangled me. And she started to scream, the bitch, to make herself look innocent in front of him. What a mess!'

'It may be worse than you think,' said Manfred, delighted by the chance of getting his own back, 'in fact, it could be very serious indeed for you.'

'What do you mean – he won't make a complaint to the police, will he?'

'No, that's not his style. I think you will find his seconds calling on you in a few hours' time. Take my advice and choose swords.'

'My God – this can't be real?'

'Gottfried can be very old-fashioned about things like honour and all that rot. I don't suppose he'll kill you, but he'll certainly maim you. That's why I suggest you insist on sabres – he'll only slice an ear off. But with pistols it might be much worse. If he aims at your knee you'll be crippled for the rest of your life. And if he became really vicious and aimed higher – at the part you intended to use on Nina . . . Well, you wouldn't want to lose that. So make it swords.'

'What shall I do!' Werner exclaimed desperately.

'There is nothing you can do except stand up boldly and take what's coming to you.'

'Suppose I went and explained that it was with Nina's consent? Then he'd see there was no point in going on with this murderous farce.'

Manfred finished dressing and stared thoughtfully at Werner.

'My dear man, you don't seem to understand the code of conduct of decent people,' he said, tongue in cheek, 'if you even hinted at any such thing Gottfried would divorce Nina and kill you for certain. Leave things as they are.

With luck it will only amount to a week or two in hospital. Then he'll be ready to shake hands and forget the whole thing.'

'There's only one thing for it! I'll pack a bag and get a taxi to the railway station before daylight. Perhaps if I stay away from Berlin for a few months it will blow over. What do you think?'

'Everyone will know that you're a coward, but you'll have a whole skin. Auf wiedersehen, Werner.'

He and Vicki laughed so much in the car on the way to her apartment that the driving was very erratic. They almost collided with a taxi as they passed the Kaiser Wilhelm Memorial Church but not even the driver's tirade of abuse sobered them. Manfred put his foot down hard and they soon left the shouting behind as they sped across the sleeping city. Vicki lived in an unfashionable part of Berlin, on the borderline between acceptable middle-class apartments and workers' tenements. She worked for a magazine, Manfred knew, but obviously she was not very well-paid.

They went into the kitchen to make coffee and lace it with brandy. Manfred noticed that one window had its roller-blind up and the other had it pulled three-quarters down. He looked out of the unscreened window to a narrow courtyard two floors below and, across that, the dark windows of the block opposite.

'It's only about two o'clock and everyone is in bed,' he said, 'you must have hardworking neighbours who need their sleep.'

He pulled the roller-blind down to shut out the unprepossessing view and would have pulled the part-closed one down too, but Vicki stopped him.

'Leave that one – it's my private peep-show.'

'What on earth can there be to look at out there?'

'I don't do the peeping – it's the man in the apartment across the yard.'

'Do you know him?'

'No, he's a little fat man, nearly bald. He started to make

102

a nuisance of himself the day I moved in. He was always at his window, leering and waving at me.'

Manfred sat on a corner of the kitchen-table and lit a cigarette.

'That seems a good reason to keep the blinds down,' he said.

'You don't understand – I'm teaching him a lesson.'

'How?'

'The idea came to me in a flash one morning after I'd been to a party. It was about seven when I got in and I came into the kitchen for a glass of water before I went to bed. And there he was, across the way, grinning and waving at me, the conceited pig. I pulled the blind down and it stuck like that, with a gap at the bottom. That was when the idea came to me. I stripped naked and moved about a bit close to the window. See what I mean? I'll show you.'

She slipped off her short evening frock and passed slowly in front of the window in her white silk stockings and high-heeled shoes. Her gingery-red tuft was at the right height to be seen below the partly-drawn blind.

'That must have cheered up his morning,' said Manfred, 'but what were you trying to achieve?'

'I suppose I wanted to make him feel bad by showing him something he'd never in his life get his hands on. Anyway, that's how it started. I turned round from time to time, to let him see my bottom, and then back to face the window so that he'd get a good eyeful. After a while I hid behind the wall and just peeped with one eye round the side of the blind to see if he was still there.'

'I'm sure he was. No bald little fat man would leave a show like that.'

'You're right. He'd opened his window to get a better view and he was holding a drying-up cloth in front of him with one hand. You can guess what he was doing with the other hand behind the cloth!'

She handed Manfred a cup of black coffee well-laced with brandy.

103

'Did that make you laugh or did it make you angry?' he asked.

'Neither. I thought to myself *Got you!* and I strolled about again in front of the blind till I thought he'd had long enough. Then I peeped round again.'

'And?'

'Then I laughed. He was slumped on his arms on the window-sill. His head was hanging down and he looked shattered, so I knew he'd done it.'

'I wonder what excuse he invented for being late at work that day?'

'That was only the beginning. Seven in the morning is no time for me to be giving free exhibitions, so I had to think of something else to keep the squeeze on him. He gets home from his work about six in the evening, when I'm getting ready to go out for the evening. So I started to put the same show on for him every evening as soon as I saw him in his apartment.'

'With the same result?'

'It never fails. The moment he spots my red fur-coat below the blind he's ready with his towel.'

'How long has this been going on?' Manfred asked in amusement.

'Nearly every day now for about three months. And I had another brain-wave. It was the time of the month when I couldn't give him his little thrill by showing myself off, so I bought the fanciest pair of knickers I could find – a bright red silk with lace and embroidery – the sort of thing you'd expect a French whore to wear. I put those out on the sill and watched from behind the other blind.'

'Did he take the bait?'

'He certainly did! I watched the whole performance from start to finish. His face got redder and redder as he played with himself behind the cloth and when he'd finished he slumped over with his bald spot pointing at me, just as if his whole body was a big pink thing going limp. That really made me laugh.'

'So what is the lesson you have taught him?' Manfred asked.

'He's still learning it. When he gets home in the evenings I give him a personal exhibition through the window below that blind. And before I go to bed, I put the fancy knickers out on the sill to get him going in the early morning before I'm awake.'

'The poor idiot must be a nervous wreck by now.'

Vicki smiled sweetly.

'I passed him in the street the other day – Sunday, it was. He looked terrible. He's lost weight and he's got dark rings round his eyes. When he recognised me coming towards him he turned away and crossed the road. So I think that he's learning his lesson.'

'Which is?'

'Not to get ideas above his station. No grubby little pig is going to think he can make eyes at *me*.'

Manfred put his cup down and pulled Vicki close enough to him to stroke the ginger tuft between her very slender thighs.

'And how long will you continue this lesson? Until he can't do it anymore?'

'Longer. He's still enjoying himself, even though it's wearing him out now it's twice a day. When he can't do it anymore, that's when the lesson will really sink in. He'll stand there at his window staring at my red-fox and his thing will be limp in his hand and useless. I'll be laughing and he'll be crying. Then he won't come to the window to stare at me and I'll have won.'

'Cruel girl! But leaving aside his dreadful manners, I can understand his fascination with this pretty thing,' said Manfred, stroking her ginger curls, 'as soon as I saw it at Ulrika's absurd party, I knew that I had to become better acquainted with you.'

'And your idea of getting better acquainted was to have me on my hands and knees on a marble slab.'

'Better than parrots in a cage,' he said, remembering her words, 'or is it? I don't know how parrots go about it.'

'I do. When I was a child my father kept a pair of parrots.'

The coffee with brandy had raised Manfred's spirits and the touch of her warm flesh was a delight.

'Tell me!'

'It's easier to show you than explain. Come into the bed-room and I'll demonstrate.'

Manfred picked her up. She was slender and weighed little. He kissed her breasts and carried her to the door.

'Which is the bed-room?'

'Second door on the right,' she said, her arms tightly round his neck. 'Wait a minute – I must put out my whore's knickers for the man opposite.'

'Give him a morning off,' said Manfred, 'you and I have more interesting games to play than that.'

Consequences

It was in early July, only a week or so after Ulrika's celebration, that Mitzi Genscher telephoned Manfred to say that she wanted to talk to him. His first thought was that she was between boyfriends and was offering to resume relations with him. The thought was not without a certain attraction – his recollections of their brief *engagement* was pleasurable enough. But he was involved with red-headed Vicki just then and her interest in the variations of sexual enjoyment was absorbing his time and energy.

'Meet me at the Café Schon for lunch,' he suggested.

'No, I want to talk to you about something very serious. I'll come to your apartment this afternoon.'

'Not this afternoon, I shall be out.'

'This evening then,' she persisted, 'it's very important.'

'I'm afraid that's not possible either.'

Nor was it. He had already arranged to pick up Vicki at seven to take her to dinner and dancing afterwards.

'Tomorrow then,' said Mitzi, 'ten o'clock in the morning.'

After a night with Vicki he expected to be sleeping most of the morning.

'Make it after lunch, Mitzi. Let's say three o'clock. What do you want to talk about?'

'I'll tell you when I see you.'

She rang off and Manfred put the telephone down. Her persistence puzzled him. Surely she could have taken the hint that he was not available and turned her attention to some other man. The answer could only be that she was short of money for the rent and food. He didn't mind helping her with that, if it was an emergency. Of course, he thought, she would then show her gratitude in the only way she could. The prospect of an afternoon of Mitzi's gratitude was not unwelcome. Mitzi with her clothes off was a big blonde doll to play with. She offered her pink and white body to her partner's desires and thoroughly enjoyed whatever was done to her – it was that which had endeared her to him. The contrast between her warm, soft and slow yielding and Vicki's demanding temperament was very marked. Vicki's physical thinness belied her wiry energy and her inventiveness in bed was astonishing – as was her insatiability. There had been nights with her when Manfred felt much like her neighbour across the courtyard – wrung-out and still trying to respond long after his body told him that it needed rest.

That being so, perhaps it was time to stop seeing Vicki and slide for a while into a more restful arrangement with Mitzi. The more he thought about it, the more pleasing a prospect it became. He conjured up a vision in his memory of the last time he made love to Mitzi, the day he had bought her the fur-coat. After lunch he took her back to her apartment and the landlady, after one look at the red-fox Mitzi was wearing, addressed Manfred as *Baron* and insisted on serving tea and little cakes in Mitzi's room. The tea went cold on the table while Manfred and Mitzi made love on the bed, she naked but wearing her new fur-coat so that the fur rubbed against his skin and the silk lining against her own. It was a long and delightful afternoon and one well worth repeating.

With these thoughts in his mind, the evening with Vicki proved less enchanting than usual. They danced and drank until about two in the morning and when they got back to her apartment, his intention was not to stay too long – just long enough for honour to be satisfied. Vicki had thought of a new twist to her cruel little game with her neighbour. She wanted Manfred to stay until seven in the morning and then make love to her in the kitchen, close to the partly-

108

drawn roller-blind, standing up and sideways on, so that the poor tormented man opposite would be incited to over-strain himself.

Manfred refused and told her he had no intention of performing in public.

'But it was public enough at Ulrika's party,' she said, 'it didn't bother you to make love to me on the marble slab with other people in the room.'

'That was different. That was for my pleasure and your pleasure. This wouldn't be. I'd never be able to do it for thinking of the man opposite staring at me the whole time.'

She grinned at him.

'I tell you what, I've got another idea. We'll stand by the blind naked when he comes to the window. He can only see a bit of you below the blind and you won't be able to see him at all. So there's no reason to be shy.'

'What then?' he asked cautiously.

'We'll just stand there, so that he sees my fox-fur and your lovely big tail, so that he knows someone else is getting what he can't get. And I'll play with you slowly – I'll make your tail stand up like a broom-stick handle and stroke it till you squirt all over my belly. That should really finish my peeping-tom off – with any luck he'll jump out of the window and break his bones.'

'Dear Vicki, what unnatural ideas you have!' he said, wondering if she could be entirely sane.

He gave her the hardest night of her life, deliberately holding back so that his energy would not be sapped, but making certain that she went all the way, time after time. He did it to her on her back, on her hands and knees, face-down and every other way that occurred to him, until her body was shiny with sweat and her red hair was plastered to her forehead and her face was thin and drawn with exhaustion. About five in the morning, with broad daylight coming in through the bed-room windows, she lay sprawled across the rumpled bed, only part-conscious. Manfred pulled her thin legs apart and spread himself over her.

'No, please,' she whispered, 'not again – I'm done for. Let me sleep.'

He thrust into her without mercy and rode her hard, ignoring her whimpering, and released his passion for the first and only time that night. When he rolled off her she lay with her eyes closed and did not move a muscle. He put his hand on her belly and her skin was cold to the touch. She was deeply unconscious.

Manfred dressed and left, determined to have no more to do with her. He was home and in bed before six and up and bathed and dressed in time for lunch. He thought it sensible to give the Geigers the afternoon off. If things worked out the way he expected with Mitzi, it would be inconvenient to have the servants in the apartment and he could take her out to dinner to show his gratitude for her gratitude.

At three the bell rang, he opened the door and there was Mitzi and beside her stood her friend Ilse Kleiber. Manfred's heart sank at the sight of Mitzi's protruding belly under her thin summer frock. Nevertheless, he greeted the two women courteously and took them into his drawing-room. Mitzi and Ilse sat side by side on the zebra-skin sofa, gloved hands in their laps, looking at him silently from under their small summer hats.

'My dear Mitzi,' he began, 'I am not sure whether congratulations are in order or not.'

'Congratulations on what?' she said sulkily.

'On your happy condition.'

'Happy! Is that what you call it?' she said shrilly, 'What do you think this is – a cushion under my clothes?'

She was on her feet suddenly, her frock hoisted up to her bosom, to display her bulging belly under thin white knickers.

'Look what you've done to me!'

Frock held high with one hand, she pulled her knickers down with the other, right down until the patch of fair hair between her thighs, so that all of her pale-skinned and swollen belly was bared to his sight. Her obvious distress, however theatrical its expression, moved Manfred to sympathy. He was off his chair and beside her in an instant, an arm round her shoulders to comfort her.

'Don't be upset, Mitzi – let us talk about this calmly.'

For some reason he did not try to explain to himself, his free hand was on her big belly, stroking it in a soothing manner. She turned her tear-stained face towards him.

'Sit down,' he suggested, 'we must discuss this. There are few problems which cannot be resolved with good will and good sense.'

'It was her good will and your lack of sense that put her in this state,' Ilse Kleiber observed acidly.

They sat down on the sofa, Ilse making room for them, and Mitzi huddled against him.

'How could this happen?' Manfred asked gently.

But it was Ilse who answered him.

'How? Have you forgotten? I'll tell you how it happened – she lay on her back and opened her legs and you got on top of her and . . .'

'You know what I mean,' Manfred interrupted.

'I don't know,' said Mitzi miserably, 'I've always been so careful. Oh Manfred, what am I going to do?'

She had dropped her frock when they sat down together but his hand was still under it, stroking the dome of her belly.

'My God!' Ilse exclaimed. 'What are you doing – trying to seduce her? Haven't you done enough damage already?'

'Shut up, Ilse!' said Mitzi. 'He has every right to stroke my belly if he wants to.'

'That's true,' said Ilse. 'After all, there's something of his inside it. The question is, what's he going to do about it, besides giving it a good feel?'

Mitzi's round and doll-like face turned to Manfred with a smile of complete trust.

'You will help me, won't you?'

The taut skin of her belly was smooth and warm and to stroke it was a pleasure that diverted Manfred's attention from the immediate problem. His hand slid down below the curve to touch the curls between her legs.

'What do you think is the best thing to do?' he asked.

'Marry her,' said Ilse immediately.

'Impossible.'

'Isn't she good enough for you?' asked Ilse sharply. 'Girls like us are all right for a quick bang but not for the gentry to marry, is that it? It would have been a different story if you'd put your friend Nina in the family way when she was dropping her knickers for you.'

'You don't know what you're talking about,' Manfred replied angrily, 'Mitzi is married already. The question doesn't arise.'

'Manfred, please don't be angry with me. Ilse means well.'

Under her loose frock her legs had moved apart on the sofa and Manfred's hand was well between them, inside her half-off underwear. Her pale blue eyes stared at him fondly.

'That's nice,' she whispered. 'It's been so long since anyone touched me.'

'Why? Didn't you want to?'

'I've been so miserable and scared since I found out. But it's all right again with you.'

'Never mind all that now,' said Ilse, 'is he going to look after you?'

'Of course he is,' said Mitzi happily.

'He hasn't said so.'

'You'll need money,' said Manfred, 'you can rely on me for that.'

'That's all right then,' said Ilse, 'I'm her witness.'

'She doesn't need a witness. My word is sacrosanct. Did I treat you badly when you helped them play that joke on me, Mitzi?'

'You were very nice to me,' she murmured, quivering with emotion as his fingers caressed the soft lips between her legs.

Ilse sat with her legs crossed tightly, as if she were experi-

112

encing the same interesting sensations between her legs as Mitzi. Her pretty face was flushed a light pink.

'You're not thinking of trying to make love to her?' she exclaimed. 'Not in her condition – four months gone!'

'That's for Mitzi to decide.'

'But in front of me!' Ilse protested, her voice jerky with emotion.

'You can wait outside.'

'But I'm her witness!'

'Then be a witness.'

'Manfred, I'm dying for it,' said Mitzi.

She pushed her white knickers down her legs and kicked them away.

'Move out of the way, Ilse,' she said quickly, 'go for a walk or something.'

No sooner was Ilse off the sofa than Mitzi spread herself along it, her back to Manfred and her frock pulled up again to her arm-pits. He understood at once and lay on his side behind her, to undo his trouser-buttons and let his hard stem emerge. Mitzi pulled her knees up towards her domed belly, a little manoeuvring found the right angle and Manfred pushed slowly into her until his belly was pressed firmly to her bottom.

'Oh yes,' she breathed, 'that's wonderful!'

He reached over her to clasp a breast while he thrust slowly and carefully with his loins. Behind him somewhere he heard Ilse gasping and fidgeting, then his attention was captured by the waves of pleasure that spread through him from his probing stem. Mitzi sighed and gurgled happily, evidently making up for lost time, but he kept himself on a tight rein so as not to discommode her in any way. His remembrance of Mitzi was that she responded very quickly and enjoyed two or three crises to his one. But that was all changed, he found, either by her physical condition or her mental state, and it was a long time before she shuddered and cried out in release. By then Manfred was clinging to his last remnant of self-control by his finger-nails almost and with a gasp of relief he jabbed quickly and discharged his passion quickly.

When he disengaged himself from her and rolled on to his back, Mitzi stayed curled up, her sighs of content almost those of the regular and slow breathing of a sleeper. It was obvious that his promise and his actions had removed a great nervous tension and she was at last resting easily.

Manfred turned his head to look for Ilse. She was sitting in an arm-chair and her skirt was pulled up high enough to show her bare thighs above her stockings. Her hand was down the front of her blue knickers and was moving busily. She caught Manfred's eye and stared glassily at him, her mouth hanging open.

'Yes, Ilse,' he said, 'do it!'

She tried to say something, but the words were blurred.

'I want to see you do it,' said Manfred, 'show me!'

Her free hand dragged her knickers down below her knees, her legs spread wider, and he saw the little patch of light brown hair between her thighs. With two joined fingers she was rubbing quickly between the parted folds of flesh there. He glanced up to her flushed face and her bulging eyes, then down again to her fluttering fingers.

'Yes, Ilse,' he said firmly. 'Yes, yes, yes! Do it for me!'

Her body convulsed in the chair, lifting her bottom off the seat as she uttered a wailing cry of garbled words and sobs. Slowly it faded to silence and stillness.

'You devil!' she said, staring at him, 'I don't know what it is, but seeing you with Mitzi gets me going every time.'

'Every time? But this is the first time you've ever seen me with her.'

'The first time I've actually seen you do it to her, maybe, but there was that time you were in her room – when Rosa and I were there.'

'What of it? You both left before anything happened.'

'Mitzi told us how you'd made her dance naked with you and I made a joke about fiancés having their rights.'

'I don't remember that.'

'You wouldn't – your only thought was to get Rosa and me out of the room so that you could make love to Mitzi.'

'It wasn't like that at all – you're romanticising the situation. I wanted to talk to her about the silly engagement business.'

'That's what you say now, but we were hardly out of the room before you had her clothes off and were at it. You can't deny that!'

'She told you that?'

'She didn't have to. My room is next to hers. I could hear her moaning and crying out through the wall. And it wasn't just once!'

'Dear Ilse,' said Manfred, grinning at her, 'you must have heard similar sounds through the wall many times when Mitzi was entertaining her men friends.'

'Plenty of times, but it never bothered me before. It was different that time. I couldn't get out of my mind the thought of you on top of her, bumping away. It drove me so frantic that I had to do what you've just seen me do. I know I shouldn't be telling you this – it will make you big-headed. You did it to her three times that evening and I had to play with myself three times to stop myself going crazy. I was a wreck the next day.'

'Ilse – I am amazed to think that I could possibly have such an effect on any woman, least of all a clever and experienced one like you.'

'Well, now you know. You must think I'm an idiot, especially after catching me at it this time.'

'Not at all. It was enchanting to watch you – and very exciting. Come here.'

Ilse was off the chair at once but, hobbled by her knickers below her knees, tripped and almost fell in her haste. She kicked her shoes off and trampled the blue underwear over her feet and was on her knees beside him. Her hands snatched at his shirt-front and underpants to bare him from chest to groins so that she could kiss his hot belly again and again. Her hand held his risen stem in a tight grasp and she mumbled words of endearment, almost to herself.

115

Manfred reached down over the edge of the zebra-skin sofa to feel between her legs and slide his fingers into her slippery depths.

'I can never resist a wet one,' he murmured.

Ilse shook and kissed his stem as if it were an object of adoration, her clenched hand moving up and down it in a frantic rhythm and, in response to her stimulation, his fingers rubbed faster in her moistness and he too was gasping as violently as she was and it was far too late to consider a change of position. Manfred's belly contracted and he spouted ecstatically into Ilse's sucking mouth. She gurgled and shuddered wildly, thrusting herself hard against his embedded fingers.

Mitzi stirred herself and rolled over carefully to face them. Ilse's head lay on Manfred's belly and his hand, removed from beneath her skirt now, rested on the back of her neck.

'I wasn't asleep you know,' said Mitzi, 'I was only resting. I knew what you were doing, but I don't mind. I know you've been hot for Manfred since the day you met him.'

'He knows that now,' Ilse answered dreamily, her tongue tickling inside his belly-button.

'You were good enough to tell me that you entertained a certain attachment for me,' said Manfred, who felt very pleased with himself, 'and however surprising I found that at first, your demonstration of affection has convinced me.'

'You devil!' said Ilse fondly.

'Isn't he wonderful!' said Mitzi proudly.

'Dear ladies, our expressions of mutual affection have resulted in a degree of disorder on so hot an afternoon. I suggest that we go to the bath-room and repair the ravages of love.'

They crowded naked together in the shower cubicle and let the warm water splash over them to take away the perspiration from their bodies. Manfred soaped his hands and began to wash Mitzi. She raised her arms and he saw that she had let the hair grow in her armpits and it was the same blonde floss as between her legs. He washed her breasts, unable to make up his mind whether they were bigger now than four months ago or whether the pink buds were getting darker in colour. He washed over her bulging belly with great care and down between her smooth thighs. Ilse, meanwhile, was scrubbing Mitzi's back vigorously, especially the round cheeks of her bottom.

'Don't get me wrong,' she said, 'but I've sometimes wondered what it's like to be a man and make love to a woman. Have you, Mitzi?'

'That's a strange idea!' said Mitzi with a giggle, 'I'm happy with things as they are.'

'You've wondered but you've never tried it?' Manfred asked, smiling at Ilse over Mitzi's wet shoulder.

'Not really. I had a friend at school who was that way inclined and sometimes we'd kiss and feel each other a bit. You know – schoolgirl stuff. Once or twice she went all the way when I had my hand in her knickers, but I never did when she played with me. Then I met a boy who couldn't keep his hands off me and before I knew it I was opening my legs for him.'

'And you've had them open ever since,' said Mitzi.

'Look who's talking,' Ilse retorted, good-naturedly. 'What I meant was not just playing about with another girl but being a man and having a great pink thing to stick in her. How does it feel, Manfred? You're the only one here who knows.'

'It feels very nice, but I don't suppose it's any nicer than being a girl and having a little slot to receive it.'

'But it must feel different, and that's what interests me.'

'I am not at all sure how your curiosity can be satisfied, Ilse, but I'll give the matter some thought,' he said with a grin.

When it was Ilse's turn to be washed she stood with her back to Manfred and leaned her wet body against him. He reached round to soap and stroke her breasts, smaller than Mitzi's and already a little slack, young as she was. By slow stages he worked his way down to her flat belly.

117

'Lower down,' she breathed.

He teased her by lathering her tuft and just above it.

'Lower!' she repeated.

Mitzi was smiling at her friend's eagerness. She put her own hand between Ilse's spread thighs and winked at Manfred.

'You want to know what it's like to be a man,' she said, 'but have you wondered what it's like to be made love to by another woman?'

'I want Manfred's hand there, not yours.'

'Close your eyes and see if you can tell the difference,' Manfred suggested.

'Stop it, you slut!' said Ilse, wriggling to get away from Mitzi's hand. Manfred tightened his hold, pinning her arms to her body and Mitzi grinned and took advantage of Ilse's predicament.

'Mitzi – I know why you're doing this,' she exclaimed, 'it's because of what I did to Manfred after he'd made love to you. But you said you didn't mind.'

'That's right. So why should you mind what I'm doing to you?'

'Mitzi, leave off! You'll make me do it!'

'Which is more than your school friend ever did.'

'What will Manfred think of us?'

'That you are an adorable pair of sluts,' he said, kissing her wet ear.

At that her protests stopped. Her wet body relaxed against him and in a short time Mitzi's attentions brought her to the critical moments and she cried out in pleasurable release. Manfred stroked her belly lightly to soothe her and soon she was herself again.

'You devils – both of you!' she declared, 'I'll pay you back for that when I get the chance.'

The two of them washed Manfred with great attention and thoroughness. For him it was pure delight to stand beneath the cascading water and feel four hands moving over his body, touching, stroking, rubbing. His stem stood rigidly to attention, making the women laugh at the sight.

They covered it with scented soap-suds and washed the suds off, but they were very careful not to precipitate a crisis.

They dried each other and moved into the main bedroom. Manfred lay with an arm round each of them, feeling like an Oriental despot in his harem. The afternoon had turned out very much better than he feared when he first opened the door and observed Mitzi's condition. The moment seemed right now that both women had softened towards him to tell them what was in his mind. Each hand cupped round a warm breast, he began.

'Now, my dears, we must discuss the situation in which Mitzi finds herself. I have already promised that she can look to me for help, but there are things we should all understand.'

'What things?' Mitzi asked.

'The truth of the matter is this, Mitzi – there is no certainty that it is I who am responsible for your condition.'

Both women would have sat up to protest, but his firm grip on them held them close to him while he continued.

'We shall examine the facts, my darlings. When I met you at my birthday party, you were with Werner Schiele. I find it impossible to believe that he had not availed himself of your good-nature. Indeed, you told me that you had been with him for some time when we had lunch together after we went shopping. I made love to you for two days, no more. After that I am sure that you found someone else quickly enough. After all, you are a very attractive woman.'

'What are you saying?' Mitzi asked timorously.

He squeezed the breast he was holding affectionately.

'I am saying that there is only a one in three chance that I am responsible. Isn't that so?'

'I'm sure it was you, Manfred. Women know these things.'

'Easy enough to say, dear Mitzi, but you cannot be sure either. What is happening in your belly may just as well be Werner's doing as mine, or the man after me. Who was he?'

119

'Dieter Bruckner. He was at your party.'

'Of course, he saw you dancing naked with me – that would certainly interest him. Does he know about the problem?'

'He threw her out weeks ago when he found out,' said Ilse. 'He's a pig.'

'And Werner, have you told him?'

'He's vanished and I can't find him.'

'That only leaves you,' said Ilse, trying to take over the negotiations again. 'You can see why we had to come here.'

'I'm not blaming you. But I don't want you to think that I'm a complete fool.'

'I was desperate,' said Mitzi. 'Please forgive me.'

'Werner Schiele is in hiding,' said Manfred, 'and I can guess where.'

'Who is he hiding from – the police?'

'He thinks he's going to be murdered by an outraged husband, but it was only a joke, I'm sure he's in Vienna. I'll be able to get hold of him through friends. I'll offer to make peace for him with Nina's husband if he'll give you a decent amount of money. He'll be miserable away from Berlin, so there's every chance he'll agree.'

'And Dieter?' Ilse asked.

'Leave him to me. I've known him long enough to be able to squeeze something out of him. There are certain private activities he keeps very quiet about in case his father finds out. So there you are – three possible fathers, three contributors towards your maintenance.'

'Oh, Manfred! What can I say,' Mitzi murmured.

'You're cleverer than I thought,' Ilse added.

'Then that's settled, dear ladies.'

'We're not ladies,' said Ilse, 'we're sluts – that's what you said.'

'Adorable sluts,' he corrected her.

She put her hand on his thigh and stroked slowly upwards.

'Being treated like a slut is more enjoyable than being treated like a lady,' she said, 'at least, I think so.'

120

'Why, how do you imagine ladies like to be treated?'

'How do I know? They always look so elegant that it's hard to imagine them without their clothes on. I mean – what grand lady would finger me in the shower the way Mitzi did?'

'My cousin Ulrika would take great pleasure in doing that to you while I held you fast.'

'She must be the exception to the rule then. You'd never get a grand lady to do what I did to you on the sofa. I'm sure that if one of them ever touched this thing of yours she'd keep her gloves on. And as for kissing it – never!'

'Dear Ilse, how wrong you are. This thing of mine, as you call it, has had the pleasure of being kissed very thoroughly by several Baronesses.'

'Did they know what to do?' she asked incredulously.

'The grand ladies you think so highly of behave exactly as you do when their clothes are off, I assure you.'

'Do you hear that, Mitzi? What do you think – you've been taken to parties where grand people go – do they carry on the way Manfred says?'

'All I know about ladies is that they go out with no knickers on.'

'No, they don't!' said Ilse, 'What a ridiculous idea! They wear expensive knickers made of silk with lace and embroidery. I've seen them in the shops.'

'The young ladies I have the honour of knowing wear no underwear,' Manfred informed her, highly amused by the conversation, 'it went out of fashion years ago.'

'Dirty little whores!' Ilse exclaimed. 'So who wears the fancy knickers in the shops?'

'Adorable little sluts like you, of course. I'll buy you half a dozen pairs each.'

'They won't fit me,' said Mitzi ruefully, but Ilse was much captivated by the suggestion and stroked his hard stem in gratitude.

'Will you watch me try them on?'

'I doubt if any of the shops would permit that.'

'I suppose not. But at least you'll help me choose them –

then I shall know what colours you like best. And afterwards you can have a private exhibition, just like you did with Mitzi in her fur-coat.'

'I didn't say I didn't want them,' said Mitzi, 'I only said they won't fit me just now. But in a few months' time they will.'

By then Ilse's attention was focussed on what she held and its possibilities.

'What *is* it like to be a man and make love to a woman with this?' she asked softly. 'Can't you explain it to me at all?'

'There's no way of describing sensations in words. But I have an idea that may help you to understand,' he said, greatly excited by her fondling.

He pulled Ilse on top of him and parted his legs so that hers were between his.

'I don't mind being on top,' she said, 'but it doesn't answer my question. I've made love like this before, you know.'

'This time will be different.'

He put his hands down between their bellies to open her and guide his stem into her.

'Raise yourself on your arms, Ilse.'

She put her hands on the bed and lifted her upper body clear of him, and only their loins were pressed together.

'Now, close your eyes and don't move,' he murmured, 'this is the time for your imagination to take over. Imagine that you're a man and that you're lying on top of a woman. You are Manfred and you're going to make love to Ilse with that strong thing you've pushed inside me. I'm Ilse lying under you and my legs are open for you and I can feel your stem inside me.'

'Ah,' she whispered, her hot belly wriggling on his.

'Bend your neck and look down between us to where we are joined – don't look anywhere else at all, just there.'

She did as he said, dropping her head before she opened her eyes. He too stared down the length of his body. Where their bellies met there were two patches of very light-brown

122

hair, his and hers, not much different in shade, linked by the short section of his column that was now inside her.

'Keep looking at that,' he said very quietly, 'you can see how your stem is going into me.'

'Oh yes!' she moaned.

'Make love to me with it – I want you to.'

Her loins began to thrust against him in short hard stabs.

'I can see it going into you!' she gasped, 'I'm making love to you, Ilse! Can you feel me inside you?'

'Yes, yes! It's so long and thick and hard – do it to me, Manfred!' he moaned, 'I want all of you in me – all of you!'

She slammed herself harder and faster against him, groaning with pleasure.

'I'm going to do it!' she shrieked, 'I'm going to fill you full!'

The crisis swept through them both at the same instant. Ilse cried out again and again as she pounded against him and he cried out with her in his pleasure and for seconds that seemed an eternity they lost their identities and neither knew which was doing it to the other.

At long last Ilse's arms gave way and she collapsed on to him and lay panting. Manfred put his arms round her and held her close.

'My God – you nearly had me off the bed with your jolting,' said Mitzi, forgotten beside them.

But neither paid any attention to her. Ilse was kissing Manfred's face and he was stroking the cheeks of her bottom to soothe and calm her.

'You're utterly fantastic,' she said, 'you really made me believe that I was making love to you! I could see myself sliding into you.'

'And is your question answered now?'

'In a way, but . . .'

Her words trailed off.

'There's no pleasing you!' said Mitzi sharply, 'He's done his best for you, so be content with that. If God had wanted you to be a man He wouldn't have given you a slit between your legs. Not that it matters, but the telephone is ringing.'

123

'Let it ring,' said Manfred, 'we're not at home to anyone.'

'It might be important. Get off him, Ilse, and let him answer the telephone.'

Manfred recognised the signs of jealousy and eased Ilse off.

'There is something far more important at this moment then answering casual telephone calls,' he said, 'come here in the middle, Mitzi, so that your two very good friends can put their arms round you and cuddle you.'

'Cuddle me! A lot of good that will do me now she's drained you dry with her silly curiosity.'

All the same, she clambered awkwardly over Manfred and lay in the middle.

'Mitzi is feeling left out of things,' he said, stroking her breasts lightly, 'She is passing through a difficult time in her life and she needs all the love and comfort her friends can give her.'

'Poor Mitzi,' said Ilse, stroking her friend's domed belly, 'I know you've got your troubles, but you have to be brave. We'll look after you, you know that. And Frau Brubecker will let you keep your room now you've got the money to pay her. So there's nothing to worry about.'

'Yes, there is!' said Mitzi, sounding as if she was about to break into tears, 'I can't make love properly any more and seeing you doing it made me realise what I was missing.'

'Only for a few months,' Ilse comforted her, 'then you'll be at it twice a night again, just like before.'

'And look what I got for it!' Mitzi complained.

Manfred put his hand between her legs and tickled her.

'That afternoon when you and I made love on the fur-coat was one of the nicest of my life,' he told her.'

'Was it?' she asked doubtfully. 'After what you said about Baronesses kissing you all over I wouldn't think that making love to me was anything special for you.'

'But you're wrong. We really liked each other, you and I, and that made all the difference. You know yourself how much better it is to make love with a man you like a lot

124

than one you like a little. The physical sensations may be the same, but the satisfaction is on another level entirely.

'It was nice with you every time, even when it was only for a joke,' she answered, mollified by his words and by his touch between her legs.

Manfred nodded to Ilse, who understood his intention and slid her hand up to Mitzi's breasts to caress them softly.

'That damned telephone is ringing again,' said Mitzi with a sigh.

'A wrong number,' Manfred assured her, his finger-tip finding her secret bud, 'pay no attention to it and it will soon stop.'

Ilse's thumbs were flicking over Mitzi's nipples, teasing them to firmness.

'It's your bell that's going to ring,' said Manfred.

The Twins

Manfred's elder brother rarely visited Berlin and even more
rarely brought his wife with him when he did. This relieved
Manfred of the decent dullness such a visit would otherwise
have entailed. On this visit they dined with the Behrendorfs
one evening, as Sigmund liked Gottfried and generally
invited him to stay with him in the country for the shooting.
Nina played the hostess impeccably and by all impressions
had been forgiven for the unfortunate incident at Ulrika's
celebration. Needless to say, there was no mention of it at
all. There were two other married couples present, not
very interesting people in Manfred's opinion, and Nina's
unmarried sister and a widowed sister of Gottfried's, to
even up the numbers.

On another day they visited cousin Ulrika for five o'clock
tea. She wore a pretty afternoon frock and looked remarkably demure, though she offended Gottfried once or twice
by the frankness of her conversation. Manfred took
Sigmund to see Oskar's production of *Three in a Bed* and
that went down well enough. And on the last night of
Sigmund's stay, Manfred took him to the White Mouse
cabaret after dinner.

It was expensive, hot and crowded, the main attraction
being its nude dancers. For himself Manfred did not find
it stimulating to watch a young woman wearing only red
shoes twirl about a stage, but Sigmund did. For most of
the time he was cut off from entertainment of that kind,
his only diversions being field sports with horses, guns and
dogs, the charms of his placid wife, and whatever he could

126

arrange in the way of discreet adultery with his neighbours' wives. For this reason, Manfred considered, it was necessary to make allowances for Sigmund when he came to Berlin and let him indulge himself.

The nude dancer twirled as gracefully as she could, her breasts rolling about to her gyrations, and she must have made a marked impression on Sigmund for, when two women of the house sat down uninvited at the table, he made them welcome and ordered another bottle of champagne at once.

The *hostesses* were pretty enough in their way, but Manfred felt no urgent desire to pay for their services. With Sigmund it was otherwise. He took a liking to the fair-haired one, chatted to her confidentially and kept filling her glass. In short, he gave every indication of wishing to make her closer acquaintance. Manfred was not surprised in the least when, after a whispered conversation with her, Sigmund turned to ask him a question.

'This young lady has graciously invited me to her apartment,' he confided, 'What do you think – is it safe to go with her?'

'She won't rob you or let her pimp murder you, Sigmund, if that's what you mean. And if you ask to see her police book, you'll know when she had her last medical inspection.'

Sigmund had by then had a fair amount to drink and brushed aside such unromantic considerations.

'Then if you have no objections, little brother, I'll be off and leave you with the other young lady.'

And off he swaggered, the blonde on his arm, leaving Manfred to pay the bill. It was not much after eleven, according to Manfred's wrist-watch, but the evening was over. Sigmund had found what he wanted and Manfred was left with half a bottle of champagne and a young woman in a tight green frock. She obviously expected him to follow his brother's lead and her hand was on his thigh to encourage him.

'Not tonight, my dear. I'm tired and I'm going home.'

127

'It's your loss. You'd soon be frisky if you came with me.'

'Some other time perhaps.

But however good his intentions were, fate had ordained that he would not sleep in his own bed that night. As he left the White Mouse he collided by accident with a girl in a little wrap and her hand-bag was knocked from her hand and spilled its contents on the ground.

'A thousand pardons, Fraulein. That was very clumsy of me.'

He squatted on his haunches to help her retrieve the multiplicity of small objects – a lipstick in a silver case, a powder compact that had burst open and scattered its powder widely, keys, rouge, a folded bundle of bank-notes, a tiny lace handkerchief and all the other paraphernalia that women carry. As she squatted beside him, Manfred saw her legs and was impressed. Her skirt had ridden up to show slender and shapely thighs in gossamer thin silk stockings. He looked at her face and found that she was very pretty and not more than about eighteen. She had a small mouth painted scarlet, eyebrows plucked to a thin arch over large blue eyes, a soft little chin – and her hair was straw-blonde and arranged in a profusion of tiny curls.

He helped her to her feet.

'May I find you a taxi?'

'Thank you, yes. I'm not going far but I'm nervous about being alone on the streets at this time of night.'

'Naturally – one reads such dreadful things in the newspapers.'

His words were from politeness only. Young women who strolled the streets at night were not usually nervous.

'I have my car here,' he said, intrigued by the girl, 'may I have the pleasure of driving you home?'

She hesitated at that and looked him over very carefully before committing herself. She must have liked what she saw, because she accepted his offer. Manfred took her arm and walked her to where he had parked, introducing himself as they went. She told him that her name was Tania

Kessler and, without being asked, explained how she came to be alone outside the cabaret. She had been there with a friend, had quarrelled with him and walked out.

As they drove off Manfred turned his charm on her, in the hope that the evening would not be such a fiasco as he had thought.

'This friend – he let you go off on your own? He must be a fool to let so beautiful a young lady walk away from him.'

'I told him I never wanted to see him again. But what about you – why were you in there? Were you looking for a woman?'

Manfred told her about his brother's visit and how he had been deserted.

'How disappointing,' she said cheerfully. 'What do you suppose your brother is doing now?'

'I can guess exactly what he is doing but I would not dare to describe it to you.'

'Do you think I'm a virgin?' she teased him. 'Tell me – what is your brother doing at this moment?'

The conversation had taken a turn which Manfred found promising.

'By now he is in bed with the woman he left with.'

'And?'

'He's not very imaginative. He'll be sprawled on her, thumping away. Unless she has shown him another possibility, of course.'

'Are you imaginative?'

Her hand touched his on the steering-wheel and he knew that the night was not over by a long way.

'I try to approach these matters in a spirit of adventure, Fraulein Tania. There is much more to making love than my brother will ever know.'

'How true that is,' she sighed. 'Do you find me attractive, Manfred?'

'You know that I do. Are you going to invite me in?'

'Wait and see.'

He parked the car outside her apartment building and

assisted her out. Standing there in the street he put his arms about her and kissed her. Her perfume was exciting and her little red mouth was soft under his. Her responsiveness emboldened him to slip a hand under her wrap and lightly clasp a small breast through the thin silk of her frock.

'Are you sure you want to come in with me?' she asked somewhat archly.

'Can there be any doubt?'

She led him up to an apartment on the second floor. The lights were out and she did not switch them on, but Manfred was able to make out that the apartment was well decorated and furnished. Either her family was well-to-do or, more probably, the friend with whom she had quarrelled had been keeping her in good style. Once in her bed-room, she switched on a bed-side lamp which cast a warm and dim glow through the room, discarded her wrap and invited him to sit beside her on a pink chaise-longue which stood by the wall opposite the bed.

Manfred kissed her at length and would have caressed her breasts again, but she stopped him and became coquettish.

'I invited you into my apartment. I didn't invite you to make love to me.'

'As far as it goes, what you say is perfectly true. But there is an unspoken understanding when a pretty girl asks a man to her bed-room late at night. A virgin might not know that – she might think that he was with her to discuss poetry or politics or Patagonia. But as you were so good as to inform me that you are not a virgin, I can only conclude that you are familiar with the conventions of meetings of this sort, young as you are.'

Tania giggled and put her hand on his thigh. It was a long and narrow hand with finger-nails lacquered scarlet to match her lipstick.

'You have a persuasive tongue,' she said. 'Before I know what's happening I'll find myself beneath you and you thumping away like your brother with his whore. That's not my idea of making love.'

130

'I'm pleased to hear it. You must tell me what pleases you.'

Her long fingers unbuttoned his trousers slowly.

'I like to know what I'm being offered before I accept it.'

'Dear Tania, you make me feel like a fruit on a market-stall being squeezed by a housewife before she buys it,' he said, enjoying the touch of her hand on his upright stem.

She put the tip of her tongue in his ear and then whispered to him.

'It's so big and hot! I'm afraid it's going to explode in my hand.'

'Not in your hand – not until we find a cosier place for it than that.'

'You promise?'

Her fingers played with him very skilfully. Her pretty face had a most serious expression on it as she observed what she was doing to him and the tip of her wet tongue played over her top lip. Manfred put his hand on her thigh, under her frock and moved it upwards, over the fine silk of her stocking and to the warm flesh above the stocking-top, where a suspender gripped. His fingers touched the lace edge of loose-legged knickers and he remembered what he had told Ilse about women who wore underwear like that.

Tania's legs parted for him and he felt higher, seeking her furry mound, only to encounter another and very tight-fitting garment inside her knickers. This puzzled him and he reached higher still until his hand closed on a long and hard bulge held firmly against her belly by what felt like a silk cache-sexe.

Instantly he wrenched his hand away and jerked Tania's skirt up to her waist with one hand while, with the other, he ripped down her underwear. He stared in disbelief at what he had exposed – a thin and hard stem rising from between her thighs! Tania was unmistakably a young man.

'Damn it to hell!' Manfred roared. 'What the devil do you think you're playing at!'

His outrage was such that he swung his arm at the creature's blonde-curled head and knocked him from the chaise-longue to the carpet.

'Of all the dirty, disgusting, swinish tricks!' he shouted, up on his feet in blind fury, 'I'll kill you!'

The boy who pretended to be a girl had landed face-down and was covering his head with his arms to protect it. Manfred, who hardly knew what he was doing, kicked him in the side.

'Horrible little pervert!'

'Don't hurt me,' the boy whimpered.

He scrambled up on his hands and knees to escape and squealed loudly when Manfred landed a hearty kick on his bottom. How long the violence would have continued before Manfred regained control of himself, who can say? Fortunately for the victim, the door opened so fast that it slammed against the wall and a figure in pink silk pyjamas rushed in.

'For God's sake leave him alone! You'll kill him!'

'Yes I will!' Manfred shouted back. 'He led me on, the little swine! I thought he was a girl!'

He rolled *Tania* over roughly with his foot while fending Silk Pyjamas off with one arm. Tania's frock was up round his waist and the ruins of his torn underwear hung round his slender thighs. There stood the unambiguous emblem of his masculinity, rising from hairless groins.

'Filthy little pig!' Manfred snarled. 'Is that a girl? I ask you!'

'Come away,' Silk Pyjamas shrilled. 'Leave him alone.'

Manfred's anger was waning. He let himself be hustled out of the room, and into another bed-room across the passage, grumbling as he went.

'Sit there,' said Silk Pyjamas, pointing to a chair, 'I'll get you a drink while you calm down.'

'Who are you?' he growled.

'I'm Ludwig's sister. You can't really have thought he was a girl – he usually brings his own kind home. Where did you meet him – in the Eldorado Bar?'

132

'Certainly not! I don't go to places like that where the men all dress up as women. He was in the *White Mouse*.'

'Albert must have taken him there as a joke. But are you sure you thought he was a girl? I mean, some men are not very honest about their amusements. They do one thing and pretend another.'

'He had breasts! I touched them.'

'You're easily fooled. They're made of soft rubber.'

Manfred took the class of brandy he was offered and thought things over. Now that his anger had dissipated the whole episode seemed ridiculous.

'You're right – I'm a complete idiot. He took me in completely. He's as pretty as any girl and the make-up was perfect. You're his sister, you said?'

'We're twins. I'm Helga and he's Ludwig, but he calls himself Tania when he dresses up as a girl.'

Manfred surveyed his companion carefully. The same size and shape as the other one, the same pale blonde hair, though straight instead of curled.

'You look remarkably alike. Please accept my apologies for disturbing you. I hope I haven't hurt him too badly.'

'There's no need for apologies. This is not the first time I've had to rescue him. Some of the men he brings home are very dangerous.'

'It must be difficult to have a brother like that.'

'He's a nice person really, and very intelligent. But when he goes out dressed as Tania, anything can happen. What's your name?'

'Manfred von Klausenberg.'

'I seem to know a lot about you, Manfred, even though we've just met.'

'Really? What do you know about me?'

'I know that you prefer girls to boys, that you like brandy, that you can afford very elegant evening clothes – and that you've got a fine-looking tail. That's four things already.'

Manfred glanced down at her words and saw that his trousers were still undone, as Ludwig had left them, and

133

that his limp *tail* was hanging out. He hurriedly made himself decent and apologised. Helga laughed and she sounded so much like *Tania* that a suspicion entered his mind.

'You say that you are Ludwig's sister?'

'His twin sister.'

'How do I know that you're not his twin brother? I've been deceived once tonight.'

Helga laughed and she sounded even more like Tania. She ran her hands downwards over her silk pyjama jacket to outline her small breasts.

'Now do you believe me?'

'They might be rubber, for all I know.'

'They might be, but they're not,' and she unbuttoned her jacket and let it hang loosely open so that he could see her small and pointed breasts.

'Now do you believe me?'

'They might be artificial ones, stuck on. How do I know?'

She stood up from the bed and untied the cord of her pyjama trousers so that they slipped down her legs and he saw her light-brown tuft and no sign of anything that should not be there.

'Well?' she asked.

'You're his sister.'

'I'm glad we've got that settled, said Helga, running her fingers through the curls she had revealed. 'You came here expecting to find one of these and you found one like your own instead. What a disappointment for you.'

'It was the worst shock I've ever had in my life, I assure you.'

'Would it be cruel to send you home disappointed now that you know that the real thing is available, I wonder?'

Manfred needed no further invitation. He discarded his jacket and sat on the bed with her, to kiss her and fondle her breasts inside her open pyjamas. They were authentic, no question about that.

'You look so much like each other,' he said, 'it's unnerving.'

'That's because he dresses and makes himself up to look like me. I'm the genuine one and he's the fake.'

There was a bump somewhere in the apartment.

'Is he all right?' Manfred asked. 'I only kicked his backside a few times.'

'Don't worry about him,' she said, pulling his hand down between her thighs, 'he likes to be beaten up. It's part of his fantasy of being a girl.'

'Surely not!'

'You wouldn't believe half of it if I told you.'

'Try me.'

'There was one night when Albert was staying with me and we were in the middle of you know what when we heard screams from Ludwig's room. I knew what it was and ran in to save him and there was this man punching him all round the room. He wasn't trying to knock him down, just hurt him. Some of them are like that – they get their thrill from beating each other or being beaten.'

'Surely this person had been given a nasty shock, as I was, and was retaliating in the same way,' said Manfred, stroking between her legs.

'It wasn't like that. They were both stark naked and they'd done it already. And while Ludwig went reeling round the room, with this man hitting him, his pecker jerked up again with every punch, till it stuck out like a handle. Every time a punch landed on him it jerked up in the air – you've never seen anything like it!'

'Incredible,' said Manfred, his fingers stirring inside Helga's warm and authentic affair.

'The fists landed on his face and body with a great slapping noise and his sticker jumped every time as if it were on a string – smack, jump, smack, jump, just like that. I grabbed the man round the waist from behind to try to stop him but he was too strong for me. He gave Ludwig a punch in the belly that doubled him over and brought him to his knees – and would you believe it – he squibbed off, halfway across the room! There was I, without a stitch on, hanging on to this gorilla to stop him hitting Ludwig – and

135

there was dear Ludwig down on his knees enjoying the thrill! Then Albert came in, having wasted all this time getting into his trousers, and he threw the man out and his clothes after him. Ah, Manfred!'

She writhed and shook and Manfred wondered how much of her sudden ecstasy was due to his fondling and how much to the story she had told him. It was clear that there was a most unusual rivalry between Helga and her twin brother and he guessed that being invited into her bed was some form of revenge on Ludwig.

When she was quiet again, he undressed and got into bed with her. Her arms closed round him, she rubbed her slender young body against his, and they embarked on a memorable night of love-making. Her climaxes came easily and she gave him little pause between them before her hands were playing with him again to rouse him to renew his attentions to her. It was only when his soldier refused to stand to attention again that she at last reluctantly let him go to sleep, her arms tightly round him as if she feared he might run away. He woke in the morning to the pleasant sensation of her hand stroking his refreshed soldier, now ready to do his duty again and this time Helga lay on top of him and did all the work, as if she were greedy for whatever affection she believed he was offering her.

Later on, they were in the kitchen, drinking coffee, when Ludwig put in an appearance. He was wearing trousers and a pullover and seemed no worse the wear for what had happened. Nor was he in the least embarrassed to find Manfred at the table with Helga, his evening jacket over the back of his chair.

'You're still here,' Ludwig said, smiling pleasantly. 'Did you sleep well?'

'Well, but not long.'

It was after ten o'clock and neither of the twins appeared to be in any hurry to go anywhere. Manfred sat and talked and listened and learned. They were runaways, as he had guessed, and had come to Berlin less than a year before from an unhappy home in Magdeburg. What they lived on

136

was not explained to him and he did not ask. Whatever it was, it enabled them to live well, for by daylight Manfred saw that the apartment was a good one and well-furnished.

Ludwig proved to be an interesting conversationalist. He made no reference to the antics of the previous night, but talked sensibly and was obviously a well-educated young man. As for Helga, Manfred liked her. She was very pretty, well-spoken and, as he had ascertained, accomplished in bed. She gave every impression of liking Manfred, but whether that was to irk her brother was impossible to say on such short acquaintance. The resemblance between the twins was remarkable when the two sat side by side – the same pretty face, the same eyes, the same build. Their hair was the same shade of straw, though Helga's was straight and Ludwig had his in little curls – the result of long and frequent labours with curlers and hot irons, no doubt. And there was one other important difference at breakfast – under his striped pullover Ludwig's chest was flat, while Helga's little breasts pushed out the front of her pink silk dressing-gown.

After the drama of that first meeting Manfred saw Helga as often as she would let him, which was not very often. He came to understand that the Albert she had mentioned who had thrown Ludwig's friend out on his ear was keeping her. It surprised him at first that she would accept invitations to dinner and to go dancing and to sleep with him when she was financially dependent on another man, but before long he became aware that she did not like Albert much at all and would be pleased if Manfred offered to replace him as paymaster. But Manfred had no wish for a commitment like that. It seemed to him more sensible to entertain her, take her shopping from time to time for frocks and other fripperies and enjoy her company in bed whenever he could, while the mysterious Albert took care of the rest.

In these weeks he also got to know Ludwig well and found him sufficiently amusing to ask along sometimes when he took Helga to the theatre or to lunch. Ludwig often talked about freedom and insisted that it was the driving need of every aware person to break free from the bonds of the past, otherwise that person's life was no more meaningful than that of a prisoner. In this he was referring to far more than his flight with Helga from their home to Berlin. The drive towards freedom was to be seen, said Ludwig, in literature and in the theatre and in painting. Liberated spirits were creating new visions of truth for those who could understand them. The first time he and Helga visited Manfred's apartment, he turned up his nose at the pictures on the walls, exactly as Max Schroeder had done on the unforgettable evening of the birthday party. Ludwig had familiarised himself with the work of modern German painters and admired them indiscriminately. He was so persuasive on this subject that he succeeded in dragging Manfred to an art-dealer on the Kurfurstendamm. Manfred stared in total incomprehension at canvases daubed with garish swathes of colour and pictures of oddly distorted people doing inexplicable things. All this, he was sure, was the outcome of a conspiracy between dealers and artists to foist rubbish on the public at high prices.

Nevertheless, Ludwig's enthusiasm and the skill of the dealer won him over and he bought the least offensive painting in the gallery. At the very least it might be a good investment, he considered.

The painting showed two naked and grossly fat women sitting at a small round table, flanking a middle-aged man who resembled a pig in evening clothes. A bottle and two empty glasses stood on the table, and an ash-tray that held a stubbed-out cigar. The colours were hideous, the complexions of the women being greenish and that of the man a muddy purple. What the significance of it might be was beyond Manfred, though he guessed that the artist, whose signature in the corner looked like Glitz, had seen some of the paintings of Toulouse-Lautrec but wasn't up to the same standard. He asked Helga what she thought of it and she was deferential towards her brother for once,

138

saying that if Ludwig said it was a master-piece, then it must be so.

Manfred paid for it, thinking that he would have preferred to have bought one of Horst's studies of Rosa nude. At least Horst painted women any man would be pleased to get hold of, not Glitz's ghastly creatures with sharks' jaws and breasts sagging down to their bellies. For that matter, he would have preferred a nude portrait of Helga by Horst. But he was half-inclined to believe the dealer when he said that the painting would appreciate greatly in value as Glitz's reputation grew to European status and then in due course to international acclaim. There were, Manfred thought, enough rich idiots in the world to bring the dealer's words true.

After he had completed the arrangements to have the painting delivered and hung, he took the twins to the Café Schon on Unter den Linden, it being late in the afternoon and Manfred feeling a need for alcoholic sustenance after spending so much money on something he didn't like. They found a table on the terrace where they could watch the passers-by on the avenue. They had been talking about painting over their drinks for perhaps ten minutes when Jenny Montrose turned into the terrace. She looked wonderfully elegant and attractive in a summer jacket and skirt of tan shantung. Manfred's heart soared as he rose to his feet to greet her.

His mouth opened wide in surprise when her companion, a short man, appeared from behind her. He was a negro with a shiny coal-black face and grinning white teeth. He was dressed in a striped blazer and a straw boater-hat.

'This is Eddie Jones,' said Jenny. 'He's from Philadelphia and he's a trumpet player. Perhaps you have heard him?'

Manfred introduced Helga and Ludwig and invited Jenny to join them. Eddie spoke almost no German at all and sat quietly with his drink while Manfred made himself pleasant to Jenny. American jazz-players had been hugely popular for the past year or two, ever since the *Chocolate Kiddies* revue had been staged in Berlin, but Manfred had

139

never before met a negro socially and was not entirely certain how to proceed. Nor did he understand why some of his intellectual friends accorded jazz some sort of cultural importance. For him it was useful to liven up a party, but not really music in any real sense.

Apart from that, there was in his mind a hazy picture of Jenny and Eddie making love. It was hard to imagine the beautiful body he had seen at Ulrika's celebration lying alongside the shiny black body of the musician, his dark hands on her white breasts. And beyond that – when he lay on her . . . presumably his stem was as black-skinned as the rest of him, and that was a strange thought.

The truth was, Manfred admitted to himself, that he was jealous. He wanted Jenny for himself and to this end he set out to be charming, not caring whether Helga was listening or not. But to his invitations to lunches, dinners, dances, theatres, Jenny was polite and friendly and regretted that she was unable to accept. Eddie, in ignorance of what was being said, grinned happily across the table at Helga. Manfred saw that he was wasting his breath – Jenny was much too involved with her fellow-countryman at present to become interested in anyone else. So he abandoned his pursuit and talked cheerfully of other things. When Jenny left, with Eddie tagging along behind, Helga gave Manfred a furious look and did not speak to him for the next half-hour. But that night, in bed, she was particularly tender and attentive towards him, as if fearing that he would disappear from her life as suddenly as he had entered it.

There was an afternoon when Manfred called at the apartment in Auguststrasse by arrangement to take Helga out. Ludwig let him in and explained that Albert had arrived unexpectedly and taken his sister to lunch.

'Then I will be on my way. Please ask her to telephone me when she returns.'

'I'm sure she'll be back soon. Stay and talk. Albert never has time for her in the afternoon.'

Manfred sat down opposite Ludwig, who was neatly dressed in an open-necked white shirt and grey trousers. It seemed a useful opportunity to find out a little more about Helga's benefactor.

'This Albert – what is his other name?'

'Grutz – Albert Grutz. He's tremendously rich, you know. He made a fortune in the big inflation, though I don't know how.'

'What sort of man is he?'

'He's very generous. To look at he's big and heavy and has a thick old-fashioned moustache. He's about fifty, I suppose. He has a big house in Grunewald Forest, though we've never seen it. I mean, he can't invite us there like you do to your apartment because he's married and has five children. The oldest son is older than I am.'

The picture of Albert that emerged was not much to Manfred's taste, even though Ludwig seemed to like him and Helga obviously found him tolerable, for reasons of her own.

'Is he liberated?' Manfred asked with a smile, referring to Ludwig's usual preoccupation.

'No, he's a prisoner of his own past. He'd like to break free but he's too old to take such a big step.'

'Do you know anyone at all who is free, in the way you mean it?'

'I am,' said Ludwig proudly.

'How so?'

'Because I can become Tania whenever I want to. When I'm Tania I can do whatever I like.'

'You are suggesting that women are in some way more free than men? I don't believe that for one moment.'

'You haven't understood me. When I put on women's clothes and become Tania, it is a spiritual experience. It is to cut the bonds with the past and to see the world in a new way.'

'But changing your clothes does not change the essential *you*, Ludwig. There are women who put on men's evening clothes, but they are still women under the starched shirt-front. The American lady we met the other day – Fraulein Montrose – I have seen her in men's clothes. But it doesn't

141

mean anything. It is like going to a fancy-dress party in disguise. You may be dressed as Frederick the Great or Julius Caesar, but you are still yourself.'

Ludwig began to describe what happened to him spiritually when he put on women's clothes, arguing that Manfred was wrong and that the personality underwent a change in accordance with the attire. Eventually he offered to prove his point if Manfred would agree to an experiment. Totally unconvinced, Manfred followed Ludwig into his bed-room, feeling slightly foolish but ready to settle the point.

Ludwig opened a wardrobe and showed him a dozen frocks hanging there, colourful, beautiful and expensive.

'Just for a moment try to imagine yourself wearing one of those instead of your suit. Touch the material and feel its delicacy – silk, satin, chiffon!'

'I cannot imagine wearing anything like that.'

'That's because you're shackled to the past, to old ideas and worn-out conventions. You have notions of what is right and what is wrong that have been taught to you by people who never tried to think for themselves. Where in nature does it say that men must wear trousers and women must wear skirts? There are countries in the world where the men wear long robes instead of trousers, and countries where the women wear tight trousers instead of frocks – you must have seen pictures of them.'

'But these are backward countries. They do not have our cultural heritage or history.'

'In the old days, our German ancestors in their forests wore tunics – the men, I mean – and what is a tunic but a short frock? And two hundred years ago, rich gentlemen wore clothes made of silk, embroidered and edged with brocade, with lace at their cuffs. You have a portrait of one of your own ancestors dressed like that – I've seen it in your apartment. Was he less a man for his silks and laces?'

'Why no – he was a military commander of great distinction. But what are you trying to prove?'

'I am trying to show you that you are a prisoner,

142

Manfred. Have you the courage to break out of your prison?'

Courage was a quality which Manfred did not lack.

'We will try this experiment in spiritual freedom,' he said, 'but don't get any odd ideas about me – remember the night when we met and what happened then.'

'I won't forget. Take your clothes off while I find something suitable for you.'

Manfred stripped down to his underpants, still feeling foolish.

'You have a good strong body,' said Ludwig. 'What a pity you are not interested in me.'

'So long as you understand that fact we shall remain friends.'

Ludwig took from the wardrobe a long evening frock of mauve satin.

'No,' he said, holding it against Manfred, 'That won't fit. You're so much bigger than I am. What else have I got . . . you'll have to take your underpants off, you know.'

Manfred removed them, wondering what on earth he was doing.

'Put this on,' and Ludwig handed him a small silk triangle with elastic straps, 'it keeps everything up out of the way.'

Manfred pulled the posing-pouch up his legs until it fitted tightly over his limp equipment and held it close against his belly. He felt better then because it stopped Ludwig from staring at that part of him.

'Good,' said Ludwig with a grin, 'now these.'

These were a pair of pale blue knickers with a band of lace round the loose legs and a pattern embroidered at the waist. Manfred struggled into them, finding them small for him, and stared at his own reflection in the long mirror.

'Now for stockings – sit on the bed.'

He sat and fumbled with the unfamiliar task. Skilled though he was in assisting young women remove their stockings, he had never attempted to help one put them back on afterwards.

'I'll show you,' said Ludwig.

Before Manfred could object, he was kneeling by him to smooth the fine silk stockings up his legs and then to slide garters with pink rosebuds up to his thighs to hold the stockings in place.

'Your legs are covered with fine blonde hair,' Ludwig observed, 'I shave my legs so that nothing shows through my stockings when I am Tania.'

'And you shave under the arms,' Manfred recalled.

'And somewhere else as well,' Ludwig added with a smile, 'did you notice that when we first met and you had your hand up my frock?'

'Why do you do that?' Manfred asked. 'Women have hair between their legs too.'

'But the shape is different,' said Ludwig, 'women's hair grows in a straight line across the top.'

'I know one who has it cut in a heart-shape,' Manfred told him, but Ludwig was not impressed.

'None of my clothes will fit you,' he said. 'What can we do? Let me think. Stand up for a moment.'

He produced from a drawer of his dressing-table an object which had led Manfred astray – a white satin brassiere with cups which were filled with soft rubber. He strapped it on Manfred's chest and it fitted extremely tightly, even with the straps adjusted to the maximum. The embarrassment Manfred had experienced at the beginning had by now vanished. Was this the start of spiritual liberation? he asked himself.

Ludwig brought out the wrap he had worn on the evening they had first met. He fixed it round Manfred's chest, under his arms, and pinned it at the back.

'That's the best I can do,' Ludwig sighed. 'Walk about slowly and get the feel of the clothes.'

Manfred took a few steps and the assortment of clothes he was wearing slid over his skin in a way that gave him strange sensations. He was glad to be wearing the tight silk pouch at that moment, to conceal an unnecessary stiffness that was making itself apparent.

144

'Well?' Ludwig asked. 'What do you think of our little experiment?'

'I'm not sure. There is an effect, but I find it hard to understand.'

'Don't confuse yourself by trying to understand.'

Manfred stopped before the long mirror and stared at his reflection. The wrap fixed round his body outlined pointed little breasts and lower down there were frilly blue knickers and silk stockings. The mirror said that this was an over-sized woman, but the head said that it was a man. The total impression was that of an outlandish creature of inde-terminate sexuality and unknown potential.

'How do you feel?' Ludwig asked softly.

'I don't know,' Manfred answered, engrossed by what he saw in the mirror.

The silk pouch inside the knickers seemed to be getting tighter and tighter. He was, he had to admit, sexually aroused, though the reason eluded him. To put on women's clothes seemed hardly reason enough to evoke feelings of langorous pleasure.

'This is only a start,' Ludwig's voice said persuasively from somewhere behind him. 'The real moment of freedom comes when you show yourself dressed as a woman in public – not to stupid people who cannot overcome their own prejudices – but to friends who know what it is to be free and who hold out their hand to you in friendship and understanding.'

'The Eldorado Bar, you mean?'

'I have many friends there . . . but even that is only a prelude to the moment when you break the shackles that hold you to the past.'

'How is that done?'

'Can't you guess?'

Ludwig was beside him, so that both images were in the mirror together. Manfred felt a hand rest on his bare back, above the blue knickers, and then a knuckle ran thrillingly along his spine.

'Freedom springs from sacrificing your old self in an act of love,' he said very softly.

'Ludwig!' a voice called from behind the two of them. 'Did Manfred call?'

Manfred whirled round, his face red, to see Helga standing at the bed-room door, still wearing her hat and gloves. She stared at him in silence for some moments and then smiled crookedly.

'There you are, Manfred. I never expected to find you playing games with Ludwig.

'It's an experiment,' he answered awkwardly.

'I'm sure it is, though I've never heard it called that before. Is the experiment still in progress?'

'It's finished.'

She walked slowly across the room towards him, the crooked smile still on her face.

'Are you sure? From what I can see inside your knickers there's some way to go yet.'

'Helga, you're spoiling everything!' Ludwig protested angrily.

'Am I spoiling your fun? How often have you spoiled mine?'

Manfred stood paralysed by shame as she approached him.

'Blue knickers! Are they really your style, Manfred?' she asked.

Her gloved hand pressed against the silk.

'Finished, you said? Only just started, I would say, from the feel of this.'

'Helga,' he said hoarsely.

'Tell me something,' she said, 'would you rather have my hand or Ludwig's hand touching you?'

With shame Manfred remembered that on the evening he had been in this room with *Tania*, Ludwig's hand had indeed stroked him where Helga was touching him now.

'Lost for words?' she asked. 'If I hadn't come home just now it would be Ludwig's hand rubbing you now.'

'It would not!' he said sharply.

146

The tightness of the silk pouch seemed to be making Manfred light-headed. He reached out to put his hands on Helga's breasts through her summer frock, hoping to make her crooked smile go away.

'That's something Ludwig can't offer you,' she said, 'his are made of rubber. Mine are the real thing – you should know that – you've played with them often enough.'

'And kissed them!' he mumbled.

Ludwig snorted in disgust and walked away from them. In the mirror Manfred saw that he had thrown himself on his bed and was lying there with a sulky expression on his face.

Helga turned her head to speak to her brother.

'Ludwig – clear out!'

'I won't! This is my room.'

'Please yourself,' she said.

Her eyes stared into Manfred's and their expression was cold as she jerked his silk knickers down to his knees, to be followed by the pouch.

'Ludwig has been telling you about spiritual liberation,' she said, 'he always goes on about it. Do you know what he means? I'll tell you – he wants to get hold of *this*!'

She was gripping Manfred's upright stem so hard that he winced.

'Isn't that true, Ludwig?' she asked over her shoulder. 'This is what you were after – take a good look at it now it's on show because that's as near to it as you'll get while I'm here.'

'You're a bitch!' said Ludwig angrily, 'The only thing you know about is lying on your back for men. You're stuck in the past – you'll never be free.'

'If you're free, I don't want to be.'

'You don't say that when Albert's here,' said Ludwig viciously.

'I thought you'd drag him into it sooner or later. Perhaps Manfred would like to know why Albert pays for this apartment and keeps us both.'

Her grip on Manfred's swollen stem was fierce but not

147

unpleasant. She tugged at it to keep his attention. Manfred shook his head in answer to her question about Albert, silently cursing himself for being drawn into this quarrel between the twins. Helga smiled at him chillingly.

'Dear Albert does all this for us because he likes us both,' she said. 'Sometimes he takes me out to dinner and sometimes he takes Tania. Understand? Sometimes he sleeps with me and sometimes he sleeps with Tania. When dear Albert is in bed he doesn't care which hand is holding his spike. And you know who Tania is because you put your hand up her skirts.'

'Shut up!' said Ludwig, 'I won't let you do this!'

'How will you stop me, *Tania*? You wanted to stay, so stay and watch. You'll see Manfred ruin a new pair of gloves in a minute.'

Indeed, her hold on Manfred was threatening to make him fire his volley.

'I won't look!' Ludwig shrilled.

'I don't care whether you look or not. He's going to do it and I'm the one he'll do it for, not you.'

'But this is my room!'

'That's why.'

Manfred growled in his throat, angry at being in so ridiculous a position. He seized Helga by the waist, took three or four steps and threw her, kicking and squealing on to the bed alongside her brother. He flipped her frock up to her waist and laughed bitterly to see that she was wearing blue silk knickers almost like those that hobbled his legs. He hooked his fingers into the waistband and ripped the flimsy material from top to bottom. Helga screamed and brought up her knees sharply to protect herself. Manfred grabbed her shins and forced her bent legs up to her breasts and then fell on her with all his weight. She screamed again when he thrust hard into her exposed entrance.

'Stop it!'

'Do it to her!' Ludwig cried in malicious glee.

Both outcries were lost in a roar of triumph from Manfred

148

as his raging stem spat its fury into Helga, only moments after he had penetrated her.

He got off her quickly and she rolled over to hide her face, her arms over her head. Manfred ripped off the wrap he was wearing, hearing the pins tear the material, the knickers and stockings and hurled them at Ludwig, no longer caring whether that one saw him naked or not. He put his own clothes on as fast as he could, saying not a word. Helga and Ludwig were both silent, and Manfred turned his back to them so that he would not have to see them.

Fully dressed at last, he went to the door, determined to have done with the twins forever. He turned, the door-knob in his hand, to inform them that he wanted no more to do with them. Helga still lay face-down on the bed, her gloved hands over her head. Ludwig had moved close to her and was comforting her, whispering close to her ear and stroking her bare bottom delicately, where the remnants of blue silk hung about her thighs. And in that instant Manfred realised that the twins were not only rivals, they were lovers.

Ludwig looked up and fixed Manfred with a look of pure hatred.

'Go away,' he said, his voice clear, 'go away! We don't need you!'

The Book

Ernst Tillich's novel was published in September and according to the reviewers it was the most important cultural event of the year. Even without the acclaim, Manfred would have bought a copy, simply because he knew Ernst, but he found it hard work to read it. In essence it was a tale of a cruel father who beat his children, tore up their books and made their lives so miserable that the eldest boy went out one dark night and drowned himself in the River Spree. This shocked the other children, two more boys and two girls, into open rebellion against their tyrannical father and provoked a scene of brawling confrontation which ended only when they pushed him out of the apartment window. The odious parent fell three floors, cursing his children, until he smashed into the pavement below and lay broken and dying in Kaiserstrasse, within sight of police headquarters. An elderly lady walking her dog fainted at the horrid sight and, as the leash slipped from her nerveless fingers, the dachshund trotted up to the dying man, cocked its leg and urinated on his blood-stained face.

Manfred's view was that the novel was melodramatic rubbish. Nor did it strike him as original – he was fairly sure he had seen much the same story produced as a play in the theatre, some years before, though he could not recall the author's name or whether it ended in the same way. Even so, in the face of widespread praise in the progressive newspapers, he decided to keep his views to himself and go to Ernst's celebration party.

From experience he knew that the standards of hospitality of intellectuals were not the same as his own. He therefore delayed his arrival until the party had been in full swing for some hours and took a bottle of good brandy with him. His hope was that the more tedious of Ernst's literary friends would have talked themselves to a standstill by the time he got there, but in this he was wrong. Ernst's drab and uncomfortable apartment was crowded with people talking at the top of their voices and the only drink left was beer.

Manfred pushed his way through the mob to congratulate Ernst, who was speechless, drunk and happy. He threw his arms round Manfred, thumped him on the back and had to be helped into a chair before he fell down.

Manfred was soon deep in conversation with someone he knew well, Kurt Niemoller, a literary critic of some renown. Kurt was a little unsteady on his feet but still talking hard about Ernst's achievement.

'The symbolism is astonishing,' he informed Manfred. 'The father dying in sight of police headquarters, a symbol of a repressive social order which, at the crucial moment, is powerless to save him! That is a master-stroke! And the dog which gives the final gesture of contempt – wonderful! There has been nothing like this since Thomas Mann's *Magic Mountain*.'

'Ernst is an old friend but I find it an exaggeration to compare his work with that of Mann.'

'You know nothing about literature,' said Kurt rudely, 'but that is to be expected – you are not engaged in the struggle.'

'What struggle?'

'The artistic struggle to create a new Germany! My God, we are living in the middle of a German Renaissance and you haven't even noticed it!'

'There's Oskar,' said Manfred, waving at the impressario to join them, 'he's deeply committed to your struggle, Kurt.'

Oskar forced his way through the crowd, dragging Magda

151

in his wake, like a small boat towed behind a steam-ship. Manfred kissed her hand and then her cheek in an affectionate manner. She was dressed in dramatic style for Ernst's intellectual party, in a short black frock with a large circular hole in the front to display her belly-button.

'I heard my name mentioned,' said Oskar, beaming at Manfred. 'Were you saying something nice about me?'

'I was explaining to Kurt that you are in the forefront of his struggle against the forces of reaction.'

'What nonsense!' said Kurt sharply. 'The plays he puts on are a disgrace. They are flimsy pretexts to get half-naked women on the stage to titillate the bourgeoisie. *Three in a Bed* was rubbish, with no artistic or social merit whatsoever, and no discernible political stance.'

Oskar's face turned slowly red with anger and Manfred stirred things up further.

'Your judgement is superficial, Kurt. *Three in a Bed* was a satire with an important social message which you missed completely. And as for political stance, surely that was obvious enough.'

Kurt stared at him suspiciously and uncertainly, wondering if he had missed something.

'Evidently the symbolism was too subtle for you,' Manfred continued. 'You need a dog to piss in your face before you understand the message. Oskar does it more cleverly and with greater intellectual depth.'

Kurt was now staring at Oskar with a puzzled expression.

'I shall speak to your editor tomorrow,' Oskar said vindictively, 'my name carries some influence. It is beyond me how he can employ the services of someone as totally imperceptive as you.'

Kurt began to make gobbling noises.

'There is the question of Oskar's next production,' said Manfred, 'it will amaze you, Kurt, if you succeed in understanding it. The symbolism lies in a group of twelve year old school-girls . . . but no, I must not give too much away.'

'I refuse to believe what you say,' said Kurt, fairly sure

at last that Manfred was making a fool of him. 'This man produces nothing but salacious and trivial spectacles for the stupid and insensitive. That was what I wrote about his last production and from what you tell me it will be equally true of his next.'

'Do you know how many people paid to see *Three in a Bed*?' Oskar demanded furiously.

Manfred winked at Magda and moved imperceptibly away from what promised to be a lengthy wrangle. She followed him and, once out of ear-shot of Oskar, she burst into laughter.

'Manfred – what a sadist you are! Oskar will lose his temper with Kurt eventually and punch him.'

They found a relatively uncrowded corner of the room, slightly shielded from the din by a large book-case. Manfred was unable to resist putting his hand on the round cut-out in Magda's frock and rubbing her bare belly.

'You are still attending to Oskar's little requirements, dear Magda?'

'Why not? He treats me very well because he is grateful. But who is attending to your requirements, Manfred? It seems a very long time since you came to visit me.'

'It's not that I do not find your games amusing, but they are very strenuous.'

'You are young and strong, not flabby like poor Oskar. If you put your hand down through the hole in my frock you will find out what I am wearing underneath.'

'You never wear anything underneath. It would be no surprise.'

'It's surprises you want, is it? I have just the thing for you – a wonderful new device that stretches you out on a frame with steel chains holding your ankles and wrists and leaving every part of you, front and back, exposed to attentions of all kinds, some of them very severe.'

'How very interesting! Has Oskar tried it?'

'He paid for it. It was designed by a person of exceptional imagination and can be used to produce some very curious results. After his first little session with it Oskar was so

153

wrung-out that he's afraid to use it again. So it stands idle and waiting for you.'

'I am tempted to investigate this new toy of yours, Magda, but I would much prefer to see you chained and helpless in it while I do unspeakable things to you.'

She took his wrist and pushed his hand down through the cut-out of her frock. His fingers closed on a furry mound that promised unknown delights.

'Tomorrow evening,' she suggested, 'Oskar won't want to see me for a day or two after tonight. He will need to recover his strength.'

Manfred withdrew his hand quickly as Oskar bustled through the crowd towards them, his face puce and his voice raised in a bellow.

'That idiot! He knows nothing about the theatre and he dares to insult me! Come along, Magda, we're leaving before I kill him.'

'Culture is a controversial subject,' said Manfred pleasantly.

'What? Yes, you're right. Thank you for trying to set that blockhead straight, even if he's too stupid to see what's in front of his nose.'

He dragged Magda away and Manfred felt someone poke him in the back. He turned to find himself facing a woman of about forty, square-headed and neckless, thick-bodied and waistless. She wore an unbecoming frock of emerald green and was flanked by two sturdy young men. Neither was older than Manfred himself, both had short and bristly hair that gave them the look of convicts. Each had on a cheap suit in dark blue and neither wore a tie.

'You're no writer,' said the woman who had poked him in the back to get his attention. 'You look too well-off to have any talent. What are you doing here?'

'I've known Ernst for years, Madame, and he invited me to his party.'

He thought it unnecessary to tell her that Ernst was the son of the village school-teacher on the Klausenburg estate,

154

or that he had borrowed the fare to Berlin from Manfred himself.

'You're some sort of capitalist,' said the woman. 'We won't need your sort forever. In the well-run society the State will pay writers a salary while they create their works, and then distribute them free.'

'Even then you will still need me, Madame.'

'For God's sake stop calling me Madame. My name's Schreker. Why will anyone need you when the State is run by the people and not by money-lenders?'

'You will need people like me to read your books, otherwise there will be no point in writing them.'

'The workers will read our books!' she declared.

'They are incapable of it.'

'We shall educate them.'

'That will take fifty years. In the meantime the only people who will read your books are other writers, after you have abolished people like me. And you're all too jealous of each other to be a satisfactory audience. I suggest that you retain me until you have educated the proletariat sufficiently to want to read books like Ernst's latest.'

'Have *you* read it?' she demanded.

'Certainly.'

'And what is your opinion of it?'

'Ernst is an old friend. Look at him over there – drunk and happy. He feels himself superior because his book has been noticed and because it will make money for him. He will be able to move to a better apartment and enjoy himself more expensively, eat in good restaurants and find more amusing girlfriends than the scrawny little creatures he finds in bookshops. All this is good. Therefore his book is a good book.'

The woman stared at him in disbelief. Her two companions, looking bored, drifted away to look for more drink. Manfred gestured at their retreating backs.

'Are they writers? They look shabby enough.'

To his surprise Fraulein Schreker chuckled at his insult.

155

'They couldn't write a laundry-list between them. But they are a great help to me in writing my books.'

'In what way, if I may ask.'

'They've got strong backs and the animal vigour of youth. That shocks your bourgeois morality, no doubt.'

'No, but why two of them? Do you need so much help with your writing?'

'Two's better than one. I never know when the mood will take me.'

'Do you pay them?'

Fraulein Schreker was so set in her frankness that she did not take the question as an insult at all, as any other woman would.

'I give them room and board and some pocket-money.'

'You are to be congratulated on your arrangements. I have met older women who have arrangements with young men for the same purpose and find it expensive.'

'That's not the same!' she said sharply, insulted at last. 'You mean rich and bored women to try to buy the illusion of love. I want no such thing from my boys. Love is total nonsense. What I ask for is physical relief so that I can get on with my work, and the quicker the better.'

'I see that you are deeply committed to the struggle to create a new Germany,' said Manfred, straight-faced as he quoted Kurt Niemoller's words to her. 'You are taking part in the new German Renaissance – a great destiny for a writer.'

'How right you are, comrade,' she answered, obviously stirred to the depths by his words, 'there is not a moment to lose!'

'May I ask about your particular working methods? They say that Marcel Proust wrote the whole of *Remembrance of Things Past* in bed.'

'Decadent French queer!' Fraulein Schreker snorted, 'I get up every morning of the week at six o'clock, put on my old dressing-gown, drink a cup of coffee and start to work. I have long bouts of intense concentration, perhaps for hours at a time. Then suddenly I am physically and

156

mentally drained and can't write another word. My wrist
and arm ache from writing and my back aches from crouch-
ing over my table, so I lie flat on the floor – did you know
that's good for an aching back? Josef or Hans, whichever
one is at hand, squats down beside me to massage my legs.'

Beneath the hem of her ugly green frock Manfred saw
that she had unusually strong calves and ankles. She saw
the direction of his glance and hitched up her skirt to show
her legs off better.

'I've always had good strong legs,' she said with satisfaction, 'I did a lot of walking in the countryside when I was
a girl. Nowadays I spend so much time sitting at my
writing-table that I've developed a broad backside. Not
that it's of any importance. Women who worry over their
appearance are stupid. What matters is what goes on in
here,' and she tapped her forehead.

'I agree that what goes on in the head is tremendously
important. On the other hand, what goes on lower down is
not without a certain interest, even to a person of your
stern principles. A moment ago you described yourself lying
on the floor with one of your assistants massaging your
legs.'

'The body has a stultifying effect on the mind unless
action is taken to prevent it,' she said ponderously. 'A few
minutes of massage takes away my fatigue, especially when
the thigh muscles are massaged firmly.'

Quite so,' Manfred agreed solemnly, 'I have noticed more
than once that women whose thighs I massage become
very lively. And when the hands go higher, they become
positively frisky.'

'I never waste time like that. One word from me and the
boy has my dressing-gown and night-dress up and is on top
of me – and in a minute or two at most I get the physical
relief I need. Then my mind is bursting with ideas and I
go back to my table and start again.'

'You have matters very well organised,' said Manfred,
appalled by what he had heard. 'Do you need this relief
frequently?'

'Two or three times a day is usually enough. If I work right through the night, as I sometimes do, then the boys take it in turn.'

'And the books that you produce in this interesting way – are they at all popular? Do they sell well?'

She stared at him in sudden fury.

'Don't you know who I am, you ignorant idiot?'

'I regret, Madame, that I rarely read modern novels, though I made an exception for Ernst. I prefer our great writers of the last generation – Thomas Mann, for example. Are your books anything like his?'

He had found the perfect insult. Fraulein Schreker turned purple with rage, swivelled on her heel and marched away. Manfred grinned and eased himself through the crowd to speak to Max Schroeder.

'What did you say to that awful woman to upset her so badly?' Max asked.

'Nothing at all. I asked her about her method of writing. Did I tell you that I've bought a grotesque painting by Glitz? You must come and tell me what you think of it.'

'There's hope for you yet. But you will find that you have a problem now, Manfred. Glitz will so overshadow those landscapes of yours and your family portraits that you will have to get rid of them.'

'Maybe, but I like those landscapes. I don't like the new picture at all. I may send it to London to be sold – a dealer told me they will pay high prices there for any modernistic rubbish.'

Max had his arm round, of all people, Rosa, the well-fleshed model who normally went about with Horst Lederer. From the way in which she cuddled herself against him, Manfred assumed that they had become close friends.

'Are you thinking of becoming a painter yourself, Max, instead of an art-critic, now that you have acquired a model?'

'A man has other uses for a fine young woman when she takes her clothes off besides painting her portrait,' he answered, and Rosa nodded in agreement.

'Max is a gentleman,' she said, 'not a lout like Horst, even if he is a good artist.'

'The fact is,' Max confided, 'I fell in love with Rosa when I kissed her bottom at your birthday party. It was a turning-point in my life.'

'As I remember, you were far from happy when you and I visited Madame Filipov. I thought you were going to hang yourself that evening.'

'That was because I would not give in to my great urge to simplify my life and thinking. I saw everything in intellectual terms and did not listen to my own heart. With Rosa everything is simple, easy and pleasant. She has a heart of gold and a well-disposed nature.'

'And a magnificent body,' said Manfred, smiling at Rosa. 'I keep meaning to drive round to Horst's studio and buy one of his paintings of her, if he has one left. I want to hang it next to Glitz's horror and see which conquers the other.'

'An interesting experiment,' said Max. 'Of course, now that I've got Rosa herself, I don't need a painting of her. She poses for me, as if for Horst, on a bed or a chair, and I can sit for hours and admire the tones of her skin, the way the light falls on her hair, the curves and planes of her body – it is better than looking at paintings, I assure you.'

'I hope that all this silent admiration leads to some bolder expression of your emotions.'

'I make sure of that,' said Rosa, 'otherwise I'd be standing about naked all day for nothing. He hasn't changed really – he only thinks he has.'

'Max – have you heard from Werner lately?'

'I had a postcard only last week from Vienna. It was a picture of the Johann Strauss memorial.'

'Did he say anything about coming back?'

'He said he would be away for Christmas. Gottfried really frightened him that night, from what I've been told. I wish I'd been there to see it. I must cultivate the acquaintance of your cousin Ulrika and get myself invited to her next orgy.'

'Did Werner give an address?'

'Yes – do you want it?'

'I want to get in touch with him urgently. I have news for him.'

'I'll telephone you tomorrow and give you the address on the postcard.'

'And I'll invite you to lunch with Ulrika. Bring Rosa with you and you'll be in her good books right away. Who else is here tonight that we know besides Oskar?'

'They're mostly struggling writers and the like. No one of importance. The American girl is here, of course.'

'Jenny? Where – I haven't seen her?'

'I saw her going into Ernst's bed-room hours ago.'

Manfred's heart sank.

'With whom?' he asked.

'They're smoking opium in there. I'm sure they won't mind if you join them. They're probably all unconscious by now.'

Manfred found his way to the bed-room. It was almost in darkness, the curtains drawn across the window and the only light from a small bedside lamp over which a woman's slip had been draped to dim it. The room was full of smoke and the sweet and heavy smell of opium. On the floor lay a cheap metal tray with a tiny glass spirit-lamp and a long-handled spoon with a small bowl. Jenny lay on the bed, naked except for her silk stockings, and a naked man lay beside her, his head on her shoulder. Two other couples, also undressed, lay on the carpet. One of the couples lay like spoons, the woman's back to the man and his arms round her, while the other couple lay at an angle to each other, the woman's head on the man's belly. Everyone appeared to be asleep.

Manfred stood at the bedside and stared down at Jenny. A strand of black hair had fallen untidily across her face. Her face was expressionless, her eyes half open and blank, a dribble of saliva from a corner of her red-painted mouth. She was exceptionally beautiful, he thought, her body a masterpiece of curves and hollows, made for love and

160

tenderness. He had seen her naked once before, at Ulrika's celebration, bent over Ulrika and whispering fondly to her while Olga Pfaff played with her. Even in those circumstances Jenny had looked proud and brimming with restrained energy. Lying here, stretched out on her back on Ernst's bed, she looked lost and vulnerable – and in some strange way, innocent. Yet she was far from innocent, Manfred told himself. She was stupefied by drugs, in wretched surroundings, throwing herself away on God knows what dirty tramps of so-called intellectuals. The thought so complicated his emotions that he wanted to weep for her and to shout in anger at the same time.

She sighed gently, her mouth open a little. Her perfectly round breasts rose and fell to her quiet breathing and Manfred's emotions became so painful that he wanted to kiss her and beat her savagely, tell her that he adored her and drag her out of the apartment by her hair.

'Stupid little cow!' he said aloud. 'To do this to yourself! You've let that disgusting and hairy swine put his grubby hands all over you! And you've opened your legs for that shrivelled monstrosity of his!'

He touched her shoulder mournfully, his finger-tips feeling the satin texture of her skin. After that it was impossible to resist trailing his fingers down over her breasts, soft and cushiony, to her pink buds.

'I would kiss them for hours if you would let me,' he said to the unconscious girl, 'But you have always been interested in someone else.'

He ran his trembling hand down to her smooth belly. She wore a narrow suspender-belt decorated with fine lace and it concealed her belly-button. He pulled the elastic belt down a little to see for himself and was pleased beyond belief by the soft oval indentation he found. He touched her tuft of jet-black hair and it was like stroking the finest astrakhan. Her thighs were slightly apart and his questing fingers touched the long lips between them. Their moistness was testimony enough to what had happened earlier before she and her companion had passed out.

'I want you more than I have ever wanted any woman before,' Manfred said softly, 'yet I hate you and despise you.'

He heard her sigh faintly again as he touched her between the thighs. He looked at her face, to see her lips move slowly, and he bent over to hear what she was saying.

'Erwin darling, do it again,' she whispered very slowly, and her long beautiful legs slid wider apart on the bed.

Manfred almost choked on his curious and painful emotions. He went round to the other side of the bed, stepping over a sleeping couple on the way. Both partners were unconscious, but the man's loins were moving in a slow rhythm against the girl's bottom, as if he dreamed that he was still making love to her.

Erwin was heavy to lift off the bed and put on the floor. At close quarters he smelled none too clean and on the forearm that had been hidden under him, there was tattooed a dagger with a snake round it. He did not wake as Manfred rolled him under the bed.

'Dirty pig,' Manfred growled. 'Sleep it off under there.'

Two souls certainly dwelled in Manfred's breast at that moment – one urging him to retreat as fast as he could from this unsavoury scene and the other encouraging him to take the revenge open to him. Emotion vanquished reason and in seconds he had his clothes off and was alongside Jenny on the lumpy bed. He stroke her breasts very lightly so as not to disturb her drugged sleep. His stem lay hard against her thigh.

'Yes . . .' she murmured, 'that's nice . . .'

Her eyes were closed and her body limp to his touch. She was in another dimension, where time had slowed down and the mind had ceased to function. But eventually her pink buds grew to firmness under his fingers and her lethargic breathing speeded up just a little. Manfred caressed her belly for a long time and then between her thighs. Her loins made tiny jerking movements and her legs slid further apart until he could find and tease the wet little bud within.

The time had come for decision – leave her or go all the

162

way. It needed no agony of mind for him to choose. He positioned himself over her with extreme care, his weight on his knees and an elbow, while he guided his leaping stem to the slippery entrance waiting for it. He loathed Jenny, he desired her, he despised her and he loved her – the conflicting passions were too much for him to either understand or deal with. But his body knew what to do.

His belly lay lightly on hers as he slid all the way into her. He kept his weight off her and stayed still – Jenny was doing everything that was necessary. Her loins lifted and fell in a slow rhythm, giving him exquisite sensations. Whether this strange love-making was pleasurable or not, he hardly knew. To Jenny it obviously was – in some remote drug-hazy recess of her mind the sensations were being felt and enjoyed, for her breathing became irregular after a time and the automatic lifting of her loins speeded up fractionally.

How long it lasted, this trance-like act of love, it would be impossible to say. Manfred's mind had lost touch with his body, as if he were drugged himself. In his mind there was a maelstrom of confusion, a mingling of guilt and desire, which tormented him. But his body was isolated from these considerations and was an automaton which was waiting for the switch to be thrown that would cause it to perform its function. Manfred was in heaven and in hell at the same time.

It was as if a bolt of lightning struck him when his body discharged its passion and his seething emotions were blotted out. He groaned and jerked while the fury spent itself in Jenny's slowly heaving body, his mouth pressed to hers and tears trickling down his own face.

She trembled under him for a very long time, her orgasmic pleasure extended by the effect of the opium far beyond the normal. Manfred waited for her to go limp again before he eased himself off her and put on his clothes. He had done what he wanted to do, but he felt no afterglow of contentment. On the contrary, he felt remorse, and shame – an emotion he had hardly ever experienced in his whole life and with which he was ill-equipped to deal. He stood at the bed-side for a last lingering look at the beautiful young woman asleep there, and his face was still wet with tears.

'Erwin, again . . .' she whispered.

If Erwin had been conscious, Manfred might well have beaten him to death then and there. But there was no satisfaction in revenge on a sleeping rival. Better to leave him where he was, under the bed, so that at least he would not respond to Jenny's whispered invitation.

Manfred rushed out of the apartment, shame-faced and speaking to no one. He wanted to be alone and he wanted to get drunk to wipe out the memory of what he had done. Two hours later he was not only drunk, he was lost. He had walked aimlessly through the streets, stopping at bars as he came to them, downing glass after glass of brandy to stop himself thinking. He found himself at last in a villain-ous-looking back street bar and stood at one of the elbow-high tables, staring morosely into his glass, when an elbow caught him in the ribs. He turned to see a young man of about his own age standing by him, poorly dressed and without a tie, but with a small metal swastika badge in the lapel button-hole of his jacket.

'Do you hear me?' the stranger said loudly. 'We don't want your sort here in your fancy clothes and flash ways. Clear out before I knock your teeth down your throat.'

A fat woman in a plain black frock came to Manfred's rescue.

'Leave him alone,' she said. 'He hasn't done you any harm. He's as much entitled to a drink as you are.'

The young man with the Nazi party badge threw off her restraining hand on his arm and shouted at Manfred.

'You've asked for it! I'll smash your face to a pulp!'

Through the haze of alcohol it dawned on Manfred that this angry stranger intended him some harm. There was no time to ask why, nor any reason either. As the young man squared up to him, his fists weaving, Manfred's torment erupted in boiling rage. He gave an ear-splitting shout, flung his half-glass of brandy into the other's face and, as his hands flew up to protect his eyes, Manfred delivered a punch to the pit of his stomach – a punch fuelled by all his frustrations. The stranger's breath escaped in a wheeze and he doubled over, clutching his stomach, positioning his chin in the right place to receive Manfred's knee hard under it. He went down with a thump and Manfred swayed towards him to trample him into the floor. The fat woman now flung herself between them, this time to restrain Manfred.

'Don't! He's too drunk to know what he's doing. He won't give you any more trouble.'

Much of Manfred's anger had been spent at the moment his fist had connected solidly with the other man's belly. He let the woman drag him to the bar and took the glass she pressed into his hand.

'Have one with me,' she said, 'don't bother about Joachim.'

'Who is he? What does he want with me?' he asked, staring at Joachim, doubled up on the dirty floor among beer-stains and cigarette ends.

'He's nobody. He only picked a fight because he's had a few too many. You look as if you've had a few yourself. What's your name?'

Some time later Manfred found himself in a small and shabby room with her. He sat on a bed, wondering how he had got there, while she took off her clothes. She was on the wrong side of forty and when her breasts appeared they were vast balloons of flabby flesh. Her belly swelled out like a beer-barrel and, below it, whatever hair she sported was lost between her over-sized thighs. Manfred stared at her in a puzzled way, waiting for her to explain why she had brought him there.

'Come on then,' she said, patting herself under the over-hang of her belly, 'this is what you've paid for. I'll help you out of your clothes.'

She had him undressed in no time and on the bed with her. The brandy was making his head buzz but he understood at last why he was with this woman. He handled her great balloons – but in vain. His usually eager stem stayed limp.

'You've had too much booze, dear. Fancy a fine young man like you walking the streets at this hour of the night, blind drunk! Had a row with your girl-friend?'

She had hold of his useless part and massaged it briskly.

'I haven't got a girl-friend.'

'Then you must have lost all your money. I can't think of what else would have got you into a state like this.'

'I've plenty of money,' he muttered as she stroked his limp stem busily.

'What then?'

For no reason at all, except perhaps the drink and his unfamiliar feeling of guilt, Manfred told her what had happened at Ernst's party. Once he started talking he was unable to stop and confessed everything.

'Opium,' said the fat woman, 'I don't hold with that. One of my regulars died only a few weeks ago from cocaine and he was ever such a gentleman. All the same, you shouldn't have jumped on the girl like that.'

'What shall I do?'

'How do I know what you should do?'

'But you know a lot about men – you must do. What do you think I should do for the best?'

'Nothing. You had your fun and now you feel bad about it. By tomorrow it won't seem so bad and inside a week you'll be laughing at yourself. Just stay away from the girl and you'll soon forget about it.'

'You think that's best?'

She grinned at him.

'You can't take her a bunch of flowers and apologise, can you? Don't be stupid. She doesn't know you've had her. She'll wake up thinking her boy-friend gave her a wonderful night. He won't remember, she'll be happy. You're the only one who's suffering.'

'That's true,' he said.

'That's more like it – there's a bit of life in your dangler

166

now. We'll soon have it ready for action and get your little business finished.'

'You're a wonder-worker,' he said, staring down the length of his naked body to where she held his thickening stem in her fist.

'Practice makes perfect. Ready for it now?'

Manfred shook his head.

'After tonight I doubt if I'll ever have the nerve to do it again,' he said mournfully.

She laughed at him.

'You remind me of a man I knew years ago. Time after time he'd come to me, always with the same long face, and he could never get it to stand up. After the third or fourth time, he told me what the trouble was. He was a married man and he was doing it to his daughter while his wife was out at work. He said that the daughter was sixteen, but I never believed him. More like twelve or thirteen, I'd say, from the way he carried on. He was eaten up with guilt about what he was doing, and terrified his wife might find out. He hadn't slept with her for years, from what I could make out.'

'And you helped him?'

That made her laugh again, a full-throated bellow.

'It's not my job to help people! I've got a living to earn. After he'd told me about his problem he managed to get it to stand up. He even got on top of me, but he couldn't do anything. Not that it mattered to me – he paid me regularly once a week just to talk and tell me what a swine he was with his daughter and how he wished he could leave her alone.'

'And did he?'

'Don't be stupid! It was the biggest thing in his life. He was crazy for his daughter. He went on doing it to her day after day and coming to me on Sundays when his wife was at home to tell me what a rotten swine he was. It made him feel better to tell me. He thought I'd understand. My God – if I'd had my way with him I'd have taken a bread-knife

167

and cut his eggs off. That would have solved his problem for him.'

'What happened to him?'

'I don't know. After being a Sunday regular for three or four months he never turned up again. I was glad to see the back of him, even though I started charging him double after he told me about the daughter. Are you ready for the big jump now – you're hard enough.'

'I've had too much to drink.'

'It's too soon after having your sleeping beauty – that's more like it. Well, I'll see that you get your money's worth.'

Her clenched hand slid up and down his stem until Manfred's belly contracted and he spattered himself in nervous spasms.

'You'll feel better after that,' the fat woman soothed him, 'I'll get a towel to wipe you with.'

'Don't go away – I need you here,' and Manfred put his arms round her and rested his head on her swollen breasts.

'I don't know your name,' he said.

'You didn't ask. It's Hanni.'

She stroked his hair clumsily.

'Such a fine young man to get himself into a state over a silly girl who's not good enough to clean his shoes. You'll be all right now.'

'I'd like to stay with you, Hanni.'

'I don't know about that. I've had a hard day and I want to get some sleep. I've got my living to earn, even if you haven't.'

'I'll give you a hundred Marks.'

'You can stay,' she said at once, 'do you want to sleep now?'

'I want to talk.'

'For a hundred Marks you can talk all night.'

She hugged him to her vast bosom and Manfred felt comforted.

'I'm not in love with this girl, you understand,' he said, 'but I am sorry for what she's doing to herself. You see, when I thought she was a lesbian, I didn't worry about her,

168

because she was with women I know – women of good family. But it's not the same now that I see she's letting thugs maul her about. Does that make sense, or am I being a fool?'

'Some women like it rough,' said Hanni, 'they get slapped around a bit and that's part of the fun. There's no sense in getting upset – everybody to their own taste.'

'I suppose you're right, but I don't like to think of this particular girl being like that.'

'Look, don't think I'm a Communist, because I'm not, but I've had a lot of men on top of me in my time and believe me, whether they're rich or poor, high-born or throat-cutters, what goes up me feels the same. It's the same for this girl of yours.'

'No, I don't believe that!'

'Look at it another way, you've been on top of well-born young ladies and you know what that's like. Now don't tell me you haven't had a bit of fun with poor girls as well. They're always ready to drop their knickers for someone like you with money enough to give them a good time. Tell the truth now.'

Manfred thought of Mitzi and Ilse and the romp in his apartment – on the sofa, in the shower and on his bed.

'Yes, but it's different for a man,' he said.

'I knew you'd say that! But tell me, if you can, that it felt any different when you had it up a common working-girl than when you had it up a young lady.'

Manfred found himself picturing the time when Ilse was lying above him, pretending to be a man and making love to him, her weight suspended on her straight arms and her breasts rolling as she thrust her loins at him. How she had made him spurt, while making believe that she was spurting into him!

'Well?' Hanni asked.

'I don't know what to think,' he murmured, his thoughts busy with Ilse.

'Yes, you do – you get the same pleasure from a poor

169

girl as a rich one. So forget about the one that bothers you and find another one.'

'There's something about that particular girl that attracts me.'

'And it doesn't take much guessing what that is. So you've sampled it and it didn't make you happy afterwards. Was it nice when you stuck this into her?' Hanni asked, her hand sliding up his thigh, 'Good God, it's standing up again already! Do you want me to hold it?'

'Yes,' he said, his eyes closed and his cheek resting on one big pillow of a breast.

As she played with him, Manfred took a nipple into his mouth and sucked at it. While the feelings of pleasure swirled through him, he retreated into a world of warm sensation, as deeply as Jenny had retreated into her opium trance. Before long he forgot that fat Hanni's hand was busy between his thighs – he forgot that she was even present. Something felt nice between his legs and something else felt nice in his mouth – and nothing else existed for him. The feelings got nicer and nicer and spread all the way through his body, so that he tingled from his curled-up toes to his sucking lips. Eventually something went off pop inside him and that was so very nice that he gurgled like a baby and after that he fell asleep, his head on a big fleshy cushion that was very comfortable.

The Film Show

When Wolfgang von Loschingen said that he was asking a few friends to a private film show, Manfred knew what to expect. On the last occasion he had been invited, back in January, there had been four of them watching pornographic films for an hour or two in Wolfgang's drawing-room, drinking his champagne and then, in a state of high exhilaration, they had taken a taxi to a small and illegal brothel in Franzosichestrasse. It specialised in Italian women, or so the proprietor claimed. Wolfgang and his friends took it over completely, told the owner to lock the door, drank a great deal more and got a real party going with the enthusiastic aid of the normally bored women.

A knockabout game of *Cavalry Action* soon established the right mood. Each young man had a naked whore mounted on his shoulders, bare thighs clamped round his neck and feet tucked under his arm-pits. The room was cleared of furniture and the couples took their positions in the corners. Wolfgang, as organiser of the revels that evening, gave the order to begin the action. He used the words of Marshal Blucher at the battle of Waterloo, words familiar to all of them from their schooldays:

'Raise high the black standard, my children! Death to the French!'

Howling the battle-cry 'Death to the French!' Manfred and the others charged towards the middle of the room, spurred on by the jabbing of high-heeled shoes in their ribs. They collided, bumped at each other with their shoulders, the use of hands being forbidden to the horses, while

171

the women shrieked with excitement, swiped at each other's breasts and tried to grab each other by the hair. After only a minute or two of noisy scrummage, Konrad was tripped and went sprawling on the floor, his rider's legs high in the air as she screamed curses in Italian.

Dismounted riders were allowed to save themselves by crawling away, but fallen horses remained on the battle-field. Wolfgang reeled from a dig in the side by an elbow, stumbled over Konrad and went down on his knees to save himself from falling head-long. His rider fell off, yelping in terror, to land upside-down on Konrad, who grabbed her and planted a smacking kiss on her belly before she wriggled free and scrambled away from the field of honour.

Manfred was left facing Hans Dietrich over the bodies of Konrad and Wolfgang. He gave a great bellow and leaped over Konrad, almost unseating his rider by the sudden attack. He strode over Wolfgang's legs and hit Hans with his shoulder, using all his weight. Hans stumbled back, almost off balance, and Manfred had victory in his grasp. But Hans' girl had Manfred's girl by her long dark hair and was tugging furiously. She leaned forward sharply to ease the pain of having her hair torn out and over-balanced Manfred. He landed on his hands and knees, the battle lost. But not quite – for the girl who pitched forward over his head butted Hans by chance in his most vulnerable spot. Hans shouted and bent double, tipping his rider forward, and she brought him down too.

Manfred found himself face-down on the floor, his face on his girl's belly, while the other girl crawled away on her hands and knees, the cheeks of her bottom wobbling comically. Wolfgang resumed command. He rose to his feet, black bow-tie under one ear, to announce with pride:

'Victory! Not a French dog left on his feet!'

A glass or two of brandy restored Hans and the party continued. Manfred proposed another game in which the men were hounds and the girls their quarry, with all parts of the establishment the hunting-ground. It was a good game, with continuous hunting-cries and shrieks of alarm.

172

When a girl was caught, she was rolled on to her back and dealt with by her captor. The house had six women in all and by midnight they had all been caught, several times over, and the hunters were at a standstill. They divided between them the colossal bill they had run up for drinks and the girls and, at the insistence of the woman in charge, for the loss of business incurred by barring the door to other clients all evening. Altogether it was a most satisfactory evening.

It was therefore with feelings of lively anticipation that Manfred arrived at Wolfgang's apartment for another such evening. The servants had been given the evening off, as usual, and Wolfgang himself opened the door and welcomed him. Konrad was already in the drawing-room, talking to a young man Manfred had not met before – the only one of them not in evening clothes. The projector had been set up on a high stand, a portable screen erected by the wall and bottles stood ready in silver ice-buckets.

The surprise was to be introduced to Frau von Loschingen.

'My beautiful aunt,' Wolfgang explained.

Manfred bowed and kissed her hand, wondering how long she would stay. She was a tall woman of about forty, handsome rather than beautiful, with a slightly beaked nose and a carefully made-up face. Her long evening gown was breath-taking. The colour was burnt orange and it was sleeveless, back-less, and slit in front right down between her breasts. It fitted very closely and displayed a figure that was still good. On the hand she extended graciously to Manfred to be kissed was a diamond ring the size of a walnut. And, he noted, another on her other hand, a matching bracelet on each wrist and diamond studs in her ears. A lady of wealth, fashion and taste, he concluded.

'What a wonderful sun-tan, Madame,' he said, 'have you been on holiday to some exotic part of the world?'

Her long arms and exposed bosom were a golden colour that was most attractive against her gown.

'I live near Lisbon,' she explained.

'Then that is the reason why I have not had the honour of making your acquaintance before, though I have known Wolfgang for years. How long have you lived abroad?'

'I left Berlin at the end of the War. I come back for a week or two each year to see if anything has changed.'

'And has it?'

'Oh yes, Berlin gets worse with every year that passes. My stay will not be a long one this time.'

'I am sorry to hear you say that. In what way are things getting worse, Madame?'

'You must call me Jutta. I suppose I seem an old woman to you but I grew up in the well-ordered Berlin of the Emperor Wilhelm. Such wonderful days they were – the balls, the dinner-parties, the opera – but the War destroyed all that. Nowadays Germany has a government of bolsheviks and anarchists. Some of the old families cling on in the hope that things will improve, but they are deceiving themselves. It will get worse, not better.'

'Do you think so?' Manfred asked.

'You have only to look around you. So-called society in Berlin now is made up of vulgar businessmen and cheap theatre actors – people of no background. I find it intolerable to find myself at the next table to a rich coal-merchant in a good restaurant. Surely you must feel the same.'

'I try not to know people like that.'

'Know them? God forbid! It is enough to see these people from nowhere usurping the places of their betters without having to *know* them.'

Wolfgang brought over the stranger in the brown-striped suit and introduced him as Franz Esschen.

'Franz brought the films we are going to see. Two completely new ones – which he guarantees are positively volcanic.'

Manfred glanced at Jutta von Loschingen and saw that she was smiling wickedly at him.

'I believe that you are shocked,' she said, 'as your friend Konrad was when he arrived and found me here. Do you

174

think that only men are interested in these amusements? Are ladies to be denied their diversions?'

'Few ladies would admit to an interest in amusements of this sort,' said Manfred with a grin.

Franz Esschen said nothing, but he was blushing.

'Hypocrisy is the failing of little people,' Jutta said, 'I heard all about Wolfgang's last film show over dinner the other evening. He claims that you had a wonderful party afterwards with some French women.'

'Italian women,' Manfred corrected her, seeing that she took it all in good humour. 'We had a game of hounds and deer that lasted for hours before we worried the deer to death.'

'If you're ready,' said Wolfgang, 'I'll top up your glasses and we'll make a start.'

'I'm ready,' said Konrad, winking at Manfred.

'Why are you here?' Manfred asked. 'What has come of your rendezvous with a certain married lady we both know well?'

'I haven't seen her all that much since Ulrika's party,' said Konrad. 'It's dangerous, with a husband who can frighten poor Werner away completely. Do you know where he is?'

'He's in Vienna. I wrote him a letter the other day, offering my services to effect a reconciliation.'

'This has the sound of a fascinating story,' said Jutta von Loschingen. 'One of you must tell me later. I smell all the ingredients of a good scandal.'

Wolfgang had refilled the glasses.

'Where will you sit, dear Aunt?'

'Here,' she answered, seating herself gracefully on the silver-brocade sofa. 'Come and sit by me, Manfred.'

The furniture had been arranged in a semi-circle facing the screen. Several possibilities were revolving in Manfred's head as he took his seat as directed. Did this surprising lady propose to accompany them later on to whatever private establishment Wolfgang had made arrangements with? It seemed possible, given her uninhibited personality. Would

175

she join in the revelry and compete with the women of the house? That would be entertaining, but very improbable. She was, Manfred decided a voyeur and she would obtain her gratification from watching the rest of them at play.

Thick curtains over the windows shut out the miserable rainy autumn evening and when Wolfgang switched off the electric lights the drawing-room was in complete darkness. Franz Esschen set the projector going and an oblong of light appeared on the screen. Eventually a lettered title came up: *Tilly Visits the Dentist*, and the film began. The scene opened on a nondescript room with a dentist's chair in the middle and a man in a long white coat facing away and doing something at a glass-fronted cabinet. A woman entered from the right of the picture, wearing a cloche hat and an outdoor coat with a strip of fur round the collar. The dentist turned to greet her, helped her out of her coat and hung it, with her hat, on a peg on the wall. Seen in full-face, he was a villainous-looking man in his forties, short-necked and dark of complexion.

'I wouldn't let him touch my teeth,' said Jutta beside Manfred. 'He looks like a cheap murderer.'

'More like a pimp, I would say,' Manfred suggested.

Tilly was in the chair, her head back against the rest and her short skirt pulled well up over her chubby knees. The best that could be said for her was that she was in her twenties, but she was too heavy-featured to be even passably pretty when seen close-up. Her make-up was plastered on thickly and not very expertly, her eye-brows untrimmed. The dentist peered into her open mouth with his little mirror and words came up on the screen: *'This is more serious than I thought, Fraulein. I must give you gas before I proceed.'* There followed a view of the dentist's hand holding a black rubber mask over Tilly's nose and mouth.

'He has dirty finger-nails!' Jutta exclaimed.

More words were displayed:

'Good, she is asleep. She is so beautiful that I cannot control myself!'

Manfred chuckled at that, feeling that it would require

176

no great effort to control himself in the presence of Fraulein Tilly, conscious or unconscious. The screen showed her from a distance, her eyes closed and seemingly asleep, her knees lolling apart and her skirt up high enough to display her stocking-tops and garters. Standing at her side, the uncontrollable dentist unbuttoned her white blouse from neck to waist to expose a pair of plump breasts. The viewpoint moved in slowly until the screen was filled by Tilly's big melons, over which the short and stubby fingers of the dentist strayed.

'Go on, man – grab a handful!' Wolfgang called out in the dark.

'Those awful nails!' said Jutta. 'If he touched me I would die!'

For a long time the screen was occupied by the dentist's hand stroking and squeezing Tilly's breasts. Manfred shifted slightly on the sofa to make himself more comfortable as his stem reacted to what he was seeing. But at last the scene faded into a longer view of the sleeping patient, her legs sprawled wider than ever. The evil dentist tugged her skirt higher and under her bottom, until he had it in folds round her waist. She was wearing knickers with short and close-fitting legs with frills round the bottoms.

'I've never seen a girl wearing those,' said Manfred.

'You've never seen a girl wearing knickers of any sort,' Konrad commented from his chair somewhere over to the right.

'I've seen one wearing a scarf round her waist,' Manfred reminded him.

'Yes, and I was the one who had the pleasure of taking it off,' Konrad retorted.

'You were not the only one that night.'

'Shut up, you two,' Wolfgang complained, 'Things are warming up.'

Indeed, the lustful dentist had his hand and much of his fore-arm down the front of Tilly's knickers, as if searching for something. Words appeared on the screen to announce his discovery:

177

'*I cannot believe it! I must see it! But how?*'

He moved out of the scene, leaving the camera to focus on the join of Tilly's legs, where a dark shadow showed through the white of her knickers. Then he was back, a pair of scissors in his hand.

'My God – he's going to shear her like a sheep!' said Konrad.

The others laughed, but their attention was seized as the dentist wielded his scissors to cut down the front of Tilly's knickers in a ragged line from waist to mound. The cut flaps fell to show her plump belly and the beginning of her curly tuft. He slid one blade under the frill round the leg of her knickers and cut carefully upwards along her fleshy thigh until he met his down-cut, and then up along the other thigh. The ruined knickers fell away to reveal a dark and bushy growth of hair that not only hid her secrets but extended for some little way down the insides of her thighs.

'What a bush!' said Konrad, 'I've never seen one like it.'

'Nor I!' Wolfgang agreed. 'Imagine running your fingers through that!'

'She has an attractive belly-button,' Manfred pointed out, 'deep and round.'

'You find that attractive, do you?' Jutta asked beside him.

In some manner Manfred could not explain, he was holding Jutta's hand on the sofa between them and her fingers were gripping hard.

'It is a special study of mine,' he told her.

Words on the screen proved that the wicked dentist was of the same mind as Konrad and Wolfgang about what he had uncovered:

'*BEAUTIFUL! It is like a fur-coat between her legs! There cannot be another like this anywhere – I must have it! But what if she wakes up?*'

'Give her more gas, you fool!' Konrad called out.

The same thought occurred to the dentist and he held the mask over Tilly's sleeping face for a second or two.

'More, you blockhead!' Konrad advised.

'He's the expert,' said Manfred, laughing. 'Do you want to kill her?'

The picture flickered and showed Tilly's parted thighs and the anxious dentist's hand between them, his middle finger sunk into her magnificent tuft to the second knuckle.

'This is getting serious,' said Konrad, 'I hope all the arrangements are made for after the film-show, Wolfgang.'

'No problem. Just shut up and watch.'

The evil-minded dentist was down on his knees between Tilly's legs, using both hands to examine her depths. Manfred became aware that Jutta had moved imperceptibly closer to him along the sofa in the dark and her thigh was pressed along his own. Their clasped hands, which had been lying on the seat between them, were now resting in her lap.

This very superior lady may have need of my services before she leaves Berlin, he thought with amusement – and why not? There's many a good tune to be played on an old violin.

The screen showed the dentist and his patient from the side, he still on his knees between her legs. He shrugged off his long white coat to display broad embroidered braces over his shoulders to hold up his trousers.

'Good Lord – what street-market did he buy those in!' Wolfgang exclaimed, but no one was listening to him.

The dentist ripped open his trouser buttons and out sprang a short and thick stem at full stretch.

'It won't be her teeth he's going to drill!' said Konrad.

Jutta was holding Manfred's wrist and rubbing his palm against her belly through the thin silk of her evening gown. He obliged her with a sensual massage, letting his fingers sink into her flesh. Meanwhile the wanton dentist had hoisted Tilly's legs up over his shoulders and, in close-up, the screen showed his stubby stem penetrating her curly tuft.

'Unbelievable!' someone murmured, but whether it was Konrad or Wolfgang was impossible to distinguish. Manfred's slow massage of Jutta's warm belly encouraged

179

her to do the same for him and her hand was pressed close over the stiffness inside his clothes.

Stubby though it may have been in reality, in close-up on the screen the dentist's drill was magnified to the length of a fore-arm and the hairy dependents below it were the size of coconuts. It slid in and out of Tilly like the piston of a railway engine, gathering speed all the time. Jutta's hand was clenched on Manfred's stem so hard as to be almost painful and her legs had parted to let him massage between her legs through the silk of her clothes.

'My God!' she gasped. 'Look!'

And well she might gasp! In the nick of time the rapist-dentist jerked his drill out and directed his outburst of lust on to Tilly's plump belly. The little audience sat speechless as they watched the climactic process to its end. Then the dentist moved away and the screen showed poor sleeping Tilly, her head lolling sideways, her melons uncovered and her bared belly streaked with the dentist's passion.

Jutta's hand left Manfred's lap and she moved silently away from him as *The End* came up on the screen. Manfred tugged his silk handkerchief from his breast-pocket and was dabbing at his perspiring forehead when Wolfgang switched on a floor-lamp in a corner behind them, imparting a soft golden glow to the room.

'More champagne, dear friends,' he suggested, 'I hope you all enjoyed the visit to the dentist.'

'Do you suppose that there are dentists who abuse their patients like that, Wolfgang?' Jutta enquired, her face flushed a delicate pink.

'They all do,' he answered cheerfully. 'Don't they, Manfred?'

'I am going to look for a woman dentist in the hope that she will take advantage of me,' he answered.

'There is a point which bothers me,' said Konrad. 'When Fraulein Tilly wakes up from the gas and stands up to leave, the tatters of her underwear will fall around her ankles. How will the dentist explain that?'

'He has a needle and thread at hand,' said Manfred.

180

'Safety-pins would be simpler,' Wolfgang suggested. 'Have you changed the reel yet, Franz?'

'Nearly ready.'

'This is thirsty work, my dear Aunt,' said Wolfgang with a grin. 'Finish your glass and let me refill it. You're going to need it.'

'I saw a film in Rome last year which would amuse you,' she said, holding out her glass. 'It was made specially for my host and it had two Cardinals doing the most interesting things to a young nun.'

'At the same time?'

'Naturally. What are we going to see next?'

'I don't know. Are you ready yet, Franz?'

'Ready.'

'Good. What's this one about?'

'You will see,' the young man in the brown-striped suit said mysteriously.

Wolfgang switched off the light and took his seat. The projector whirred and the title appeared on the screen: *The Nudist Club*. Wolfgang groaned loudly in the dark.

'Not another nudist epic! We've seen dozens of them.'

'Not like this one,' said Franz.

The opening scene was of park-land with trees and shrubbery. Half a dozen people lay on the grass, taking the sun. They were too distant to discern more than that some of them were men and some were women. More scenes of the same sort followed, from different angles, all distant, and then a sequence of nudists swimming in a lake.

'What did I say!' Wolfgang exclaimed. 'This is boring! Put something else on, Franz, before we fall asleep.'

'Wait a moment – it gets better.'

After what seemed like a long time filled with harmless nudists splashing about in the water, the scene changed abruptly to show a woman lying on a towel on the grass, her bare back and bottom to the audience. She sat up slowly and turned full-face to sit cross-legged and smiling. She was thin, but her breasts were over-sized and out of proportion to the rest of her body.

181

'Well, at least it's not Tilly again,' Konrad commented.

'How can you be sure?' Wolfgang asked, 'She might have gone on a diet.'

'Tilly had an enormous tuft.'

'She could have clipped it. The dentist might have clipped it for her before she left.'

'This girl does not wear knickers with frills,' said Manfred. 'That proves it is not Tilly.'

'And what about her belly-button?' Jutta asked, 'Is that different?'

'As you can observe, this girl's is round and slightly protruding, not deep-set like Tilly's.'

On the screen the nudist took a comb from somewhere and combed her hair, keeping her elbows well up to give an unimpeded view of her breasts rolling about to her movements.

'A good pair,' said Konrad judiciously, 'if you put your face between those and shook your head you'd knock yourself out.'

The scene faded to one of a man, seen from behind, down on his knees to peer through a big knot-hole in a wooden fence. After a time words came up on the screen to indicate his thoughts:

'What fantastic breasts she has! I wish I had the courage to talk to her.'

'Go on, idiot, she's waiting for you,' said Wolfgang.

The naked man reappeared in side-view, his eye pressed to the fence and his stem standing up boldly. There was a tattoo on his arm of a dagger and a snake.

'Good God! It's Erwin!' Manfred exclaimed.

'You know him?' Jutta asked in disbelief.

'I think it's someone I met at a friend's party. Konrad – you were there at Ernst's – do you recognise him?'

'There were so many down-and-out intellectuals there – how can I be expected to remember them? Are you sure?'

'I'll tell you when I get a better look at his face.'

But the man was gone and the view was of the girl nudist. She was sitting with her knees up and apart and was continuing her grooming by combing the hair between her legs.

'The dentist should have thought of that,' said Wolfgang, 'Tilly really had something to comb! Auntie dear – do you comb between your legs when you are dressing for a party?'

'Naturally – everybody does.'

Words on the screen revealed the girl's state of mind:

'I wish a nice young man would come and talk to me. It is healthy to sit in the sun, but I am lonely.'

The words drew hoots of laughter from the audience, which continued even more loudly when the scene changed to show the man behind the fence. His face was not in sight, only his lower half, and his clenched fist was sliding up and down his upright stem.

'Do you recognise him now?' Konrad asked, causing more ribald laughter.

Before Manfred could retort, dramatic developments on the screen gave rise to more laughter. The man rose to his feet and pushed his rigid stem through the knot-hole. His whole body was pressed close to the fence and his face was turned sideways towards the viewers.

'That's him!' said Manfred, 'that's Erwin!'

The scene shifted to the other side of the fence. Erwin's stem stuck through the knot-hole, looking forlorn and ridiculous. But he had evidently done the right thing, for there followed a view of the girl, her face registering surprise as she caught sight of the unexpected projection. She rose from her towel and went to the fence.

'Give it a sharp pull and see if he squeals!' Wolfgang called out.

The girl had other plans. She knelt by the fence and stroked Erwin's projection. She tickled the underside with one finger to make it jump and, satisfied by her examination, moved close to the fence and enclosed Erwin's stem between her big fleshy globes. Her expression changed to one of rapture.

'That's more like it,' said Konrad, 'I wouldn't object to having mine wrapped up warm in those.'

Jutta's hand was back in Manfred's lap and she stroked up and down through his clothes. He put his palm on her thigh and caressed it slowly in a gesture of appreciation.

The viewpoint was from above the girl's right shoulder, looking down on the action. She squeezed her breasts together with her hands, sandwiching Erwin's stem, and rubbed herself up and down against it. The head popped in and out of sight like a tortoise's head out of its shell and Manfred heard Jutta sighing faintly in the dark. The film seemed to be affecting her more than anyone else.

The scene continued until Erwin discharged his passion in a torrent up the girl's chest to her throat.

'What a boring film!' said Wolfgang, 'I knew it would be as soon as I saw the title. You'll have to do better than that, Franz.'

He spoke too soon. Instead of calming Erwin down, the experience cured him of his shyness. The film continued, and Erwin was over the fence and the girl down on her hands and knees on the grass while he mounted her dog-fashion. He pounded away for some time before the scene changed to a close-up of the girl's face. Her eyes were closed and her mouth was moving. Words appeared on the screen for the benefit of those unable to lip-read:

'Yes! Do it to me! Faster! Faster!'

Her face filled the entire screen and it was obvious that she was nearing the critical moments. Her head jerked up and down like the head of a puppet and her lips drew back in a grimace that showed her teeth. For the first time since the film started the little audience was totally silent, caught up in the girl's mounting excitement. They saw raw and naked lust in her face and they felt it themselves. Jutta's hand was so demanding in Manfred's lap that he feared she might bring about an accident in his trousers.

On the screen the girl's face screwed itself up, her eyes blinked open to stare blindly and her mouth gaped wide in a silent scream of orgasmic release. For ten seconds that seemed like an eternity the image of her ecstatic face dominated the audience and then slowly the viewpoint receded to bring her shoulders and arms into sight, and further back still to show her heavy breasts hanging beneath her, and further still, until she was wholly in view, her head drooping in exhaustion and Erwin slumped along her back.

The screen went dark abruptly and Franz switched off the projector. Jutta's hand left Manfred's tormented lap, not a moment too soon in his opinion. He sensed and heard her moving beside him on the sofa and wondered if the incredible close-up of the girl's face had communicated itself so forcefully to her that she had experienced a vicarious release herself.

Some little time passed in silence before Wolfgang roused himself to switch on the single lamp in the corner. Manfred blinked at the sudden illumination, discreet though it was, and then blinked again in astonishment. Jutta was no longer on the sofa beside him. She sat on the floor, her back against an unoccupied arm-chair, where they all could see her. Her beautiful evening gown lay discarded across the sofa near Manfred and she was naked but for flesh-coloured silk stockings and high-heeled shoes.

She sat with one knee up and the other bent and flat on the Persian carpet, showing off her sleek thighs and the tuft of glossy brown hair between them.

She has a good body for a woman of forty, Manfred thought. Her breasts were very well-shaped, small and still firm, with prominent red-brown buds. Her whole body, from forehead to red-painted toe-nails, was sun-tanned a rich golden colour, proof enough that she did not trouble herself with swim-suits.

The four young men stared at her in silence, not wanting to dispel the enchantment. Jutta too said nothing, her expression one of pride as she drank in their wordless admiration. She sat straight-backed and unmoving, like a living statue, one diamond-ringed hand on her upraised knee. Manfred took the initiative. He rose to his feet and stripped off his evening clothes and flung them away from him until he stood naked and his hard stem pointed in the direction of the woman waiting for him. The other men

185

stared in silence, entranced by the drama of the transition from flickering images on the screen to flesh and blood reality. Jutta gazed calmly at Manfred, as if assessing the breadth of his shoulders and his muscular thighs, before letting her look linger on his out-thrust stem.

He squatted on the carpet, close enough to lean forward and kiss her breasts and to stroke the insides of her thighs above her stockings, where the skin felt like fine satin. He forgot that anyone else was present and that his friends were watching in hushed silence. He caressed Jutta between the thighs, running his fingers through the well-groomed tuft of hair and over the protruding folds of flesh. Still she didn't move, nor did her expression change.

Manfred put his hands in her smooth arm-pits and lifted her so that she sat on the edge of the arm-chair and he could move in close on his knees. She uttered a long throaty sigh as he penetrated her and then was silent again. Her dark-brown eyes stared down between their bodies at the fleshy link that joined them and slid to and fro in a stately rhythm. Manfred knew that he would not last very long and he wanted to make the most of this unexpected opportunity. He looked at Jutta's face, trying to read what was in her eyes, but they told him nothing, and soon he was too far gone to focus clearly. His loins bucked furiously to release his passion and Jutta shook in pleasure, but even then she remained silent, though her finger-nails dug deep into the flesh of his shoulders.

'That was charming,' she said eventually, 'you caught my mood exactly.'

Manfred smiled at her and drew away. There was an impatient hand on his shoulder and Konrad's voice telling him to move out of the way. He did so and saw Konrad take Jutta by the hand and pull her off the chair, to take her back to the silver-brocade sofa and spread her on her back.

It was a short, sharp performance once Konrad was on top of her. Her legs twined over his waist, one silk stocking hanging round an ankle, as Konrad pummelled her like a

186

clock-work toy run wild. Jutta seemed to enjoy it well enough and the sound of her panting mingled with Konrad's. Her high-heeled shoes drummed against Konrad's heaving bottom as they reached their climactic moments together.

Konrad was still twitching when Wolfgang dragged him bodily off Jutta and took his place on top of her. In his haste to undress he had forgotten his black silk socks. He sank his long thin stem between Jutta's upraised thighs and groped avidly for her breasts and Manfred found himself wondering if it counted as incest for Wolfgang to make love to his aunt. And did it matter anyway? Both participants gave every sign of enjoying what they were doing, which surely was the only consideration of any importance.

Wolfgang displayed a most vigorous style of love-making. Once embedded in his dear Auntie he twisted and jerked and sighed and moaned. The outcome was not long delayed. Wolfgang's wailing rose to a crescendo and Jutta gave voice herself for the first time, crying out and gasping. Clasped in each other's arms they rolled about on the sofa in spasmodic ecstasy, legs flailing and kicking, their combined outcry thrilling and impressive.

As the bouncing of the interlocked bodies on the sofa slowed down, Manfred glanced round the room for Franz Esschen, whose turn to gratify Jutta had arrived. He was slumped in an arm-chair by the projector, naked as the rest of them, his eyes closed and his legs splayed. It was all too apparent that his passion had overcome his patience. There was a long wet trickle down his belly and his stem hung limply between his thighs.

Wolfgang climbed off Jutta and looked round. He saw Franz's condition and grinned.

'I am sorry to disappoint you,' he said to Jutta, 'Franz couldn't wait.'

Jutta sat up and glared over the back of the sofa at poor disgraced Franz.

'Useless swine!' she said. 'His sort are never any good when you need them.'

Manfred got up from the carpet and said that it would be impolite to disappoint a lady of her expectations. Although he had judged Wolfgang's love-making to lack style, the truth was that the moaning and thrashing about had aroused him strongly again. His stem stood hard and glistening in the golden lamp-light and, standing with his shoulders back and his back straight, he knew that he made a good impression. Jutta was off the sofa at once, both stockings now round her ankles. She balanced herself with a hand on Manfred's shoulder while she removed her shoes and stockings, then threw herself into his arms, trapping his upright stem between their bellies.

'Dear Manfred – you have such style!'

'You are in a more vigorous mood now than when we started,' he said, smiling at her.

'These boys have excited me to the point of madness! But they have not satisfied me – will you do that?'

'I shall do my best!'

'You must do more than that! I want to be destroyed!'

Manfred let go of her for a moment and whirled the nearest arm-chair round so that its back was towards them, seized her by the shoulders and flung her roughly against it. She gasped as the padded back caught her across the belly and pitched forward, her head hanging down towards the cushioned seat. Manfred planted himself solidly behind her bottom and kicked her ankles apart with his bare foot to expose the split mound under her belly. The dark-brown hair was plastered wetly to the open fleshy lips. He stabbed a thumb deeply into it and she cried out in shock.

'This could take a regiment of Grenadiers, one after the other,' he said brutally. 'What can three of us hope to achieve? It will swallow us up!'

Jutta shrieked in pleasure as his rigid thumb twisted inside her. She was not a woman to lie on her back, he judged, being far too skilled in the ways of love for so unimaginative an attitude. That she had received Konrad and Wolfgang in that way was due, he believed, to her verdict that they were too young to know better and her desire was too impetuous to delay its gratification by showing them alternatives. She squealed in delight again as he forced both thumbs deep into her wetness.

Manfred glanced up from what he was doing and became vaguely aware that Konrad was sitting on the floor, arms round his knees, and Wolfgang was lying on the abandoned sofa, and both of them were staring intently at what he was doing to Jutta. Even Franz had emerged from his torpor and was gazing glassy-eyed.

Jutta screamed loudly, her head jerked up and her hands clawed at the chair cushions. Before her orgasmic convulsions stopped, Manfred removed his thumbs and plunged his stem into her, so fiercely that his belly smacked against her bare bottom. He ravaged her fast and hard, so over-wrought that he did not hear her continuous shrieks or notice that her body was flopping up and down as if she were a hare shaken and worried in the jaws of a hound. He sank his finger-nails into the flesh of her bottom and pulled the cheeks apart to expose her little knot of muscle. He saw it clench and unclench and he jammed his slippery thumb into it.

His belly contracted, he roared wordlessly in triumph and exploded into Jutta, slamming himself against her bottom as he stabbed and stabbed, almost as if he were trying to kill her. Her screams of pleasure rose to a nerve-wracking peak and stopped abruptly. After that she hung over the chair-back like a rag-doll.

When Manfred regained his senses he glanced at his friends and was puzzled by the expressions on their faces.

'Holy God!' said Wolfgang from the sofa. 'Is she dead?'

'Never better in her life,' said Manfred proudly, it occurring to him that the expression he had seen was that of awe.

He disengaged himself from Jutta, picked her up and carried her to the sofa, where Wolfgang scrambled out of the way and helped to arrange her comfortably with a cushion under her head.

'A glass of brandy would be good,' Manfred suggested.

189

'She certainly needs it,' Wolfgang agreed, going to the sideboard where the bottles stood.

'Not her, you idiot, me,' said Manfred.

He sat on the carpet and leaned back against the sofa where Jutta lay, pleased with himself. Wolfgang brought the brandy and he swallowed half of it in one gulp.

'And for me,' said Jutta behind him, her voice weak.

Manfred cradled her head in his arm and raised it while she sipped at the glass. Her eyes were languorous as she looked up at him.

'Satisfactory?' he asked with a grin.

'You've destroyed me. It was fantastic.'

'You'd better sleep here tonight,' Wolfgang suggested.

She nodded drowsily. Manfred picked her up again and followed Wolfgang to a bed-room. Jutta was already half-asleep when he settled her in the bed and covered her over. He switched off the light and went back to the drawing-room, to find Konrad and Franz dressing. Wolfgang had put on a long crimson silk dressing-gown with a golden cord round the waist. Manfred put on his underwear and sat down to drink another glass of brandy.

'I must congratulate you,' said Konrad, 'Your perform-ance was heroic – stupendous! I could hear Wagner's music thundering away in the background while you were banging away at her.'

'What a pity we couldn't have filmed it,' Wolfgang said with a broad grin, 'It was better than anything we saw on the screen, wasn't it, Franz?'

'If I'd known what was going to happen, I'd have asked my friend in the film business to be here with his camera,' Franz answered, taking him seriously. 'We had enough actors!'

'Where do they get the actors from for your films?' Konrad asked.

'They're not actors. Everything you see is real and everyone knows how to do that. They pick young whores for the job and pay them a few Marks.'

'And the men?'

190

'Some of them are students and some are just out of work and want to earn a little money – like the one this gentleman recognised. What did you say his name was?'

'Erwin. I don't know his last name. I think he's some sort of unsuccessful writer, but he may be a criminal.'

'It was a shame that you couldn't oblige my aunt, Franz,' said Wolfgang, 'It was expected of you and you failed her.'

'It was watching the three of you go first – I couldn't hold out. Before I knew what was happening I went off like a water-pistol.'

'It's watching pornographic films all the time that does it,' said Wolfgang, grinning, 'Perhaps you should go into another business before you become incapable with women.'

Manfred waited a couple of days before he made a formal call upon Jutta. In an elegant light grey overcoat and a matching Homburg hat he walked along the avenue of the Unter den Linden under a grey and lowering sky and turned in under the awning of the Adlon Hotel. The doorman saluted him in military style and stood to attention. The dark-suited receptionist bowed when he enquired for Frau von Loschingen, and a uniformed page-boy in white gloves conducted him to Jutta's suite. Her personal maid, in regulation black frock and starched apron took his visiting-card and went to enquire if Madame would receive him. She returned to admit him and take his hat and coat.

Jutta was in the sitting-room of the suite, a large and airy room with arrangements of flowers, even this late in the year, standing on almost every flat surface. She was not alone, he saw with a flicker of annoyance. Franz Esschen, purveyor of unusual films, rose to his feet and bowed in a surprisingly deferential way as Manfred entered the room. Manfred nodded to him and kissed Jutta's hand. She was not wearing her diamonds so early in the day, merely sapphires on each hand. She greeted him in a friendly but reserved manner and instructed the maid to bring more tea with lemon.

191

'It is kind of you to call. I thought of going for a walk in the Tiergarten this afternoon but then Herr Esschen arrived and here I am.'

'Are you engaged for dinner this evening, may I ask?'

She nodded.

'Your visits to Berlin must be busy social occasions, I realise,' he said pleasantly.

'I try to keep up with my friends.'

Franz Esschen, sitting opposite Jutta on an elaborately carved chair, seemed to be uncomfortable, perhaps even embarrassed. He did not have the look of a man who had made any progress in her affections. The maid served tea to Manfred and Jutta told her that Herr Esschen was leaving and to see him out. Franz stood up, pale of face, and took his leave hurriedly.

'That's better,' Jutta said, 'I do not feel at ease with that young man. I am glad that you came, Manfred.'

'I suppose he called to apologise for his failure the other evening.'

'I don't like him,' she said.

Manfred thought it better to change the subject and asked where she bought her wonderful clothes. She was wearing a beautifully-styled costume of jacket and skirt in delicate lime-green.

'In Paris, of course,' she said. 'The women here dress like frumps. Do you like this costume?'

'The colour is perfect with your hair and complexion, even though it conceals your superb sun-tan. To see you golden all over was exquisite. Nothing is less appealing than a woman with tanned shoulders and legs with a white body between. In Lisbon you are able to set aside the petty consideration of wearing a swim-suit.'

'That is true, but what you saw was not acquired in Portugal but in Sicily. I have been there most of the summer and I am on my way back to Lisbon with this diversion to Berlin to see my friends here.'

'Sicily? How interesting. You have friends there too, I'm sure.'

192

'Quite a few – and one in particular, a friend from the old days in Berlin who has lived in Sicily since the end of the War.'

'A connoisseur of antiques, perhaps. I have read that there are very fine Greek ruins in Sicily.'

Jutta chuckled in an exciting throaty way.

'His interest is less in Greek temples than in young Sicilian boys. He lives not far from Taormina, in a house on the high cliffs above the sea, surrounded by groves of olives and lemons and figs – the whole landscape is amazingly beautiful.'

'He perceives some quality in Sicilian boys which is not present in German boys, does he?' Manfred asked dryly. 'It can hardly be a question of availability. Our local variety parade up and down the Kurfurstendamm every evening to look for customers.'

'Exactly! That's why he lives where he does. A vulgar parade of boys offering themselves for sale would be very offensive to him. In Sicily he lives among children of nature, unspoiled by our decadent civilisation. He poses them in the famous Greek ruins and takes photographs – and his pictures are works of art. He recreates the ancient world so well that it is as if you saw the youth of Classical Greece brought back to life.'

'An unusual interest for a man of leisure.'

'You shall judge for yourself.'

Jutta went out of the sitting-room for a moment and came back with a sheaf of large photographic prints. Manfred sat beside her on the sofa and took the first picture she offered him. It showed a boy, leaning against a rock-face in a casual attitude, a reed-flute in his hand. He was curly-haired, naked and bare-foot. His personal flute, not the one in his hand, seemed exceptionally well-grown for a boy of his age and hung heavily between his sturdy thighs.

'There!' said Jutta with enthusiasm, 'The very image of a young shepherd, such as the old Greek poets wrote about! Or he could be a young Pan, resting by the sun-drenched rocks, as self-contained and yet as wary as a young animal.

193

He listens and watches. He may take fright at the far-off sound of a human voice and skip lightly away into the olive-grove. But if he hears only the sound of bees and the distant bleat of a sheep, he will raise his reed-flute to his lips and play a thrilling melody that hints of gods and goddesses in repose and the deep indescribable tranquillity of nature undisturbed by man.'

Manfred was so struck by her words that he wondered if she was translating from some poet unfamiliar to him.

'Your sensitivity to the secret meaning of this picture is worthy of the highest praise,' he said. 'You have made me realise that it is not just a boy with no clothes on.'

Jutta's dark-brown eyes stared fixedly at him.

'We have allowed our lives to become confused and misdirected, my dear Manfred. The noise and distractions of cities and so-called society have robbed us of our God-given sensibilities towards nature and its truths. Do you not feel this?'

'You put it so clearly.'

She showed him the rest of the photographs, other boys posed in other places – against an antique ruined stone column, under a tree, sprawled on a flight of worn stone steps, on the sea-shore by a wooden boat – all of them naked and displaying their pubescent masculinity boldly. It was to the first picture she returned when she explained further.

'These pretty boys do not understand that they are living an idyllic life. To *understand* is a mental process. But they *feel* it in their hearts. This boy, for example, is wholly natural and wholly himself, because he knows nothing else. And therefore he is happy in a way which you and I cannot share. He eats and sleeps and loves as the mood takes him.'

'He is a little too young to know the delights and torments of love,' Manfred objected.

'Not at all,' said Jutta, her red-painted mouth curving in a slow smile.

'He is well-developed, I agree. Perhaps his flute is not always as docile as when your friend took this photograph.'

194

'I have seen it far from docile,' she said, and laughed.

It was impossible to mistake the delicate pink flush of her cheeks. Manfred unbuttoned her elegant little jacket and found, as he had expected, that she wore nothing under it. He stroked her small firm breasts with pleasure.

'This is what that fool Esschen came here for,' he said playfully.

'No he didn't – he had something else in mind, though I suppose he would have been pleased if I had let him touch me.'

'What did he come for then?'

'How well do you know him?' she countered.

'Not at all. I met him for the first time at Wolfgang's and I'm sure he was there only because he brought the films.'

'He's a blackmailer,' said Jutta calmly.

'A what?'

Manfred was so amazed that he withdrew his hand from its agreeable task.

'He came here to demand money. If I refused to pay, he threatened to get in touch with my husband and tell him what we did at the film-show – you and I, Konrad and I – and above all, my nephew and I.'

'Good God! What a swine! What did you say?'

'I informed him that he would be wasting his time and postage stamp to write to my husband, except that it might amuse him. He has no illusions about me.'

'And he doesn't mind?'

'He has his own amusements. It was he who first took me to Sicily, years ago. In our collection at Lisbon there are many very diverting photographs of Klaus misbehaving with peasant boys.'

'Esschen must have been greatly disconcerted, to say the least.'

Jutta reached for his hand and drew it back to her breasts.

'It's not the first time I've dealt with blackmailers,' she said as Manfred teased her nipples to firmness, 'I knew that young man was a crook the moment I set eyes on him. I

195

must warn Wolfgang before I leave, otherwise he might pay him in a misguided attempt to protect my honour. Do you have photographs of special moments, Manfred?'

'Not really – only half a dozen pictures of girls I've known.'

'Naked, of course.'

'Of course. But tell me something – even though you distrusted Kessler on sight, you would have let him make love to you if he had been up to it.'

'That's different,' she said, 'trusting and liking have nothing to do with that.'

Her hand was at his trouser-buttons, freeing his stem.

'Will you do something for me?' she murmured, stroking it slowly.

'Anything – you have only to name it.'

'That silly film we saw – you remember the close-up of the girl's face filling the screen at the end?'

'Remember it! I dreamed about it last night and woke up in the state you see me in now.'

'I want a picture of my face like that. I'm sure I looked exactly like her when you had me doubled over the chair and destroyed me. I want you to do that for me again so that a photograph can be taken of my expression. Will you do that for me?'

'But who is to take this photograph?'

'I have made enquiries and I've located a man with a small studio where he does portraits and birthday photographs and that sort of thing. He'll do it.'

'Can he be trusted?'

'He can be bought. Will you do it for me, Manfred?'

'On one condition.'

'And what is that?'

'That you give me a large print of it to remember you by until your next visit to Berlin.'

The Education of Girls

Hildegard Buschendorf was a pleasant enough woman, cheerful, talkative, fair-haired and overweight, with the prominent bosom and backside which Manfred associated with women of his mother's generation. That was a little unfair, for Frau Buschendorf could hardly be forty yet, but her plain way of dressing and her overblown figure placed her quite clearly for him.

He met her at a lunch given by his Aunt Dorothea in her house on Bellevue-strasse. The purpose of the lunch, as he quickly made out, was so that he should make the acquaintance of Fraulein von Ettlinger and her mother. Aunt Dorothea never lost an opportunity to try to marry Manfred off to suitable young ladies and she had invited some of her other friends in order to disguise her motives. Fraulein von Ettlinger was a pretty enough young lady of eighteen, though too subdued for Manfred's taste. He was polite and charming, made a note of her telephone number without committing himself to calling her, and thought no more about her.

It was raining hard that afternoon and Manfred's aunt, aware of his lack of interest in the young lady she was promoting, saddled him with the task of driving Frau Buschendorf home, she living right across the other side of Berlin. On the journey she admired his Mercedes volubly, praised his driving skill and told him a little about herself. She was a widow, her husband being of a military family, and he had met his end in the service of the Fatherland in 1916. All very sad – and very familiar.

As they passed through Alexander Platz they saw a fight in the road – about a dozen men brawling, spilling over the pavement and dangerously near the traffic. Some of them were in the brown uniforms of the Nazi Party, some of them in ordinary workmen's clothes. They were all shouting as they punched and kicked at each other. One man was lying in the gutter in the rain, face-down and evidently unconscious.

'My God, what are they doing!' Frau Buschendorf exclaimed, clutching Manfred's arm in terror. 'Why don't the police stop them?'

'They are settling a political disagreement,' said Manfred thoughtfully.

'They'll kill each other! Look – there's another one on the ground and they're kicking him!'

'Perhaps it would be for the best if they did kill each other, dear lady.'

He drove away as fast as he could. When they arrived at Frau Buschendorf's apartment, she invited him in to meet her children and he, with nothing else to do that afternoon, accepted. The children proved to be two daughters, one about sixteen and the other some years younger. Manfred wondered wryly whether this was the second try that day at getting him interested in a suitable young lady. The two girls were dressed alike, in white blouses, grey pleated skirts and white knee-socks, which he took to be their school uniform. They were both extremely well-mannered and sat quietly with their mother and her guest in the old-fashioned drawing-room, while Frau Buschendorf told Manfred how clever they both were, as mothers do.

He paid little attention as she rambled on, his interest caught by the older girl, Monika. She was cast in the same mould as her mother – the same solid bone-structure and breadth of hip. At her age she presented a slightly heavy attractiveness, but no doubt she would look much like her mother in another twenty years. The little girl, Angelika, resembled her mother in facial features and would develop in the same way as her sister in time, though as yet there was no indication of a bosom under her blouse.

His attention was dragged back to Frau Buschendorf's monologue by the unexpected word *discipline*.

'. . . so important for growing girls,' she was saying. 'Otherwise they run wild these days. I've seen it happen with my friends' girls and it leads to the most dreadful scandal and disgrace. I'm sure you know what I mean.'

Manfred nodded solemnly, without the least idea what she meant.

'My late and dear husband's brother Gunther has been a great help to me. He deals with the girls firmly and they respect him for it.'

'Is he too a military man, Madame?'

'In his youth, just as his brother was. He left the Army after the War and went into business. I never understood the details, of course, but he has done extremely well for himself. He has always been too busy to marry and so, in a sense, we became his family. He has been a great comfort and support to me. He understands what duty means, you see – something which the young people today seem not to care about. We miss him sadly.'

'May I ask what has happened to him?'

'Nothing has happened to him, thank God. His business has taken him to Spain. He imports and exports, you understand. He has been away for nearly three months now and I hope he will be back soon. He is a good influence on my girls.'

'By his example, you mean?' Manfred asked, not at all impressed by this absent paragon of virtue.

'That, of course, and also his method of disciplining them.'

Manfred glanced at Monika and Angelika, sitting demurely side by side on the heavy old sofa. They were looking attentively at their mother and there was nothing to be gleaned from their expressions.

'This method, Madame – what is it?'

199

'The only method that works with young girls – a strong hand.'

He was almost sure that he caught a flicker of amusement on Monika's pretty face.

'I see that you understand me,' said Frau Buschendorf, 'Gunther's method is a strong hand across their bottoms.'

'He beats these charming children?' Manfred asked, aghast.

'Certainly not! Do you think we are barbarians to beat our children? He has a regular routine of smacking them once a week.'

Manfred could hardly believe what he was hearing. He addressed himself to the older girl.

'What do you think of these weekly smackings, Fraulein Monika?'

'It is for our own good, Herr von Klausenberg. It doesn't hurt much and it is soon over.'

'You are fond of your uncle?'

Both girls nodded at once.

'You see,' said their mother, beaming, 'they miss their Uncle Gunther now he is away. Perhaps I should have remarried years ago to give them a father, but so many fine young men never came back from the War! And with Gunther to stand by me, I felt no need.'

Frau Buschendorf's recital of the problems of a woman alone with children to bring up became dreary and Manfred decided to take his leave. He was not listening to what she was saying, his thoughts set on the idea of sixteen-year-old Monika having her bottom smacked by Uncle Gunther. He nodded and smiled from time to time when Frau Buschendorf looked at him for a response and was surprised when she fell silent and she and her daughters stared at him expectantly.

'I beg your pardon – my thoughts were wandering.'

'So you agree?'

'Oh yes,' he answered vaguely, having no idea of what he had agreed to and thinking it of no consequence anyway, now that he was about to go.

'Then we will proceed at once.'

'I fear I may have misunderstood you, dear lady. What are we to proceed with?'

'To administer the discipline my daughters have missed for three months. I shall be most grateful to you.'

Manfred stared at her in amazement.

'You ask me, a stranger to your home, to punish your daughters? Have they behaved so badly? The idea is unthinkable.'

'I have explained myself badly – there is no question of behaving badly. My girls are very well-behaved. The discipline is a reminder to continue to behave well in future. Isn't that right, children?'

'Yes, Mama,' they said in unison.

Manfred was perplexed as how to escape from this ridiculous situation – and as to how he had got into it. Finally his sense of humour asserted itself and he decided to oblige Frau Buschendorf by giving the girls a quick slap on the backside and make his departure quickly.

'I am at your service, Madame. Please explain what I am to do.'

'Thank you – we are truly grateful, aren't we, girls?'

'Yes, Mama.'

'There is a necessary routine,' Frau Buschendorf explained, 'Monika receives ten smacks because she is nearly grown up. Angelika receives six smacks because she is still only a child.'

'Could you not carry out this domestic routine yourself?' Manfred asked.

'That would be to miss the point. They must be disciplined by a man, not by their mother.'

'Why is that?'

'To remind them of their place.'

Manfred gave up trying to make sense of the proposition.

'I have no experience of domestic routines, but I shall do my best.'

'There, girls! I knew that Herr von Klausenburg was a kind-hearted gentleman as soon as I met him.'

She rose from her chair, Manfred stood up and the girls vacated the sofa.

'It is better if you remove your jacket,' Frau Buschendorf advised, 'Your actions must not be hindered. A strong and steady hand is the main thing.'

Manfred took off his jacket and watched Monika fold it neatly and lay it on a chair.

'We always start with Monika,' said Frau Buschendorf. 'As the eldest it is her right. And it is her duty to show her sister how to conduct herself properly. Correctness is essential.'

'I'm sure it is,' said Manfred, wondering if she were slightly deranged.

'Monika, prepare yourself,' her mother ordered.

What Manfred expected to happen was that the girl would bend over and touch her toes while she was spanked. His expectations proved to be wrong. Monika hoisted her pleated skirt to show her thighs and white knickers, lay on her back on the sofa and raised her knees to her chest. The position exposed her bottom, drawn taut by the raising of her legs. Before he had recovered from this first surprise, another followed. Monika hooked her thumbs in the sides of her knickers and wriggled them down over her bottom and on to her thighs. Manfred stared at the smooth cheeks she had bared.

'The discipline is carried out on the bare flesh,' Frau Buschendorf explained. 'It is more effective like that because it humbles the recipient.'

'Just so,' said Manfred, now convinced that he was dealing with someone not quite sane, 'But the position is awkward. Why must it be so?'

'Surely that is obvious. If she bent over she would not be able to see your face. It is of the utmost importance that the girls see the face of the man and know that he is not angry with them but carrying out his task in a proper spirit of duty. Now, if you are ready, please deliver ten smacks.'

He looked at Monika's face to see how she was taking all this. Her eyes were wide open and she was gazing steadily at him, her expression giving no hint of her feelings. He stepped up to the sofa and smacked one cheek of her bottom, not at all hard.

'One!' Frau Buschendorf counted aloud.

He smacked the other cheek and heard 'Two!' From his vantage point above Monika he had a perfect view, not only of her smooth-skinned bottom but, more interesting, of the pouting split between her thighs and its light fleece of brown hair. He thought it was very pretty and continued to look at it as he continued the smacking, stopping when Frau Buschendorf said loudly 'Ten!'

The younger girl had been standing throughout at the end of the sofa, leaning against it and staring at her sister's bottom, now blushing faintly pink from the smacks.

'Excellently done,' said Frau Buschendorf, 'What do you say now, Monika?'

'Thank you very much, Herr von Klausenberg, for teaching me what I have to learn, I promise that I shall remember this lesson and profit by it,' said Monika, her words evidently a formula used on these occasions.

'Give her your hand,' said Frau Buschendorf.

Manfred held out his hand, thinking to help the girl to rise, and found instead that she kissed it. Altogether, he thought, a very strange family.

Monika got off the sofa, pulled up her knickers and smoothed her grey skirt down.

'Angelika, your turn, my little angel,' said Frau Buschendorf fondly.

The smaller girl placed herself in the same position, knees up and knickers down, to present a taut little bottom. Manfred smacked it very lightly, amused by the hairless little slit between her legs. He was not at all sure at what age girls' tufts started to grow but he guessed that it was at the same time that their breasts started to show and for little Angelika the time was not yet. She went through the same formula of thanking him, word-perfect, and of kissing his hand, before she scrambled off the sofa and stood, skirt held up while she rubbed her bottom as if he had really hurt her.

'I am pleased with the way you have behaved,' Frau Buschendorf told her daughters. 'Off to your room now and read your school-books until dinner-time.'

Manfred smiled and bowed as both girls gave him a little curtsy before leaving the drawing-room.

'My dear brother-in-law says it is necessary for women to be reminded of their place. You see the truth of this in the good manners of my girls.'

'He must be a remarkable man,' said Manfred cautiously.

'He is, in every way. And you have been so understanding and so very helpful that I feel I can confide in you further.'

Manfred inclined his head, not knowing what to say.

'Every week, after the girls have been dealt with and sent to their room, Gunther treats me in exactly the same way.'

'But you are a grown woman – don't you resent being treated like a child?'

'I welcome it,' she answered, pink-cheeked and vehement.

A mental picture of plump Frau Buschendorf on the sofa with her knees up and her bottom being smacked almost made Manfred laugh. He contained himself with an effort, wondering if he could prolong the joke.

'If I can assist in any way . . .' he said.

It was no joke – she seized upon his words instantly.

'You would be doing me a very great favour!'

Before his startled eyes, she was on the sofa, skirt up round her waist and knees on her bosom, displaying a large round bottom encased in dove-grey knickers. She pulled them down and let Manfred see her white cheeks and the prominent fleshy lips between her heavy thighs.

'Ten?' he asked.

'Twenty – it's always twenty for me.'

Manfred took his position by her side and swung his hand hard at the target offered to him.

'One!' she gasped.

He continued, landing his smacks on each cheek in turn, trying to make it sting. The massive cheeks wobbled as he struck and their pale skin flushed red after the third or fourth blow. By the time he reached ten Frau Buschendorf was sighing loudly between her counting and her legs were trembling wildly.

Manfred too was breathing faster. Without being aware of it, he had become aroused. What had started as a joke on his part had ceased to be only that and was taking on a very different aspect. By the count of twenty his stem was standing upright in his trousers. Immediately after the final smack, which rang out resoundingly, Frau Buschendorf seized the hand that had disciplined her and pressed her mouth to it.

'Thank you, thank you,' she exclaimed, her face as glowing red as her bare bottom. 'You have a strong hand and a willing heart.'

Manfred wondered whether he had laid it on too hard – the red marks on her bottom were very bright. He laid his hand gently on one of the afflicted spots to see if it felt hot to the touch.

'Is that painful?' he asked, breathing quickly.

'Discipline must hurt, or it has no meaning,' she murmured, her eyes half-closed.

Manfred's finger-tips had somehow found their way between her raised legs. While he was lightly stroking one reddened cheek to ease its pain, his finger-tips were tickling the thinly-haired and pouting lips exposed to him.

'After your brother-in-law has spanked you, what does he do next?'

'He completes the lesson,' she said softly.

'And how is that done?'

'He reminds me in the most forceful way possible that I am a woman and that I must at all times remember my duty. Do you understand what I am saying?'

'I believe that I do. Shall I proceed?'

'If you would be so kind.'

He knelt on the sofa, unbuttoned his trousers and tucked

his bent knees under her bottom to raise it. Frau Buschendorf strained her thighs as far apart as the knickers round them would permit and sighed when he used his fingers to open the thick lips presented to him. His stem slid in easily, the smacking having prepared her for what was to come. He looked at her face and saw so greedy an expression on it that he leaned forward and plunged deeply before going at her with a will. Nothing about this strange woman surprised him any more, not even when she began to count quickly to his jabbing: 'One, two, three, four, five, six, seven, eight, nine . . .'

He was soon so engrossed in what he was doing that he no longer heard her voice. He had been aroused more than he knew by the variety of female charms that had been displayed for him and smacking Frau Buschendorf's bottom while staring at her split peach had wound him up like a spring. He went off like an alarm-clock, rocking the heavy old sofa under them with his impetus. When his spring finally ran down and Frau Buschendorf stopped squirming, he sat back on his heels and grinned. She reached for his hand and kissed it.

'It's months since I was disciplined by a man,' she said. 'Thank you, dear Manfred, if I may call you that.'

To cut short what seemed an excessive show of gratitude for so easy a favour, Manfred asked her how high her counting had gone.

'I lost count at four hundred and something.'

'I suppose you always lose count at some point.'

'Not exactly. With Gunther I always reach six hundred and something before he reaches the culmination of his discipline. After that I relax and experience the deep pleasure that comes from accepting my destiny. But you are younger and stronger than he is and you drove everything out of my head before you were finished. I am sorry, but I cannot tell you the final count. It's wrong of me, I know.'

'Why on earth should I want to know?'

'Gunther insists that it is part of the discipline to make me count for him. He always asks afterwards.'

'He is an unusual man. Personally I am more interested in pleasure for its own sake.'

'That is the failing of many young people nowadays. It was otherwise once.'

'Maybe it was. But you are educating your daughters in the old ways of submission and duty and the world no longer sets the same value on these things.'

'The old ways are best,' she said firmly.

'We must move with the times or we shall be left behind as relics,' said Manfred, as he climbed off the sofa and buttoned his trousers.

'We are passing through a time of moral laxity and rebellion by young people, that's what Gunther says, but they will exhaust themselves by their excesses and the old ways will come back,' she said stubbornly.

She stretched out her legs along the sofa, her frock still up round her waist, showing off the plump article Manfred had just made good use of.

'The pendulum may swing,' he answered, 'but nothing is ever the same again.'

'Only wait. You will see.'

'Suppose that I prove to you that pleasure for its own sake is far to be preferred to the shadowy pleasures of duty and obedience – will that make you change your mind?'

'How can you prove that?'

She got off the sofa to pull up her silk knickers and smooth out the creases in her frock.

Manfred thought for a moment or two.

'Come to my apartment on Thursday afternoon,' he said. 'About three in the afternoon. One of us will be proved right and one wrong.'

Thursday was when Manfred's servants were free after lunch for the rest of the day. Not that he had any qualms about them seeing his visitors, married or unmarried. Many was the time that Geiger had brought him his morning coffee and found a young lady cuddled up beside him in bed. His instructions on such occasions were to bring a second cup. There was one memorable morning when he had brought in the coffee just as Nina was perched above Manfred, giving him a special morning greeting, though that was in the days before she married Gottfried.

In the matter of Frau Buschendorf it was different, Manfred considered. She was, after all, twenty years older than himself and much more bound by convention. Delicacy suggested that it would be needlessly embarrassing to her to subject her to the scrutiny of the servants. When she arrived he could not fail to note her smile of approval at his thoughtfulness. He helped her out of her coat and took her straight to his bedroom, there being no reason he could see for elaborate courtesies first. She knew what she had come for, he knew what she had come for – matters might as well proceed without delay.

She was wearing a woollen frock in shades of dark blue and cream and, by the look of her, had come straight from the hair-dresser. Her only make-up was a little powder on her cheeks, but even that was more than she had worn when he met her at Aunt Dorothea's lunch party. As soon as Manfred tried to get her out of her clothes, she blushed and asked him to turn away while she undressed herself. This coquettishness was in such marked contrast to the way in which she had exposed herself to him to be *disciplined* in her own home that it was clear that she felt herself to be on unsure terms with him. He stared out of the window for a few minutes until she said that she was ready, then turned to find her in bed, with only her head showing. He shed his jacket and shoes but, before he could continue, she brought her naked arms out of the bed and asked him to hold her.

This unnatural modesty on the part of a woman who had already allowed him the most intimate access to herself made Manfred slightly impatient. Moreover, this encounter was to be on his terms, not hers – that was the whole point of it. He flicked back the covers and saw her fully naked for the first time. It seemed to him then that Hildegard Buschendorf was the most naked-looking woman he had ever set eyes on and he sought to explain this to himself as he lay beside her and fondled her big soft breasts. After all, he told himself, a naked woman is a naked woman, a head, a body, two arms, two legs, two of these and one of those. Why should Hildegard create this impression of being more naked than a naked woman generally looks? In his mind's eye he compared her with other recent guests in this same bed.

Partly it was to do with her physical size, he decided. Hildegard had so much more flesh to expose than, for example, Vicki Schwabe, who was slender, or even Jutta von Loschingen, who was small-breasted and firm all over. Hildegard was heavy-boned and solidly built, with wonderfully plump thighs, a belly that curved roundly and, of course, her over-sized breasts, each a double handful in itself. But in addition to sheer size, Hildegard's colouring had something to do with the impression of ultra-nakedness. Her hair was chestnut-brown and her skin was extremely pale, a creamy-white with the merest touch of flesh-tone in it. Against this alabaster appearance the pinkness of her nipples was in high contrast. And there was something else – she had little hair between her legs, as he had noticed before when she took up her extraordinary posture on the sofa to be smacked. There was only a sparse covering of brown over the fleshy lips down there and the effect was to make her seem more exposed than, one might say, Helga, who had a fine curly tuft.

All in all, to make love to Hildegard was like gorging oneself on a huge Black Forest gateau – there was so much to enjoy and it was all so rich and creamy! Manfred stroked and felt her all over, thinking as he did that her brother-in-law Gunther must be mad to confine himself to his uncomfortable in-and-out and deny himself the pleasure of all this warm flesh.

For a woman unused to so much handling – or perhaps because of that – Hildegard enjoyed it enormously. She sighed and squirmed, her legs trembled and, when his hand was between them, her belly quivered and heaved. Manfred sat up to get his clothes off and multiply her pleasures by pressing her body to his, but at once she took hold of his arm and pulled him back down beside her.

'Please . . . keep your clothes on.'

'But why? It is so much nicer to be naked together.'

'It couldn't be nicer than it is now. It is right for me to be undressed to submit to you, but you must be strong and demanding.'

'Damnation! That's not the idea at all! Forget this strong man and weak woman nonsense for once. We are two human beings, giving each other pleasure.'

'My way is better. Touch me again and remember how you disciplined me. It was because I was submissive that you were so forceful.'

'What makes you think that?'

'Because you did it so hard and fast! It was wonderful.'

Manfred stroked her belly and then down between her thighs.

'It can be better than that,' he told her.

'What could possibly be better than lying on a submissive woman and exerting your strength? And what could be better for a woman than to feel the weight of a man crushing her as he thrusts into her body and tries to split her open?'

Manfred began to feel baffled by this extraordinary woman – extraordinary to him, that is. He was excited enough from handling her to follow her suggestion, to climb on top of her and do what she wanted. But that would be to admit defeat. He approached the point in another way.

'I understand what you mean, Hildegard. I shall be strong and force you to submit to me. That is what discipline is about, yes?'

'Oh, yes!'

'After I smacked your bottom the other day you thanked me and kissed my hand. Why did you do that?'

'It is correct to kiss the hand that punishes you.'

'But after I had, in your words, split you open, you did

not kiss the instrument of punishment. That seems to me to be most incorrect.'

As the import of his words sank in, her eyes opened wide and she stared at him unbelievingly.

'I never thought . . . but Gunther has never suggested . . .'

'Search your conscience,' said Manfred firmly, 'Perhaps he is so shocked by your dereliction of duty that he cannot bring himself to speak of it. Have you considered that?'

'I don't know what to say,' she muttered uneasily.

'I suggest that you begin with an apology.'

That was something she had been taught to understand.

'I ask you most sincerely to forgive me. Believe me, there was no slight intended. It never entered my mind.'

She looked as if she was about to burst into tears. Manfred spoke sharply.

'Your apology is unacceptable until you have put matters right.'

'You mean that you want me to . . .' but she was unable to say the words.

'It is not what I want that is important here, it is what is correct. Your sincerity can only be demonstrated by your actions.'

She looked so confused that Manfred found it hard not to smile. He rolled on to his back beside her and put his hands behind his head.

'I am waiting.'

Hildegard sat up slowly and unbuttoned his trousers with awkward fingers.

'Never in my life . . .' she began, then trailed off.

There was a pause while she gathered her courage to pull up his shirt. She gasped and almost drew away when his hard stem jerked out through the slit in his underwear.

'You flinch from your duty,' Manfred reproached her.

She took a deep breath, bent her neck and leaned down to kiss his twitching stem. Once committed, she did not skimp her duty and he felt her kisses from the head to the root of his stiffness.

She raised her head to look at him.

'Is my apology accepted?' she asked timidly.

'I believe that you are sincere. It would make matters better between us if you proved your submission to this instrument of discipline beyond the mere formality of what you have done so far.'

Hildegard took his meaning. She turned round on the bed to face him, took his stem in her hand and kissed it repeatedly. After a while she said breathlessly:

'This is so strange that you will not believe me. I was married for six years and I have two children. And for the past six or seven years Gunther has been disciplining me weekly. Yet this is the first time I have ever touched this part of a man, or even seen it properly.'

'How is that possible?'

'My husband always came to bed in a long night-shirt and embraced me in the dark. I never once saw him naked.'

'But your brother-in-law – with him you are in your drawing-room and it is not dark – how could you not observe what he uses?'

'When he makes me lie with my knees up to be smacked, I can see little more than his head and shoulders. And afterwards he puts it away before letting me move. At times I catch a glimpse of pink flesh, but no more than that.'

'There is much for you to learn. Now that you see how a man is made, what is your opinion?' Manfred said, amused by her confession and yet sorry for her.

Hildegard stroked her new discovery thoughtfully.

'I've often been to look at the old Greek statues in museums, but they have little things hanging down, not in the least like the big hard things I have felt inside my body. You will laugh at me, but last year I bought a book in one of those dreadful little shops that sell books and pictures about sexual matters. It was so embarrassing to go in – I nearly died of shame.'

'What did you buy?'

'A book of pictures of young men, all aroused. It was a

212

tremendous shock for me to see the different sizes and shapes. But it was very educational.'

'My poor Hildegard, the men you have known have treated you very oddly. They seem to have given you little and asked for little.'

'How can you say that? They gave me all they had and I did the same. What more can any woman give than admittance to her body?'

'I shall try to enlighten you before you leave.'

'But it all comes to the same thing in the end,' she said. 'Whether we are dressed or undressed, in the light or in the dark, whether we touch each other or not, it leads to the same joining together of the man and the woman for a minute or two.'

'That is like saying that all meals are the same because they consist of putting food into your mouth.'

Her hand still held his stem but she had no idea of how to handle it. He showed her how to clasp it and move her hand up and down.

'I do not understand,' she said, 'this must be a poor substitute for putting it where it should really be. Would you not rather have it there than in my hand?'

'This is not a substitute at all,' Manfred sighed, 'the two pleasures are only slightly related. No one has ever told you that in love-making only part of the pleasure is between the legs. The rest is in the mind. The touch of your hand produces another sort of pleasure in the mind from the pleasure I would feel if I were inside you.'

'Surely not,' she said.

Before Manfred could attempt any further explanation, the inevitable happened. His loins jerked upwards from the bed and he poured his stream of passion through Hildegard's busy hand on to his white shirt-front.

'My God!' she exclaimed, her hand moving faster, 'I never guessed!'

He took her wrist to halt her movements.

'What didn't you guess, dear Hildegard?'

'I had no idea of how tremendous a destiny it is to be a

man! To see how this wonderful part reared itself up and flung out its torrent! It was awe-inspiring! I never knew!'

Manfred almost despaired. Perhaps she had been too well-trained in her role of submissive female to be rescued now. His well-intentioned attempt to remove the mystery from what a man's stem did when it was inside her had produced the very opposite result. She sat staring at it as it softened as if she had received a divine revelation.

He got off the bed, stripped completely and stood to let her look at him.

'See, Hildegard – I am no marble statue in a museum. I am a living man made of flesh and bones. Now you know what a naked man looks like. Forget your picture book and fix the real thing in your mind.'

She lay propped on one elbow, staring at him.

'You are more like the statues than the picture book, Manfred.'

'Why do you say that?'

'In the pictures the young men are all hard and strong. You are small now like the statues. It was better before, when I held you.'

'A temporary condition,' he said, laughing. 'Soon I shall be like your pictures again.'

She rolled on to her back and smiled. Manfred got back on to the bed, parted her fleshy legs widely and lay between them. He stroked the protruding lips between her thighs.

'There is something I am trying to explain to you, but you have not yet understood me.'

'I know I'm not clever,' she sighed. 'Tell me again and I'll try to understand.'

'I doubt whether words will convey it. What I am trying to get you to grasp is that this warm slot between your legs is every bit as important as anything a man has.'

'That can't possibly be true,' she objected. 'You have a proud and arrogant thing – now that you've let me stroke yours I know how wonderful it is.'

Manfred stopped listening to her nonsense. He opened her widely with his fingers and tickled her exposed pink button. After a little while her legs began to shake and she gasped loudly.

'Ah, no! Not with your fingers – do it the correct way!'

'There is no such thing as a correct way, Hildegard. You must have been played with like this before when your husband took off his night-shirt.'

'Never!'

Manfred worked slowly, determined to make her experience more than she was used to. She moaned softly and rolled her head from side to side on the pillow.

'What did he do to you – at least he took off your night-gown?'

'No,' she moaned, 'no . . . he stroked my breasts through it . . . he never put his hands on my body . . .'

'And then?'

'He had me pull my night-gown up to my waist and he lay on top of me and did what men do . . . this is not possible . . . you must stop!'

Her plump body was shaking all over and Manfred was certain that she had never before felt such wild sensations of pleasure and she was half afraid of them. Her curved belly rose and fell to her panting. Manfred put his hands on her thighs to force them further apart, bent his neck and touched the tip of his tongue to her slippery bud.

'No!' she screamed. 'It's too much!'

She tried to slither away from him. Manfred used his strength to pin her thighs flat to the bed while his tongue flicked over her sensitive button. The conclusion was spectacular – her thighs overcame the pressure of his hands in a spasmodic upwards jerk and clamped round his head. Her body convulsed as if in a seizure and, though his ears were muffled by her legs, he could still hear her staccato screaming. The outburst grew louder and with a final window-rattling 'Uh!' she collapsed as completely as if she had been shot dead.

Manfred sat up and looked at her. For a moment he thought that her climactic release had been so extreme that she had fainted, as Magda had done when she nearly

215

knocked his brains out with her spiked helmet. But Hilde-gard's pink-tipped breasts were rising and falling regularly to her breathing and her eyes were open. He moved up the bed to cradle her head in his arm.

'What have you done to me?' she asked softly.

'I hope I've shown you what the plump little delight between your legs is capable of.'

'But it can't always be like that . . . it would be too much.'

'The women I know expect pleasure like that two or three times a day and sometimes more. You will soon come to expect the same.'

'I feel so content . . . and so sleepy. Is that dreadful of me? I know you must want your pleasure, but would you mind waiting a little?'

Manfred saw that as real progress. Half an hour ago she would have parted her legs and let him do as he pleased, however she felt. Some of her submissiveness seemed to have evaporated.

'Sleep for a while,' he said, 'I'll wake you later.'

He covered her over and watched as she turned on her side and dozed off. It occurred to him that brother-in-law Gunther was in for a surprise when he returned from Spain. Hildegard was not likely to revert to her former role, legs up on her chest, to give Gunther a quick dip. It would be sensible to show her a few ways in which she could reverse places with Gunther and keep him up to the mark.

So musing, Manfred put on his black and silver dressing-gown and left her to sleep. He was in the kitchen drinking a bottle of beer when he heard the door-bell. He ignored it for a while, but the ringing was persistent. He went down the hall to get rid of the unwelcome caller, flung the door wide and saw, to his astonishment, Jenny Montrose in a long mink coat and a hat to match. She was smiling in a most friendly way, but the smile faded from her face when she saw his dressing-gown and bare feet.

'I'm sorry,' she said, her German tinged with her soft

216

foreign accent, 'I've disturbed you. I saw your car outside and guessed you were home.'

'Please come in,' Manfred said quickly, his heart racing at what this visit might portend, 'I am delighted to see you.'

'Are you sure I'm not disturbing you?' she asked, her finely-drawn eyebrows rising.

'Excuse my appearance. The servants are out today and I was sleeping off the effects of a party last night,' he lied.

He hung her fur coat in the hall and took her into the drawing-room. She looked enchanting in her fur hat and a cream-coloured frock that had a large red rose embroidered over one breast.

'May I offer you something – tea, coffee, a drink? And then I will get dressed and we can talk.'

Plans were evolving in his head. As soon as Jenny was settled he would get Hildegard up and dressed and out by the service door on some pretext or other.

'Nothing, thank you,' said Jenny. 'Are you sure that this is not an inconvenient time?'

'Not in the least. It takes me a little time to collect my wits when I wake up. If you will excuse me, I will dress and be back in a couple of minutes.'

'There's no need for that,' she said, with a smile that sent his heart fluttering. 'That's a beautiful dressing-gown.'

'But I've got bare feet – at least let me go and put my slippers on.'

Jenny kicked off her shiny black crocodile-skin shoes.

'That makes us equal,' she said. 'What else haven't you got on?'

Manfred's dream had come true. Here, sitting in his own drawing-room, was the girl he most desired in the whole world. He had been drawn to her since Ulrika's absurd celebration in the Steam-bath, however ambiguous her actions that night. And this attraction had made it impossible to resist making love to her at Ernst's party, when she was unconscious, though the psychological impact on him of that episode had been so intolerable that he had

217

suppressed his feelings towards her and had deliberately not tried to see her again. Now she had come to him, a warm smile on her beautiful face, and she had not come to drink tea. Fate had ordained this momentous event, he had no doubt of that.

'What else haven't I got on,' he repeated, turning on all his considerable charm. 'A hat, of course – but please keep yours on – it suits you so well. I'm sure I can think of something else for you to take off.'

Her eyes were shining and she looked amused.

'You're asking yourself why I'm here,' she said, 'I'm not sure myself. Who needs reasons, anyway? This may come as a surprise to you but I've been dreaming about you lately – isn't that strange?'

'Flattering, I would rather say. What sort of dreams?'

'Exciting ones. That's what I don't understand. Do you ever dream about me?'

'I never remember my dreams when I wake up, but I'm sure that I have. What do I do in these dreams of yours?'

'You make love to me. But I don't make love to you. I lie there and let you do it, as if I'm paralysed. That's not my style at all – what do you make of it? Do you think I ought to go and talk to one of those Viennese professors who grope about in people's minds?'

'What do they know about it? Are your dreams pleasant or not?'

'They're marvellous. I enjoy them.'

'You don't need an old Viennese charlatan, you need me, Jenny.'

'That's what I thought, so here I am.'

'To tell me about your dreams?'

'To make love with you and find out if it's as good as when I dream about it,' and she hitched up her frock to display a long smooth thigh while she undid her suspender.

'Manfred?' said a nervous voice behind him. 'Are you there?'

It was Hildegard, standing in the door-way, all pink and

218

white and naked. She stared briefly at Jenny with goggling eyes, turned and fled, her big bottom wobbling.

'It was an inconvenient time after all,' said Jenny curtly, refastening her suspender and picking up her shoes.

'Don't go – I can explain.'

'No need,' she said, making for the door.

'If you only knew what that poor lady has suffered at the hands of uncaring men,' he babbled, hurrying after her.

Jenny had her mink coat over her arm and her hand on the door handle.

'I didn't know you made a living as a gigolo, Manfred. You'd better get back to the bed-room and earn your money.'

And she was gone, without even an 'Auf wiedersehen'.

He telephoned her several times that day and the next, but the moment he mentioned his name the servant answering the telephone told him that Fraulein Montrose was out. He wrote her a letter, but it sounded so feeble that he threw it in the waste-paper basket. In the end he decided that it was better to let some time elapse before he tried to repair the damage. He had no intention of seeing Hildegard again, even though he knew it was unjust to be angry with her. All the same, if she had not been with him that afternoon, he might by now be the happiest man in the world.

As things were, Jenny would be forgetting whatever disappointment she had suffered in the arms of another man. Those beautiful pointed breasts Manfred had touched when she lay drugged on Ernst's bed – some other man was kissing them! The warm sanctuary under her fine astrakhan tuft – some other man's hand was on it! Someone like Erwin, perhaps, unwashed, uncultured, some small criminal or pimp perhaps, the dregs of the gutter! Manfred tortured himself with jealous images and got so drunk at home for two nights running that his servants had to put him to bed.

After that he regained control of himself and learned patience. He was at home one afternoon, lying on the zebra-skin sofa with his jacket off and tie loose, reading an illustrated magazine, when Frau Geiger announced that he had a visitor.

'Who?' he asked, starting up hopefully.

'Fraulein Buschendorf.'

He could think of no sensible reason why Hildegard should pretend to be unmarried, but it sounded stupid enough to be in character for her. She had come to apologise, of course, but Manfred had no wish to see her.

'Please tell Frau Buschendorf that I am out.'

'No, Fraulein Buschendorf, Herr Manfred – a young lady.'

'Then show her in. Bring tea and whatever cake we have.'

'There's hazelnut cream layer-cake and coffee cream. I baked them this morning.'

'Then bring them both.'

He had his jacket on and was straightening his tie when Frau Geiger ushered in Monika, the sixteen year old daughter. She was dressed in school-girl style as he had seen her before, plain white blouse and pleated grey skirt.

'Fraulein Monika, how good of you to call! Please sit down and we'll have tea and cake. Is today a holiday?'

'I wanted to talk to you, Herr von Klausenberg,' she said primly.

They sat opposite each other and Frau Geiger served them. Manfred asked politely about Monika's mother and sister and she replied as politely. But no sooner was Frau Geiger out of the room than she broached the subject of her visit.

'Why does Mama let Uncle Gunther smack us?' she asked, coming straight to the point without the least sign of shyness.

'You must ask her that. It would be wrong for me to interfere.'

'You don't have to treat me like a child. Why did you smack me when Mama asked you to?'

'I'm not sure that I know. I was so surprised by the

request that I was prepared to do anything to escape from your home.'

'But you didn't escape. You stayed and smacked Mama's bottom as well.'

Manfred looked at her in alarm.

'If you find that difficult to understand, Monika, so do I. Were you listening at the door?'

'I always do. And look through the key-hole. I saw what you did to her. Uncle Gunther does the same.'

'So your Mama told me. What can I say? This is what happens between grown-ups – and things like it. It may seem odd to you now but in another year or two you'll know much more about it.'

Monika put her cup down and stared at him boldly.

'I know all about it now. I told you I'm not a child. Did you enjoy smacking my bottom?'

'To be truthful, I hardly recall what my emotions were.'

'That's not truthful at all. You had a good look at me, didn't you, when my knickers were down.'

Manfred stopped trying to play the responsible adult and grinned at Monika.

'You're a very pretty girl – I couldn't help myself. I hope you'll forgive me.'

'That's all right,' she said, grinning back at him. 'It was nice when you looked at me. Much nicer than when Uncle Gunther does. Do you want to look at me now?'

'Dear Monika, the suggestion is a tempting one but I don't think it would be a sensible thing to do.'

'Why not – if you want to?'

'Because you're only sixteen and problems could arise which neither of us want.'

'I'm not a virgin,' she told him proudly.

'Uncle Gunther?'

'No, silly! He never touches me. All the girls in my class at school have boyfriends. We all do it, you know.'

'Your Mama would not be pleased if she found out.'

'Who's going to tell her? She's got these old-fashioned ideas about girls knowing their duty, whatever that is. She expects me to be a virgin till my wedding-day, that's how out-of-date she is. She stopped talking to Frau Hammel in the apartment above us when she found out a man friend visits her when Herr Hammel is out. But she lets Uncle Gunther do it to her and pretends it's something to do with her duty. I think she's a hypocrite, even though she's my mother.'

'Children usually judge their parents harshly,' said Manfred. 'But we ought to remember that they grew up in a different sort of world from ours and were taught different values. The main thing is to live and let live.'

'Even hypocrites?'

'Your mother loves you, I'm sure of that. Her ways are not your ways. Why not do what you want and leave her in peace to do what she wants?'

'I suppose you're right. I'm glad I can talk to you. Why do people do such strange things? I mean, like Mama having her bottom smacked before Uncle Gunther does it to her?'

'There is only one true explanation of why men and women do strange things together. It is because they enjoy it.'

'But it doesn't look comfortable, the way they do it. Well, you should know – was it?'

'Comfort is of no great importance in such moments. People do the oddest things when they make love.'

'I don't,' said Monika sturdily.

'You can't have been doing it all that long,' Manfred pointed out. 'You are still at the stage when simple straightforward love-making is new and thrilling. How do you know that in five years from now you won't be experimenting in all sorts of comical ways?'

'Like what?'

'Monika, you did not come here for a lesson in sexual education.'

'But I did!'

'Then I must disappoint you. The only way to find out

is to try things yourself, not hear about them from someone else.'

'Do you do strange things when you make love?'

'To the person involved, nothing seems strange,' he said hastily, suppressing memories of nights with Magda and Vicki and half a dozen others.

'So it didn't seem strange with Mama?'

'I was doing what she wanted rather than expressing any particular wish of my own.'

'Do you always do what women want?' she persisted.

'I try to be as obliging as possible.'

'Will you do what I want if I take my knickers off?'

'What is it that you want?' he asked, grinning at the way she was trying to get him into a corner from which he could not escape.

'I want to be stroked. My boyfriend is so impatient that he doesn't feel me properly.'

Poor girl, Manfred thought, for all her seeming precocity she is going down the same road as her mother. Everything changes and nothing changes!

'And if I do, will you go away and pretend that you were never here?'

'If you ask me to.'

Monika knew that she had won, though not why. She made straight for the sofa, took her white cotton knickers off and lay down full-length with her skirt pulled up to bare the tuft of light brown hair he had seen before. Manfred lay on the sofa with her, his arm under her head, and kissed her lightly while he stroked her belly and thighs.

'That's right,' she said, her eyes staring at him, 'you know how to do it – I knew you would.'

His fingers eased between her thighs to touch the warm lips there.

'What's your boy-friend's name?'

'Heinz. We meet after school and go for a walk in the park. He's very nice really and I like him a lot, but he does it too fast. By now he'd be on top of me and ramming away.'

223

Manfred warmed to his task. He bent her top knee upwards to part her legs so that he could caress inside her little fleshy folds.

'I hope that proper precautions are taken,' he said, 'otherwise your Mama will find out that you're not a virgin if your little belly starts to swell.'

'No chance of that! I only let him do it when he's wearing one of those rubber things. You're making me feel nice all over.'

'You're moist already – you have a passionate nature, Monika.'

'Do you think so?' she murmured. 'I want to do it all the time, if that's what you mean.'

He felt her hand pressed to his trousers, where his stem stood stiffly.

'I'm nearly there,' she whispered. 'Slow down a bit!'

He teased her tiny bud very slowly and lightly, but the quivering of her body against him increased until she gasped, 'Now!'

Her throes lasted only two or three seconds and then her eyes were open and staring at him again.

'That was fantastic. You really know how to play with girls.'

'I'm glad you enjoyed it.'

'Are you going to do it properly now?' she asked.

Her fingers were unbuttoning his trousers and Manfred gave up resisting and let her pull his hard stem out.

'It's a lot bigger than Heinz's,' she said. 'You won't hurt me, will you?'

Manfred smiled reassuringly at her while he guided his hardness to the right spot and pushed gently. It was a tight fit, but not an uncomfortable one, and at about the half-way mark he stopped.

'Does that hurt?' he asked.

'No, it feels very nice.'

He undid her school blouse, found a slip underneath and pulled it out of the waist-band of her skirt so that he could play with her breasts. Nor were they that small – in fact,

224

at sixteen Monika had breasts as well-developed as those of many a grown woman.

'I love having them felt,' she informed him.

'By the time you're eighteen or nineteen you're going to have wonderful big breasts, Monika,' he said, tickling her nipples to make them firm.

Down below, he was easing himself in and out in a gentle rhythm that gave pleasure without problems.

'Do you like big ones?' she asked.

'I like big ones and little ones and middle-sized ones and fat ones and pointed ones – all of them.'

'I'm nearly there again,' said Monika, 'I love the way you do it. Are you nearly there?'

'Yes,' Manfred sighed.

'Be careful – I don't want you to give me a baby!'

Her words reminded him of Mitzi and the time he had made love to her on this same sofa, her back towards him while he stroked her swollen belly and thrust into her from behind. At once Manfred's belly contracted like a fist and he jerked himself free from Monika in the nick of time and spurted up her bare belly.

'Oh!' she squealed, 'You've done it!'

His fingers found her wet little slit and before his ecstatic spasms ended she was gasping and shaking against him.

When it was over, he kissed her breasts delicately, then her mouth, and got up to button his trousers. He gave her his handkerchief to dry her belly before she scrambled off the sofa and put on her knickers.

He thought it wiser to see her to the door himself so that Frau Geiger would not observe the pink glow on her face and deduce what had been going on.

'Auf wiedersehen, Monika.'

'Can I come back tomorrow afternoon?' she asked.

225

New Year's Eve

The Bruckners' parties were celebrated far and wide for the lavishness of the hospitality and to be invited was a prize greatly sought after, most particularly their New Year's Eve party, when the wealthy mingled with the fashionable and the dull were lost to sight in the crowd. Socially, of course, Heidi Bruckner was immeasurably superior to her husband, she being a daughter of old General von Dahlenburg, while Bruno Bruckner was from nowhere in particular. But he had the money and she used it to establish the Bruckner family in the society of the new Republic, with the ruthless streak her much-honoured father had displayed as a young Major at the siege of Paris in 1871.

The guests on New Year's Eve would be a carefully selected mixture, Manfred knew, when he received his vast gold-edged card of invitation, and a few telephone calls round his friends told him which of them had been similarly honoured. There would be Bruckner's most important business contacts with their overfed and overdressed wives and daughters. And whichever Government officials were important to his current and future enterprises. There would be people from the theatre and publishing, to give a tinge of culture to the proceedings – a mistake really, since people like that usually passed out drunk after an hour or two of the legendary hospitality. Fortunately there would also be a number of young people of good family to add tone to the event and they would supply the zest which the party would otherwise lack. To keep this throng happy and busy there would be oceans of French champagne to

226

drink, mountains of delicious snacks, music, dancing till dawn, and whatever form of entertainment Frau Bruckner had been told was all the rage just then.

The house was out in Grunewald Forest and the drive up to it was jammed solid on both sides with parked cars, mostly large, dark and sleek. Manfred was forced to leave his rakish tourer some distance away and march briskly up the drive in the freezing night air, thankful for his heavy leather overcoat and gloves. There was a little crowd of uniformed chauffeurs near the house, laughing and smoking, but they fell silent and stood up straight as Manfred passed them.

Those who liked the Bauhaus style found the grand salon of the house impressive. It was vast and high-ceilinged, taking the space of two storeys vertically, and it had a balcony with a silver-grill front across one whole end of the room. The floor was black parquet, some incredibly expensive wood that had been polished to an amazing gloss and the walls almost disappeared behind large geometric-design paintings, of the type Manfred found boring. A grand piano and a hired jazz-band of six men were lost in a corner of this huge zeppelin-hangar of a salon and the thirty or forty men and women dancing the Charleston and the thirty or forty others standing about to talk and drink went only partway to making the room look occupied.

Dieter Bruckner, son of the house, looked slightly drunk already. He wore a most elegant dinner-jacket of midnight blue and had diamond-studs in his starched shirt-front.

'Manfred!' he said, throwing his arms round him in a bear-hug, 'how are you, you dog? I've heard all about what happened at Wolfgang's film-show – why wasn't I there?'

'I expected you to be there. Were you away?'

'It was my own fault – he invited me but I had a dinner-date that evening with a little ballerina and I thought that would be more interesting. But now I've heard about how you all piled on top of Wolfgang's aunt – I could shoot myself!'

'How was the ballerina?'

'So-so. How was the aunt?'

'Fantastic! Where is your Mama, Dieter, I must present my greetings.'

'She's over there somewhere being polite to some of the old man's boring friends. Listen, there are some marvellous girls here tonight – take your pick, but leave one for me.'

Manfred grinned and made his way towards his hostess. Frau Bruckner was a large and handsome blonde woman of fifty or thereabouts. She had been a friend of Manfred's mother during the years she lived in Berlin, when Manfred's father had been alive. He bowed and kissed her hand and said the usual polite things and she smiled appreciatively at him and patted his cheek in a maternal fashion.

'Have you met Herr Grutz and his wife?' she asked. 'And Mr and Mrs Montrose?'

Jenny's father was an imposing man of about sixty, tall, strongly-built and with a well-trimmed mane of curly white hair. His hand-shake was firm and frank and his smile bland. It was his wife who took Manfred by surprise. She was blonde and beautiful, had a gloriously-proportioned figure which her ultra-fashionable frock did little to disguise, and she was no more than two or three years older than Jenny. Manfred kissed her hand with pleasure and was rewarded with a glowing smile.

'I have the honour of knowing your daughter, Madame,' he said. 'Is she here tonight?'

'My step-daughter,' she corrected him, 'She's having dinner with friends and they're all coming on here afterwards.'

Manfred noted that Montrose's genial expression hardened at the mention of his daughter. Perhaps he was not entirely unaware of her unorthodox friendships. The name Grutz struck an echo in Manfred's memory.

'Herr *Albert* Grutz?' he asked, shaking hands.

'That is so. Have we met before?'

'No, but I have heard of you.'

Albert Grutz was not at all what Manfred had expected.

He was a tall and heavy man with stooping shoulders, and he had a humorous expression in his deep-set eyes.

'Who could have been talking about me?' he asked, 'I don't know anyone.'

'Ludwig Kessler has a high opinion of you.'

Grutz eyed him warily for a moment and stood back to let him kiss Frau Grutz's hand, an action which seemed to disconcert her. She wore an expensive black evening frock and a three-strand diamond choker, but whatever her attractions had been thirty years before, they were now sadly faded. A dull hausfrau, Manfred thought – no wonder Grutz seeks amusement elsewhere, even though his style in amusement would appear bizarre to most.

The jazz-band played with lunatic exhilaration, couples danced, Manfred circulated, looking for his friends. He soon came across Max Schroeder, with a very pretty girl on his arm.

'Fritzi von Gerstenberg,' said Max, introducing them, and Manfred wondered, though briefly, what had happened to the great passion for Rosa and the peace of mind Max claimed she had brought him. Fritzi looked no more than nineteen and, whatever her talents, the art of soothing a troubled soul was not likely to be among them.

'I have stumbled across the secret of life, the world and the universe,' said Max, interpreting Manfred's quizzical look at Fritzi.

'That sounds very useful, Max. Are you allowed to tell me or are you sworn to silence?'

'It is too precious to reveal casually to the ignorant mob, but you are my dearest friend and so I shall tell you. But you must promise not to pass it on.'

'I swear! Tell me.'

'Then listen carefully. *Nothing is true or real except what I decide is true and real.*'

'I'm real!' his girl objected. 'Or do you think you were only dreaming this afternoon?'

'Of course you are real – I have decided so. By the way, Manfred, have you seen the lady Werner brought back with

229

him from Vienna? I haven't yet decided whether she is real or not.'

'I had lunch with him the other day and he didn't say a word about a lady from Vienna.'

'Obviously he wouldn't – not to you. You keep on taking his girl-friends away from him. They're dancing over there – come and meet her.'

When the band paused Manfred made the acquaintance of Wolfgang's new friend, Countess Liesl von Lorincz-Androsch, a dark-haired and ivory-complexioned beauty approaching thirty. There was a worried look in Wolfgang's eye when he introduced them and Manfred patted his arm reassuringly.

'Have you spoken to Gottfried?' he asked.

'Not exactly. I nodded to him and to Nina when we arrived, but that's all.'

'There's nothing to worry about now. I've made peace for you. And now if you will excuse me, I want to find Jenny Montrose.'

'I hoped you were going to ask me to dance,' said the Countess, and Werner's expression became glacial.

'I would be honoured – but a little later, if Werner permits.'

Guests were arriving all the time and the enormous salon was beginning to fill up. Somewhere in this mob of laughing, drinking, dancing men and women was Jenny and, with any luck, the disaster of her visit to Manfred's apartment might be forgotten and a new start made. Or so he hoped. But before he found her, Albert Grutz appeared from nowhere, linked arms with him and marched him out into the entrance hall. It was empty but for the man-servant stationed at the door to admit more guests and three or four maid-servants to take coats and hats.

'A few words with you, Herr von Klausenberg. I gathered that you know young Ludwig Kessler. That's your business, of course, not mine. I'm an easy-going sort, anyone will tell you that. I'd rather do someone a good turn than a bad one. I don't lose my temper except under

230

extreme provocation. But . . . if certain little pastimes of mine became public gossip, I would get very annoyed. You understand me? And if any malicious tittle-tattle came to the ears of my wife or business colleagues, I would take steps to make sure that the instigator of vicious lies had reason to be sorry he was ever born. Do I make myself clear?'

'You have no reason to fear anything from me. My interest was in Helga, not Ludwig, and it was fleeting, I can assure you. I haven't seen either of them for months.'

'That may be so, but a closed mouth makes no enemies, if you catch my meaning. See here, young man, I'm not stupid enough or vain enough to think that either of those two stays at home and reads a good book when I'm not around. What they get up to doesn't bother me in the least, but I expect and demand discretion where I'm concerned.'

'With every right,' said Manfred. 'So would I, in your position.'

'A man's amusements are his own business. As long as we understand each other there will be no glass broken.'

'Agreed. But tell me something, if you will, Herr Grutz, unless you think it is not a fit subject for discussion, in view of the circumstances – did you know that Helga and Ludwig are lovers?'

'No! I don't believe it – they're as jealous of each other as two dogs over a bone. What makes you say that – did you see something?'

'I didn't see them making love, if that's what you mean. The last time I saw the twins – back in August I think it was – there were strong indications of an unusual attachment under their rivalry. Enough to convince me, at least.'

'Well I'm damned!' said Grutz, staring thoughtfully at him, 'If that's right, then some fascinating possibilities present themselves. I'm grateful to you. Now you mention it . . . there were signs and I missed them. Well, well!'

'How would you go about settling accounts with someone who harmed your private interests?' Manfred asked, out of idle curiosity.

'No great problem, my boy. Have you any idea of how many political murders there have been in the last few years?'

'No. The newspapers carry small items about people found shot or beaten to death. The Red Front murder National Socialists and the National Socialists return the compliment. I can't recall reading of anyone being arrested.'

'The police know when it is not in their own interests to investigate too thoroughly. And almost any violent death in the streets can be written off as another act of political vengeance.'

'You have useful allies, Herr Grutz, but not with the Communists, I imagine.'

'One hand washes the other, as the saying goes. I'm glad we had this little talk. I like to clear up misunderstandings. And my next visit to the twins may be of remarkable interest now that you have opened my eyes.'

'Perhaps in return you can tell me about something.'

'What do you want to know?' said Grutz, his manner cautious again.

'The American banker, Montrose – no doubt you are acquainted with him.'

'And what is your interest in him?'

'Not in him. I found his young wife charming.'

'Ah yes, of course,' said Grutz with the ghost of a grin, 'You must understand that I have no personal knowledge of any irregularity – and any such suggestion would be scandalous. But it has been whispered that Frau Montrose may perhaps be susceptible to the blandishments of good-looking young dogs like you, though I'm sure the utmost tact and discretion would be called for. If there is any truth in the whisper, that is.'

'Do you find her charming yourself?'

'She's far too old for my taste – she must be at least twenty-five.'

'And the daughter,' Manfred continued, seizing the opportunity.

232

'I've met her at dinner-parties with her parents. She and her step-mother don't get on together, that's all I know.'

Manfred thanked his informant and made his way back into the salon, just as Gottfried and Nina stopped dancing. They greeted him effusively.

'Dance with Nina,' said Gottfried, 'I need a drink and time to get my breath back. Who was that you were having a private conference with in the hall?'

'A business friend of Bruckner. You wouldn't like him, Gottfried.'

'I'm damned sure I wouldn't. Did he give you anything useful for the Stock Exchange?'

'Nothing. His sort always keep things to themselves.'

Manfred danced with Nina. She was in white, with seed-pearls sewn in whorls on her bodice and skirt, and she was in a very good mood.

'All quiet on the Western Front?' said Manfred cheerfully.

'Peace and marital harmony,' she said, 'even Werner has been forgiven. There's no need to stay away from me – Gottfried knows everything.'

'What do you mean, everything? What is there for him to know?'

'I confessed that you and I have been madly in love for years and have to see each other. Gottfried was very understanding.'

'Good God!' Manfred exclaimed, stumbling and almost falling over. 'Why did you tell him nonsense like that?'

'He was getting suspicious about Konrad – it really was most trying. He kept on pestering me about having a lover and in the end I confessed that it was you.'

'Nina – it's not true!'

'What's that got to do with it? Gottfried likes you. He simply said *That's all right then* and since then there hasn't been a cross word.'

'But this is monstrous! You have an affair with Konrad and I get the blame!'

'As long as he thinks it's you there isn't any blame. That's the whole point.'

'I've never understood Gottfried and now I never shall.'

'There's nothing much to understand. We're happily married and we suit each other. He likes to sleep with me, but there's a little actress he visits that he thinks I don't know about.'

'One of Oskar's troupe?'

'Right – an odd-looking little creature named Magda Nebel. Have you met her?'

'If she was at Oskar's first-night party I suppose I must have seen her,' Manfred answered vaguely, trying to imagine stolid Gottfried strung up on Magda's special device with the thin steel chains, but the effort of imagination was beyond him.

'Speaking of Konrad, he's not here tonight,' he said, 'I wonder why he wasn't invited.'

'If you want my opinion, Gottfried had something to do with that. He doesn't like him.'

'Even though he thinks I'm your lover, not Konrad?'

'Konrad and I parted company weeks ago, darling,' said Nina. 'He was simply too possessive and boring. He started to question me about whether I'd slept with my own husband! Can you imagine?'

'So who is in favour with you at the moment, Nina dear?'

'That's what I've been telling you, if you'd only listen – no one is. You and I can be good friends again, the way we used to be. And since Gottfried thinks we are anyway, there won't be any problems. Isn't that wonderful?'

'Darling Nina, you astonish me. I hardly know what to say.'

'You don't have to say anything. We'll have some marvellous times together, like the old days. How about the day after tomorrow? I'm free all afternoon. We could meet for lunch and then go to your apartment.'

Manfred stared thoughtfully at the beautiful young woman he was dancing with, trying to remember how it had been when he was head-over-heels in love with her –

not so very long ago. The frantic emotions of those days had gone past recall. All that remained was the memory of how very exciting it had been to make love to her, and that was something he could remember about a good many women.

'Nina – before we plunge into another affair I think it only right to tell you that I'm not desperately in love with you and I know that you're not in love with me. We've both changed.'

'Naturally we've changed. We've grown up since then. We don't have to be desperately in love to have a wonderful love affair – you know that as well as I do.'

'Much the same was said of marriage in the days when parents arranged them without consulting their children.'

'I don't see what that's got to do with it, but I do know that you still want me, whether you're in love with me or not. You proved that at Ulrika's party, when you jumped on me the second Konrad's back was turned. Deny that if you can!'

'Speaking of Ulrika – there she is, making a late and dramatic entrance. Come on.'

He led Nina off the dance-floor to where Ulrika stood at the top of the two broad black marble steps which led down into the salon. Her frock was of crimson chiffon, so short that the hem barely reached to her knees, so skimpy of bodice that her arms, shoulders and almost her entire bosom was uncovered, and so flimsy that her nipples were plainly visible through it. She was posing, one knee thrust forwards, one hand on her hip and, in the other, an ivory cigarette-holder almost as long as her forearm.

'Disgraceful!' a woman said loudly as Manfred passed her. 'That woman is no better than a whore!'

'But a magnificent one,' said the man with her.

Manfred halted to turn towards the couple and give them a polite smile.

'Excuse me, but I could not help overhearing what you said, Madame. I must inform you that Fraulein Heuss is my cousin. She is not a whore, she is a lesbian.'

235

The woman, who was not more than thirty herself, blushed.

'Well, really!' she said. 'Am I to be insulted like this! Heinrich – do something!'

The man stared hard at Manfred for a moment, winked almost imperceptibly, and led his wife away, still complaining. Nina giggled and took hold of Manfred's arm cosily.

'Do you know who that was?' she asked, her tone indicating that the couple had been of great importance.

'No, nor do I care,' he answered, leading her to the steps. 'Ulrika, you look fantastic!'

At close quarters the dark shadow through her flimsy frock made it very obvious that Ulrika's only other items of clothing were her shoes and stockings.

'Thank you, darling,' she said, holding out her hand to be kissed, 'I'm on the prowl tonight.'

'Why is that?'

'I intend to start the New Year with a new lover to bring me luck. Nina, dear, from the way you're hanging onto Manfred I can guess that the two of you have decided to get together again. Old friends are the best – is that it?'

A man-servant approached them with a tray of glasses and stood silent, pretending not to notice Ulrika's near-nakedness. She took a glass of champagne, emptied it in one swallow and gave the man so dazzling a smile that he almost dropped his tray.

'Yes, old friends are the best,' Nina agreed. Don't you find it so?'

'Old friends are like old clothes,' said Ulrika. 'They're comfortable but they don't make you feel beautiful and desirable any more.'

'There are plenty of beautiful women here tonight,' said Manfred, grinning at his outrageous cousin, 'but whether any of them are interested in your advances, who can say?'

'I can say,' Ulrika answered with confidence, 'One look at a woman and I know whether I'm wasting my time or not. Naturally I prefer those who have never made love

236

with another woman before – there's the thrill of seducing them away from their husbands or boy-friends.'

Gottfried joined them on the marble steps, his monocle tightly in his eye and a vaguely drunken expression on his face. He bowed stiffly over Ulrika's hand and, unseen by him, she smiled knowingly at Manfred and Nina.

'I'm planning a special party in a few weeks from now, Gottfried,' she said sweetly, 'I hope you will come – and bring Nina, of course. It will be spectacular.'

Gottfried's genial look vanished at once.

'Thank you,' he said cautiously, 'if we are in Berlin at the time . . . please excuse me, there is someone I want Nina to meet over there.'

He dragged Nina away and Ulrika and Manfred laughed together.

'Who is that marvellous creature over there by the band?' Ulrika asked. 'The young blonde in the white frock – do you know her?'

'That's Wolfgang's sister, Lotti. She's nineteen and she's engaged to be married.'

'You must introduce us. I feel the hand of destiny on me, my dear.'

'It's not the hand of destiny you want between your legs. You shall meet her, but I'd bet a thousand Marks to a Mark that you'll get nowhere with Lotti.'

'It's a bet. You think I'm ugly and charmless, do you?'

'Darling, I think you are sensational, but I'm a man.'

'Raise the stakes then – five thousand Marks to five Marks – how's that?'

'You're so sure of yourself? The odds should be the other way round. Still, a bet is a bet. Tell me something – was it easy to get Jenny Montrose into your bed?'

'She's so eager to try anything and everything that she seduced me. I could hardly believe it was her first time with a woman. There is something touching about Americans in Europe – it's as if they try to catch up on the whole of our history and culture in two weeks.'

237

'They have so little history or culture of their own. Do you classify an affair with you as history or culture?'

Ulrika smiled grandly.

'To make love with me is a cultural experience of historical significance,' she answered. 'Did you find her the same – eager to the point of frenzy?'

Manfred chose his words carefully, still privately ashamed of what he had done to Jenny at Ernst's party.

'We almost got together once, but it went wrong.'

'What! But you must have been lovers – she always asks about you when I meet her anywhere. Are you telling me the truth?'

'I've no reason to lie. Come and meet Lotti.'

Before that could happen, the entertainment began, with a fanfare from the band and a request to clear the centre of the floor. Frau Bruckner had engaged the services of a troupe of of dancers to perform what was announced as 'The Dance of the Seven Veils'. The music struck up and into the salon tripped half a dozen pretty young women, stark naked and bare-foot, to circle round in modified ballet movements, mainly designed to give the fashionable audience ample opportunity to stare at their breasts and bellies and backsides. In due course the lead dancer appeared, equally naked but trailing panels of transparent chiffon about her as she went through her routine.

Manfred and Ulrika were standing near a wall, in the circle of spectators. Manfred put his arm lightly round his cousin's waist and whispered close to his ear.

'What is the point of bringing a cabaret act into a private party? Especially a mixed party of this sort – if it were a men-only function I could understand it. But here it strikes me as the height of vulgarity.'

'Don't be a prude, darling, I'm enjoying it. You see the girl second from the right – the one with her arms above her head – I'm going to have her. I can never resist plump little breasts like hers.'

'I thought you wanted Lotti?'

'Of course I do, but if her fiancé is here she won't come

238

home with me tonight. Once you've introduced us I shall give her a day to think about me and then invite her to lunch. The little dancer will do for tonight.'

Manfred slid his hand gently from Ulrika's hip up to her breast and stroked it cautiously through the very thin chiffon of her frock. He felt the nipple go firm at his touch.

'You're a beast,' Ulrika whispered. 'But I forgive you – I know I'm irresistible.'

'You owe me something if what you said about playing with me when we were children is true.'

'Young as you were, your little thing stood up stiffly enough even then.'

'And is doing now,' he whispered. 'How about coming home with me tonight?'

'Don't be silly, darling, I've no interest in your stiff little thing now.'

'It's not so little any more.'

'I know – I saw it at my Steam-bath party. Why don't you find Nina and show it to her – she knows what to do with it.'

The dance ended to hearty applause from the spectators and the dancers filed away. Ulrika went after them and Manfred got himself another drink and thought that for him it was a disappointing party. After several glasses of champagne he became more cheerful and towards midnight he was dancing with a girl he had been introduced to – a very pretty fair-haired girl of about twenty named Romy Spengler. Like him she was a little drunk and when the music stopped abruptly, she fell laughing into his arms.

Bruno Bruckner and his wife were on the balcony that ran across one end of the salon. He addressed his guests in a loud and confident voice.

'Ladies and gentlemen – in two minutes it will be midnight!'

A line of servants filed into the salon carrying loaded trays and there was a rush to get another drink. In the scramble at least one glass smashed on the parquet. Manfred forced his way into the crowd.

239

'There!' he said, returning to Romy. 'One for you and one for me – though some of it was spilled when an idiot pushed me.'

The guests were looking up at the Bruckners on their balcony, glasses ready. Herr Bruckner was staring at his gold wrist-watch.

'Happy New Year!' he shouted happily and the salon rang with the cry as the guests shouted back and emptied their glasses.

There followed a positive orgy of kissing, hand-shaking and back-slapping. Manfred kissed Romy on both cheeks and she put her long thin arms round his neck and pulled his mouth to hers. The feel of her body squeezed close to his was very enjoyable and made him realise that the party might not be a complete disappointment after all.

'Ladies and gentlemen – and dear friends and colleagues,' Bruckner called out, 'permit me to say a few words on this important occasion . . .'

The few words proved to be a speech, both long and dull, in which Bruckner went into some detail about the problems which still beset the national economy. This was, no doubt, only a prelude to a proposed explanation of what was to be done in the New Year. But before he had even completed his analysis of the problems, Romy took Manfred's hand and tugged at it. Hand in hand they slid stealthily through the crowd staring up at the balcony until they could dart unnoticed through a side-door of the salon, the entrance through which the servants had been bringing champagne and food all evening.

'What a boring man!' said Romy. 'He asks us to a party and rants at us as if we were his board of directors.'

She was in Manfred's arms again and they kissed hotly.

'Unpardonable,' he agreed.

'Especially when there is something of colossal importance to do,' she added.

'Which is?'

'There is only one way to get the New Year off to a good start. Where can we go?'

They were in a passage that led to the kitchens and no one was in sight, the servants being immobilised in the salon to receive the benefit of their employer's view of the state of the economy, along with the guests. But through a door at the end of the passage there was the sound of singing and merriment, the kitchen-staff having escaped the ordeal. Halfway towards the kitchen Manfred found a door leading on to the back-stairs and led Romy up until they came out in a broad corridor with Persian rugs and doors along each side.

'Bedrooms,' said Romy, 'Just what we're looking for!'

The nearest door took them into a large and sumptuously furnished room, with pearl-grey walls and more of the geometric paintings. More usefully, it had a large and low double bed with a pink satin cover.

'Ghastly!' said Manfred, staring at the pictures. 'He must buy them wholesale.

'Who cares?' Romy chortled and threw herself bodily on to the bed, bounced and giggled uncontrollably.

A moment later Manfred was beside her, hugging and kissing her. She undid something at the side of her strapless frock and pulled the bodice down to show him her pointed little breasts and Manfred kissed them hungrily.

'At last!' she said. 'We've lost ten minutes of 1929 already!'

She rolled away from him on to her back, knees up, and raised herself on her shoulder-blades and high-heeled shoes to pull her copper-coloured frock up round her narrow waist, so revealing her lack of underwear. Manfred slid down the bed and kissed the fleshy little lips below her light-brown tuft.

'Don't keep me waiting at a time like this,' she urged.

Manfred was between her parted knees, his trousers unbuttoned. He lay on her quickly and slid his hard member deep into the warm little recess waiting for it. Romy squealed in pleasure and, at that very moment, a woman's voice cried out in outrage.

'What is going on here!'

241

It was a stupid question, in view of their position on the bed. Manfred scrambled off the girl, tucking his manhood out of sight and doing up his trousers, while she pulled her frock down hurriedly and sat up. There stood Frau Bruckner herself, hand on the door-knob, her face flushed dark red.

'I can't believe my own eyes!' she exclaimed. 'You, Romy! What would your father say if he knew of this! And as for you, Manfred, I am astounded that you should abuse my hospitality so grossly!'

Romy kept sensibly silent, but Manfred felt impelled to offer some sort of excuse. He rose to his feet and bowed slightly to Frau Bruckner.

'Madame, I fear I am guilty of an unpardonable breach of good manners. But I must ask you not to blame Fraulein Spengler, since it was I who brought her here. She is a little drunk from your excellent champagne and was unaware of my intentions. The blame rests entirely on me, I assure you.'

'Very well,' said Frau Bruckner grimly, 'I will take your word for that. Romy, you may go and no more will be said. But I must ask you to conduct yourself more decently while you are in my house.'

'Yes, Frau Bruckner,' said Romy demurely, jumping off the bed.

'You will remain here, Manfred,' Frau Bruckner continued unrelentingly, 'Romy may be young enough to act foolishly after a glass or two of champagne, but that is hardly true of you. I have more to say to you on this matter.'

She moved away from the door to let Romy scuttle out, still fastening the bodice of her frock. Then, to Manfred's slight alarm, she crossed the room to the dressing-table by the far wall and sat down to examine her make-up in the mirror.

'This is *your* room?' he asked, his heart sinking, 'I had no idea – what must you think of me!'

'Think of you? I think that you are a young man of

unusual courtesy. I wish my son Dieter had manners half as good as yours. I don't know how I prevented myself bursting out laughing when you told me that little slut didn't know what you brought her here for. But the lie did you credit. Do you know her well?'

Frau Bruckner was patting her hair in the mirror and her manner had changed remarkably for the better.

'I don't know her at all,' said Manfred, 'someone introduced us tonight. The time seemed appropriate to make her closer acquaintance.'

'Closer acquaintance! What a polite way you have of putting things. You had her sprawled across my bed and you were on top of her – that's really what I call closer acquaintance!'

Manfred sat down on the bed, much relieved by Frau Bruckner's attitude, and lit a cigarette from his gold case.

'Perhaps I am old-fashioned, Madame, but I find coarseness of expression unpleasing.'

She turned on her pink satin-topped bench to face him.

'Always?' she asked. 'Surely not.'

'I am not sure that I understand you.'

'And I'm sure that you do, my dear. There are some situations in which the use of coarse expressions can be very exciting.'

'So I understand. But is this a suitable topic of conversation between us, dear lady, especially in your bed-room?'

'What better place? And my name is Heidi, as I'm sure you know.'

'If your husband were to surprise us here, as you surprised me, I do not know what I would say to him. I could hardly claim that I had dragged you to your own bedroom, unaware of my intentions.'

'I locked the door when Romy left. No one will surprise us.'

She stood up, undid the fastening of her long gown and crossed her arms to pull it over her head. Manfred's feelings were extremely complicated at that moment. The brief episode with Romy had stirred his blood and some urgent relief was necessary – but it had never entered his head that the woman offering the relief might be his friend Dieter's mother.

Frau Bruckner wore no brassiere and had no need of one, her breasts being surprisingly small and flat. She stepped out of her lace-trimmed black silk knickers and stood for his judgment in her stockings and suspender-belt. She was a big woman, broad of hip and solid of belly, but neither flabby nor sagging. Her remarkably healthy-looking pink flesh looked everywhere firm and appealing.

Her most unusual feature lay between her thighs. Her mound was shaved – or plucked – completely smooth so that her long vertical slit was totally exposed. Manfred stared in fascination – he had never before seen a hairless woman. Frau Bruckner walked slowly towards him.

'You like the look of my Fotze,' she said softly.

From a lady of her age and position, the common word startled Manfred and made his stem twitch in his trousers. When she halted immediately in front of where he sat on the bed he reached out to run his fingers over the smooth flesh between her legs.

'Why do you have no hair?'

'For a simple and shameful reason. My husband can't keep his hands off little girls. The only way I can get him into bed with me at all is to be like one.'

'Is it important to get him into your bed?' Manfred asked, delighted by the feel of her soft flesh under his hand. 'You must have friends to make you happy, Heidi.'

'Several, but I don't want Bruno to escape from me completely. I have to keep some hold on him by offering him something he can't get elsewhere. He can't do much more than play about with his little girls, but with me he can let himself go with no fear of the consequences.'

She came a step nearer, straddled his knees and sat down on his lap. While she was busy with his trouser buttons Manfred stroked her breasts. Small and flat as they were, they were pleasant to the touch and her large nipples quickly lost their softness under his fingers.

244

'So you brought that little whore Romy Spengler up here to celebrate the New Year,' she said, smiling at him. 'And now you're celebrating it with me instead. What do you think of that?'

Her fingers played very expertly with his stem and at that moment Manfred felt no particular regret about the change of partners. He could catch up with Romy later after he had finished with Heidi.

'The New Year is starting with a surprise,' he answered. 'That must be a good sign.'

'Do *you* like little girls?' she asked, not listening to him.

'Only grown-up girls.'

'How about boys?' she murmured, obviously excited by the sight of his stiffness.

Manfred smiled and teased her nipples.

'What a question! You have the proof in your hand of what I like.'

'What do you want to do with it?'

'I want to put it in your Fotze, Heidi.'

Her breath hissed between her teeth in excitement at the word. She pushed him down on to his back and heaved herself forward to get his stem into the soft bare lips between her legs and sink down on it.

'You've got what you wanted,' she gasped. 'Now you're going to give me my New Year present!'

She rode up and down on him, very agile for a woman of her size. Manfred took her engorged nipples between thumbs and forefingers to squeeze them and encourage her efforts.

'Tell me what we're doing,' Heidi panted.

He told her, using the most brutal and coarse expression for the act in which they were engaged.

'Ah!' she moaned, 'say it again!'

He said it again, over and over, as she slammed against him and brought on her climactic convulsions so fiercely that Manfred's back arched off the bed as his crisis swept through him.

Afterwards Heidi scrambled off him quickly and he sat

245

up to rearrange his clothes decently. He would have kissed her and caressed her pink flesh for a moment or two as a mark of gratitude and respect, but she had retreated to the bench before her dressing-table and was sitting there facing him with her knees pressed tightly together.

'You must go downstairs and back to the party before you are missed,' she said, 'I shall be some little time.'

'Is anything wrong?' he asked curiously.

'I don't know what came over me. It must have been the sight of you with that little slut Romy. My God, you're young enough to be my son!'

'Don't you like young men, Heidi. I mean, what about your special friends, the ones who make you happy while Herr Bruckner is off pursuing his own amusements – are none of them young?'

'They're a good deal older than you and I can trust them. What have I done! This will be gossipped all over Berlin by tomorrow.'

Manfred knelt by her feet and put his hands on her bare shoulders.

'No one but you and I will ever know how we celebrated the New Year together, I give you my word.'

'Thank you,' she said, 'I know I can trust you.'

Manfred leaned forward to kiss her mouth gently, then her flat breasts. She stroked his hair and he parted her knees reassuringly to kiss her belly and the smooth lips between her thighs.

'A happy New Year,' he said, getting to his feet.

'And to you, Manfred. May it bring you everything you wish for yourself.'

Which was all very well, he thought as he made his way down the broad main staircase towards the sound of music and noisy hilarity, but what had taken place in Heidi's bedroom was not what he had wanted for himself in the New Year. The quick act of love with her was by no means as agreeable as it would have been with Romy. With Romy underneath him they would have giggled together like naughty children while their loins thrust at each other and

246

it would have been innocent and natural – a game. But with Heidi Bruckner it was not like that at all. She had used him to bolster her own waning confidence in herself and had suffered pangs of ridiculous remorse afterwards. In retrospect Manfred was irritated by what he had allowed to happen.

The salon was like a beer-garden. Everyone was dancing to the frantic music of the jazz group, laughing and shouting as if they were totally drunk. As they probably were. The heat was over-powering and the smell of cigar-smoke, perfume and perspiring bodies nauseating. Manfred felt that he had had enough – it had been a disappointing party after all. The servants seemed nearly as drunk as the guests and in the room near the entrance hall where the hats and coats had been taken, he found a footman on top of a maidservant, the two of them hard at it on top of a pile of very expensive fur-coats. Without disturbing them Manfred found his black leather overcoat and left the house.

Outside it was freezing cold, with the threat of snow in the air. The sky was over-clouded but there was enough light from the windows of the house to illuminate the drive between the double row of parked cars. He was thirty or forty paces from the front door when he heard scuffling ahead of him and low voices. At first he thought it might be the chauffeurs, but commonsense told him that they were in the kitchens, getting drunk and making advances to the female staff. His curiosity was aroused and he moved forward silently and slowly towards the sound and stopped behind a huge limousine to peer over its top. He saw two figures ahead of him and their position admitted no ambiguity as to what they were doing. One of them was sprawled face-down over the bonnet of the next parked car in the line, feet apart on the ground, trousers down, to show a pale gleam of flesh. The other stood close up between his companion's legs and leaned forward to make thrusting movements with his loins. Manfred heard him say 'Fantastic!' and recognised the voice of Dieter Bruckner.

Astounded is too mild a word for Manfred's state of mind

247

at that moment. He had known Dieter for years and was well acquainted with at least half a dozen women Dieter had been with. There had never been the slightest hint that he was interested in young men. Yet here he was, battering away at the rear end of one! And to judge from the vigour of his onslaught and his exclamations of pleasure, he was thoroughly enjoying the experience.

This is unbelievable, Manfred said to himself – either I am drunker than I thought or Dieter is blind drunk and doesn't know what he's doing. But neither hypothesis fitted the facts. However drunk Dieter might be, he could hardly mistake a man for a woman at such close quarters. What on earth could it be like, this imitation love-making, Manfred wondered – this exchange of the curved and tender body of a woman for whatever paltry substitute another man could offer? He remembered Ludwig dressed up as a girl and his own violent reaction at the moment of discovery.

Dieter gasped loudly as his crisis arrived. His partner writhed on the shiny car bonnet and cried out and at once Manfred knew the truth. It was Jenny Montrose in men's evening clothes lying face-down on the car with her trousers round her knees! Black rage exploded in Manfred's heart and he ran round the limousine which had concealed him, seized Dieter by the hair and spun him round, away from Jenny. In the faint light Dieter's expression was one of shock, as well it might be, his mouth hung open and his eyes bulged from his face. His trousers were open to let his hard stem stick out, still dribbling feebly.

'You swine!' Manfred bellowed and punched Dieter in the face, sending him staggering backwards.

'Manfred! Have you gone mad?' he yelped. 'What's the matter with you?'

'Get out of my sight before I murder you!' Manfred shouted.

There was a dark trickle of blood from Dieter's nose. He brought his fists up to defend himself and threw a punch at Manfred's head. Manfred blocked it and punched him hard over the heart and, as he staggered, followed it with a punch to the chin that knocked Dieter over backwards.

'Out of my sight!' he shouted again, waiting for Dieter to get up so that he could knock him down again. But Dieter wanted no more. He got up slowly, backed away a few steps, then turned and lurched away into the dark. Manfred swung round to confront Jenny, who was off the car bonnet and fastening her trouser buttons.

'What the hell is going on?' she demanded, surprise causing her to lapse into English. Manfred took her by the throat, pulled open the car door and hurled her inside. He heard her cursing as he scrambled in after her and slammed the door behind him. She had fallen half across the back seat of the car and half on the floor.

'What the hell do you think you're doing?' she said furiously, still speaking in English.

'Bitch!' Manfred shouted, dragging her upright. 'Dirty whore of a bitch!'

She recognised him at last.

'Ah, it's Herr von Gigolo,' she said in German. 'Drunk as usual! You've got the wrong woman. I don't pay for it.'

Manfred slapped her face, left and right, growling in his throat, like a dog on the attack. Without hesitation she slapped his face, hard enough to hurt. Manfred grabbed her arms and they wrestled on the car seat, she trying to knee him between the legs, until he found himself kissing her. For a while she struggled furiously but then she relaxed and returned the kiss.

'Why didn't you say that's what you wanted?' she asked, easing herself from his clutch, 'I thought you were trying to hurt me.'

She tugged at the gold studs in her starched shirt-front until she had it open from bow-tie to waist. Manfred pulled the shirt wide open to kiss her bare breasts voraciously.

'That's better,' she said. 'All that flitting about and kissing the hand and mealy-mouthed politeness – why didn't you push me on my back months ago and do this?'

'I didn't want it like this,' he growled against her flesh.

249

He hooked his fingers in the waist-band of her trousers and ripped the buttons open.

'Are you always this wild?' she gasped.

His hand clenched tightly over her furry mound and two fingers were deep into the warm wetness of her earlier love-making.

'My God!' she moaned as his fingers ravished her. 'Not so fast . . . wait!'

But he didn't wait and soon she gave a long throaty wail and shook hard against him. Even before her crisis was over he dragged her trousers down her long legs with impatient hands until he had them off completely and could push her on her back and heave himself on top of her, one leg along the car-seat and one on the floor. He tore his own trousers open as roughly as he had treated hers and, two seconds later, penetrated her with a lunge that made her cry out.

'It's like being raped!' she gasped while he slammed into her, his mind a red haze, 'slow down!'

Her complaints trailed off as she was caught up in the fierceness of his passion and she jerked and squirmed beneath his thrashing body, her hands clutching at his hair to pull his mouth down to hers. A thunderous stroke seemed to rip through Manfred and he screamed in ecstasy, his rage draining away with his passion.

When he came to himself again he asked Jenny if she was all right, some recollection of her wailing making him anxious that she might not be.

'I'm dead and in Heaven,' she said faintly.

She put her arms round his neck and kissed him again and again.

'I think I must confess that I may be in love with you, Jenny, boring though that may be for both of us.'

'I don't care whether you are or not – you're not going to escape from me after that. What don't you take me home – or is there another fat old hausfrau waiting in your bedroom for you?'

'Come and see for yourself.'

He rolled off her awkwardly in the confined space and they got out of the car. Jenny had her trousers draped over her arm and presented a slightly comical appearance in her black tail-coat and crumpled shirt.

'No point in putting them on again,' she said, 'it's not a long drive. Come to think of it, the owner of this handsome vehicle deserves to have them as a souvenir of what took place here tonight.'

She threw her trousers into the back of the car and slammed the door. Manfred picked up the long leather coat he had dropped when he attacked Dieter and put it round her shoulders to keep the cold wind off her while they walked down the long line of parked cars to his tourer. Jenny looked at it approvingly and asked him to put the top down.

'And if we die of cold?' he asked.

'Then we'll die happy – what more do you want?'

With the hood down and an icy wind over the top of the wind-screen they drove away from the Bruckners' house and towards the city centre. The Kurfurstendamm was jammed with people, arms linked, singing and laughing and idiotically happy that a New Year had begun. Jenny shrugged the overcoat off her shoulders and stood up, clinging to the windscreen with one hand, to wave and shout greetings at the people on the pavement, while the wind pulled her undone shirt open to expose her shapely breasts.

'You are the most beautiful woman in the world!' Manfred shouted to her, 'and I am crazy about you!'

She sat down to take his face in her hands and kiss him, so distracting him that the car wobbled halfway across the road and brought a blare of car-horns from traffic going in the other direction.

'Don't kill us!' she said, 'We've too much to say to each other.'

Then she was up again, perching on the back of the seat while she struggled out of her tail-coat.

'What are you doing?' Manfred shrieked.

251

'I can't stand these silly clothes! I want you to know I'm a woman.'

She bundled the tail-coat up and hurled it at two policemen standing on the pavement. One of them waved and the other shouted and Manfred put his foot down hard to get away from them. He looked up at Jenny and saw that she was pulling her shirt over her head. She sat there, her black hair tousled by the wind, her face glowing, naked except for a tiny suspender-belt and silk stockings, the shirt trailing out behind her like a banner as she held it high. On the pavement people pointed and cheered.

'Don't freeze to death now!' Manfred called to her, 'I need you!'

'I'm on fire for the first time in my life!' she called back. 'Happy New Year, Manfred!'